Change Up

ELLEY ARDEN

CRIMSON
ROMANCE™

Published by
Crimson Romance
an imprint of F+W Media, Inc.
10151 Carver Road, Suite 200
Blue Ash, OH 45242. U.S.A.
www.crimsonromance.com

ISBN 10: 1-4405-9150-4
ISBN 13: 978-1-4405-9150-1
eISBN 10: 1-4405-9151-2
eISBN 13: 978-1-4405-9151-8

Cover art © iStock/PeopleImages.

*To anyone who has ever been touched by
the emotional turmoil and destruction of Alzheimer's.*

Prologue

Rachel Reed sat at her sleek black desk in her corner office over-looking city hall, complete with its statue of William Penn, and tried not to worry. Any time your boss came to town it was nerve-racking. This time wasn't any different. At least it shouldn't have been. Nothing had changed since the last time he'd been here. All systems were go on the abandoned warehouse being converted into residential space. Closings were complete on the land assemblage in downtown Philadelphia, and tenants in all ten buildings were being relocated efficiently.

She maniacally strummed her squared-off fingernails on the desk. *Think, think, think.* Was she missing anything? Was there any reason he'd be back in town so soon after his last visit? Had she made a mistake?

She just about shattered the intercom button with an overenthusiastic press as she summoned her executive assistant, Liv Butler, into the office.

"What's up?" Liv asked, bright and confident, like any young and hungry EA should be.

"Something is wrong," Rachel said, clicking through screen after screen of monthly status reports. "I can feel it. We've met all our objectives, correct?"

"Yep," Liv said, her face in her tablet. "Wait. Maybe he's coming in for your birthday. The big four-O."

Rachel looked up in time to see Liv's brows bob in jest and ignored it. Forty wasn't a big deal unless you were using it to measure professional success—as in being able to call yourself a multimillionaire by the time you turned forty. Rachel could do that, so forty could come and go without any fanfare, like all the rest. "My birthday is not for another week," she said dismissively.

"Besides, that's too sentimental a reason for him to come in. We've never had that kind of relationship."

"Maybe he's retiring."

Never. He might've been sixty-five, but he had the focus and determination of a man half his age. "Liv, we're talking about a man who texts me at three a.m. to alter directives and clarify goals. He won't sleep, let alone retire." Although those texts had been far and few between lately.

Something was definitely wrong.

Rachel spent the next ninety minutes strumming like a madwoman, rereading texts and emails, replaying conversations in her head, trying desperately to come up with something—anything—that would warrant this visit. But everything was perfect on her end … until the intercom sounded again.

"They're here," Liv said.

They?

What the heck was Rachel in for?

The door opened, and her father walked in, followed by her mother. For as long as Rachel had been heading up the Philadelphia offices of Reed Commercial Real Estate Services, her mother had never stepped foot inside this building.

Maybe the impromptu visit was about her birthday after all. As weird as that would be.

Rachel stood, steadied her stride, muffled her surprise, and gave them the requisite greetings—a handshake for her father, who had been her business mentor and boss since she'd graduated from UPenn what seemed like a lifetime ago, and a hug for her mother, whom she saw once a year at Christmas—if her work schedule permitted. The greetings were even more stilted than usual.

"What brings you to Philadelphia?" she asked, knowing it wasn't business if her mother was in the mix. Jackie Reed preferred defined gender roles. Men worked. Women took care of them. Rachel couldn't think of a more miserable existence.

"Let's sit," her father said.

Those two little words tilted the world on its axis.

Rachel didn't hesitate to do as she was told. When your boss said jump, you asked how high. When your boss was your father, you didn't have to ask; you already knew. Still, her heart doubled its beat.

Once she was seated behind her desk, she studied her father, who couldn't seem to make eye contact with her. Danny Reed looked well: wrinkle-free skin a healthy shade of pink, salt-and-pepper hair as thick as always, tailored suit coat the perfect fit. When silence stretched on, she turned her attention to Jackie, who appeared every bit as put together as usual: neither a gray hair on her sleekly bobbed head nor a mark on her pancaked and painted face. Flowers and pastels were topped off with pearls. So why the long faces?

"We're sitting," Rachel said. "Now what?"

"Darling," Jackie started, finally looking at Rachel, only to be cut off by Danny.

"I have Alzheimer's," he said.

Rachel's breath hitched. Her father had never been one to beat around the bush. His assuredness and directness had made them all millions. But this time, she wished he'd built up to it. *Alzheimer's*. How was that possible? He looked great. He sounded great.

"Are you sure?" she asked.

"Positive," her mother said, tears glistening in her eyes, and Rachel had the foreign impulse to get touchy-feely. It didn't have time to flourish, though, because her father took control of the conversation again.

"We have work to do," he said, and he whipped out the leather-bound legal pad that accompanied him on every business trip.

But Rachel was still stuck on the news. *Alzheimer's*. When did he find out? What were his symptoms? How were they treating the disease?

"The attorneys should be here at four," he said. "You will have special power of attorney to make business deals on my behalf. These papers"—he slid the legal pad toward her—"detail my wishes. I simply ask that you follow them to a T."

She stared at the inch-thick stack of typed pages tucked in the inner pocket, her mind reeling. Surely power of attorney was a bit extreme. He sounded fine. He seemed competent.

"Rachel," her mother said. "Are you okay … with all of this?"

"Of course she's okay." Danny's brusque tone said the same thing it always did: Rachel was tough. His hand-groomed foot soldier. She could handle anything.

"I'm fine," Rachel said. "Just processing."

"Process this," her father said, tapping the folio again. "Everything you need to know is in there. I'll help as much as I can, but before it's too late, you need to have the legal power to execute these plans without my signature."

It made sense, except none of it made sense. He still didn't look like a man dealing with Alzheimer's disease. "Dad …" She paused as she leafed through the thick stack of pages.

And then something caught her eye. "You want me to sell the baseball team?" Oh, how she'd bit her tongue when she'd discovered three Christmases ago her father was considering a multimillion-dollar vanity project to bring independent baseball to her hometown of Arlington, Pennsylvania. The only thing that had kept her quiet at the time was her belief he would come to his senses and see how owning a barely professional baseball team in a league that had no affiliation with the MLB wasn't a good investment.

"But they haven't even had their first season." He was asking her to sell a team on speculation? She was a commercial real estate broker, not a magician.

More details flashed at her from the pages in her father's notebook. She was going to have to spearhead the remaining preparations for the inaugural season? "Dad," she said again, "I don't know anything about running a baseball team."

She'd been to her fair share of sporting events thanks to company season tickets and colleagues who needed to be schmoozed, and baseball was by far her favorite because of the atmosphere and the zen-like pace of the game, but enjoying the game was a far cry from understanding the business.

"You won't have to run it. The personnel we hire will run it. They are all listed in the folder." He sighed, a rare show of weakness, and she felt ridiculous for worrying about her workload when he was facing … Alzheimer's.

That word pulled the proverbial rug from underneath her.

"It's a lot," he continued. "I know it is. But it's probably the last thing I'm ever going to ask of you."

Rachel hated the lump that formed in her throat, hated that she couldn't think of confident words to displace it. She nodded.

"It's not the hereditary kind," her mother said suddenly. "So that's good news. Dr. Rictor said you and Helen Anne only have a slight increase in risk."

What a lovely thought. Not that on some level Rachel wasn't already worrying about it, but talking about it made it all the more real. *A slight increase in risk.* That was supposed to make her feel better.

It didn't. So she did what she always did when emotions threatened to swallow her whole. She looked at her father and, with a definitive nod and a slap of her hand to the leather-bound folder, said, "I can handle this. You have my word."

Chapter One

Rachel looked at the magazine-worthy house in which she'd been raised looming up before her and beat back the apprehension that accompanied her on every trip to Arlington. It felt especially funny being here in late February. Strange even. There were no evergreen wreaths or red bows on the Georgian-style windows, no garland winding around the thick pillars. In fact, the huge white house looked … lifeless.

She swallowed against the lump that had plagued her for more than a month now, ever since her parents' impromptu trip to Philadelphia, and pushed out of her BMW ready to work. Unlike the occasional Christmas visit, this trip was about business. She didn't need to be apprehensive about that. On the contrary, she needed to be focused, so they could make the most out of this face-to-face meeting and she could get back to the work that awaited her in Philadelphia.

Once Rachel was on the porch, she rang the bell, but when no one answered, she wondered if it was broken. She knocked. Then decided she should knock louder. Finally, she jiggled the handle, figuring the fourteen years she'd lived here as a child entitled her to let herself in.

Locked. Her apprehension turned into full-blown heartburn.

Before she could fully process how odd this was, considering her father knew she was coming because they had a nine o'clock meeting with a tree-cutting expert from Pittsburgh, the distinct sound of metal sliding against metal told her the bolt lock was opening and soon after so would the door.

"Rachel!" Her mother gasped as she clutched a pink terry robe around her throat. "What in the world?" She patted a few flyaway hairs at the top of her head and made a face. "I'm not even dressed. This is such a surprise!"

For a split second, Rachel thought maybe she had the wrong day or at least the wrong time and reached for her phone in the front pocket of her satchel. "Dad and I have a meeting …"

"Rachel!" There he was, dressed in a fluffy white robe with a Pittsburgh Pirates logo on the breast pocket. His slippers made an uneven shuffling sound as he walked down the wide hallway with a goofy grin on his face. "What a wonderful surprise!"

"That's just what I was saying," Rachel's mother said.

Was she dreaming this? Maybe she was having some sort of out-of-body experience brought on by unprocessed stress. Except the cold, late-February air chilled her to the bone, and she knew that couldn't be true. "This shouldn't be a surprise," she said to her father. "We're meeting with Wes Allen today about the trees. That's today, right?" She whipped out her phone and confirmed what she'd already known to be true, and then she looked at her father again. He seemed confused, so she elaborated. "The meeting is today at nine o'clock. The details were in my Friday update. Didn't you get my email?"

His brows scrunched together at the top of his nose. "No. I … I don't remember the last time I checked my email. I … What's the date?"

"February 21," Jackie said softly.

"Oh," her father said absently, frowning briefly before his face brightened. " Wonderful! Pitchers and catchers reported on February 17."

Rachel's shoulders slumped. He could remember a random date like that but not the meeting they had scheduled for today?

"Spring training is my favorite time of year," he continued. "The Buccos have quite the bullpen this season. Liriano, Martinez …" Then he quieted and rubbed his fingertips over his forehead in an agitated fashion. "Liriano, Martinez …" He dropped his hand

and fumbled for something in the pocket of his robe. "Where's my phone? I need to find my phone." He turned and shuffled away, leaving Rachel standing on the porch, staring after him in disbelief.

"He's been having a rough couple days," her mother said, and when Rachel looked at her, she saw tears.

"Why didn't you tell me?"

"I didn't know you were supposed to be meeting someone."

"I wasn't talking about the meeting, Mom. I'm talking about …" No matter what she did, she couldn't get the word *Alzheimer's* to come out of her mouth. "I'm talking about his health. Why didn't you tell me he was getting worse? This can't be normal. I saw you not even two months ago, and he was fine."

Jackie sighed. "He wasn't fine. He just hides it well. But I agree, this is worse than usual. He has an appointment with Dr. Rictor on Monday."

Off and on these last weeks, Rachel had thought of reaching out for more information about her father's treatment, but with her usual responsibilities in Philadelphia coupled with the scope of work to get this team up and running—and sold—she'd chosen to leave those details to her mother and sister, Helen Anne. Obviously that hadn't been the smartest thing to do.

She glanced down the empty hallway. "He needs to see someone who will be more aggressive with treatment, because this is not okay. Mom …" She leveled her mother with a serious look. "Let me take him to Philadelphia. I'll find the best neurologists."

Jackie shook her head. "Your father likes Dr. Rictor. We trust him, and we can't keep running to Philadelphia every time he needs to see a doctor. It's …" The tears fell. "It's a lot to handle, Rachel. I'm doing the best I can."

Crap. "Where's Helen Anne?" After all, her sister was living in this house, too.

"She's at church with Macy."

"No, I mean where is she while all of this is going on? Is she helping you, or is she hiding in that little bookstore of hers?"

"Of course she's helping," Jackie said defensively. "But I don't want Macy …" Her voice broke with a small sob when she mentioned Rachel's ten-year-old niece. "The divorce has already been hard enough on her."

Rachel's shoulders slumped under the weighty realization that things with her father were more serious than she'd wanted to admit. Worse, if she were a decent daughter, she wouldn't be passing the buck off to her sister—she would be here more often to help out.

Again, the long list of business tasks facing her scrolled through her head, and she wished she'd brought her executive assistant along because even if Rachel wanted to be more involved in her father's care, she didn't see how she could make time to be everywhere at once. The sheer magnitude of her to-do list was daunting.

"I should go check on him," Jackie said.

Rachel hesitated at the threshold to the house. "Okay. I'll call and check on him later. I don't want to be late for my meeting." The business side of things was where she was needed most, especially now.

She would carry on and do everything on her own—just like she'd promised her father.

• • •

Sam Sutter heard something moving in the dense patch of trees behind his house. Something big. He glanced back at his thirteen-year-old Lab mix, who was sprawled on her belly on the lawn, mauling her Sunday-morning soup bone, and figured that whatever it was, it couldn't be too ominous if Babe didn't care. But still … the heavy rumble clawed at his common sense and had him rethinking his usual walk in the woods. He didn't want any trouble.

He was just about to turn around and head back to the house when he heard faint voices. Now that was curious. Splitting a box shrub in two, Sam peered deeper into the forest that separated his property from the far edges of the old community college, but he couldn't see a dang thing other than more bark and leaves. What was going on in there?

Right about now, everyone in bucolic Arlington, Pennsylvania, was split between three places: the Catholic Church, the Presbyterian Church, or the Pancake Palace. Well, almost everyone. He was here, like he was every Sunday since he'd walked away from a budding baseball career and bought his mother's favorite log house on the end of her favorite wooded cul-de-sac.

He glanced at the shockingly blue sky like he did every time he thought of his mother and damn near jumped a foot back from the forest's edge when a god-awful clanging sent the birds fleeing the treetops.

Finally, Babe abandoned her bone and bolted past him into the thick of things. *Dumb dog,* he thought affectionately. Every other animal was running in the opposite direction.

Sam hesitated for only a second and then followed her. "Babe!" He whistled. Her barking was sure to scare away whatever was left of the birds. He looked overhead like he expected the mass exodus to continue. But there wasn't a hint of movement anywhere. Just an eerie stillness punctuated by Babe's incessant barking. And with every step, his desire to turn around and avoid whatever was going on grew.

"Babe!" He whistled again and cut around the rock-rimmed fire pit he and his father would put to good use later tonight. There was nothing like two guys nursing a six-pack and chilling under the stars. Buying this house had been the best thing Sam had done with the money he'd made from playing baseball. But those thoughts never came without the wish that he'd done so sooner—soon enough for his mother to have sat around that fire, too.

He rushed an apologetic glance skyward before he hurdled over the thick trunk of a fallen tree on his sprint toward an agitated Babe. It sounded like she had something cornered. Normally, he would've guessed a squirrel or a possum, because it was a little too early in the year for it to be a fawn, but he remembered those voices. Babe normally wasn't weird with people.

He cleared another patch of trees, and sure enough, Babe had something cornered: two people and a bright-red pickup truck towing a dozer on a trailer.

"Hey!" he yelled to his dog, and this time, he clapped. "Get over here!"

Babe looked at him, looked back at the pair who Sam was sizing up, and trotted remorsefully back to his side, where she sat.

One of the people beside the truck was a woman. And not just any woman. "Rachel Reed," he said, darn-near accusatory, recognizing her immediately despite the five or so years that had passed since the last time he'd seen her. She wore tailored, tan dress pants and a tight, white sweater, looking like a Wall Street pinup. "You're a little overdressed for a hike and awfully far from Philly, aren't you?"

A blinding smile jumped off her sun-kissed face, making her noted resemblance to Cameron Diaz even more undeniable. "Little Sammy Sutter! What are you doing here?"

"I live here," he said, gesturing in the direction of his house beyond the trees and deciding to let the "little Sammy" quip slide while they were in the presence of a stranger. "Sam Sutter," he said instead, emphasizing the adult version of his name and reaching a hand toward the broad man standing beside Rachel. "I don't believe we've met."

"Wes Allen."

"Wes is from Pittsburgh," Rachel said. "He's helping me out with a little project."

In the woods. On a Sunday. Sam glanced at the dozer, and the hairs on the back of his neck rose. "I thought all your projects were in Philly these days."

"They are. Technically this is …" She hesitated. "My father's project."

The baseball team. Sam slipped the tips of his fingers into his blue-jean pockets and nodded slowly, adopting the devil-may-care attitude he'd perfected since walking away from a Chicago Cubs affiliate team ten years ago. But his insides twisted. And that was before he noticed the Allen Tree Cutting logo on Wes's truck.

"How's Luke?" Rachel asked.

"Married."

A wicked little smile tipped her ruby lips. "Better him than me."

Absolutely. Sam's older brother was working for the family landscaping business and expecting his third child with Mandy. It was a simple, happy life. The kind of life their mother had wanted for both of them. The kind of life Luke never would've had with Miss High-Achiever here, living in some sterile Philadelphia condo surrounded by smog and cement.

Rachel had never been right for Luke. Sam's thoughts flashed back to the summer before eighth grade, Luke's senior year of high school. At the Sutter family's Labor Day picnic, Luke had sat on a picnic table bench making goofy eyes at Rachel all day instead of playing Wiffle Ball with the rest of them. They'd been just as nauseating together that whole year, much to Sam's chagrin, with his brother following Rachel around like a lapdog. Until the next Labor Day, when she'd dumped Luke the night before she left for college. Rachel Reed had made it clear she was heading places, and Luke was no longer good enough to bask in her shadow.

Looking at her through the lens of twenty years, Sam found the woman to be just as beautiful and just as irritating as ever.

Stomping all over his clearing, eyeing up his trees like she owned the place.

"Well, I don't want to keep you from your Sunday morning," she said, her tone clearly dismissive. "It was nice seeing you. Tell Luke I said hello." Again with that uppity smile.

This was the part where Sam should have politely told Rachel it was nice to see her, too, then gone on his merry way. But a warbler sounded overhead and settled a few branches above the truck.

Listen to the birds, his mother used to say. *They know when something's up.* Of course, she'd been talking about the weather, but still … it stuck with him. Sort of took on new meaning today.

Sam glanced at that damn logo on the truck again, and he couldn't stop himself. "You're not planning on cutting down these trees are you?"

"Just a little fact-finding mission," she said. "Nothing for you to worry about."

He found it hard to believe anyone needed a bulldozer on a fact-finding mission. "Some of these trees are more than two hundred years old."

"Some of these trees are impeding a parking lot expansion."

He scoffed. Damn city people and their concrete jungle obsession. "Some of these trees are on my property." But for the life of him he couldn't remember exactly where the property line ended. He also couldn't recall a damn thing about zoning ordinances and setbacks.

The warbler squawked again.

"I know exactly where your trees start and end," she said confidently. He didn't trust her, and that was before she tilted her head and regarded him through narrowed eyes. "You, of all people, must be excited about my father bringing professional baseball to Arlington."

Here we go. Sam shrugged. "I don't really follow baseball these days."

"That's a shame. Sam used to play for the ..." She looked from Wes back to Sam. "The Cubs, right?"

Sam nodded once and added, "Never made it out of the minors." Why sugarcoat it? Chasing "the bigs" in a rusty bus, believing he was the next big thing, had caused him to miss out on a lot of things. He was still trying to make up for some of them.

Again he thought of his mother, and this time the guilt was almost too much to swallow.

"What are you doing now?" Rachel asked, surprising him, not because he expected her to keep tabs on his career, but because she'd never been the kind to care much about other people—at least that had been his experience when she'd labeled him "whiny little Sammy" who was always trying to come between her and Luke.

"I'm working for my dad," he said with little genuine interest in keeping this conversation going.

"Just like me."

Except he wasn't like her, and he couldn't leave that assumption hanging between them. "We're nothing alike, Rachel. For starters, I would never even think about cutting down these trees. That would be a really shitty thing to do."

She shrugged. "What can I say, Sammy? Progress can be painful, but in the end, it's the best thing for everyone."

"Because the best thing for you is the best thing for everyone?" He scoffed. She hadn't changed one bit in twenty years. "Try telling that to the birds." Sam looked at the wide-eyed man taking this all in beside her and nodded curtly. "Nice to meet you."

But that was a lie. It would only be nice if the guy drove back to Pittsburgh without touching a single tree. If one trunk fell ... Sam hated to even think about it. Thank God his nature-loving mother wasn't alive to see this.

He wandered off with Babe beside him and the warbler overhead, craving the usual Sunday peace and quiet, but he kept hearing phantom chainsaws and wood chippers. How much parking did the Reeds need? Surely they wouldn't cut down all of this. He reached out and let almond-shaped leaves tickle his palm. But what if they did? What if he had to say goodbye to Sunday walks and evening fireside chats with his dad? And what if he had to look out his kitchen window and see a baseball stadium every damn day? He stopped. Babe stopped, too.

That was *not* going to happen.

• • •

"Whoa! That's one heck of a house," Liv said as Rachel, for the second time in as many days, guided her BMW down the winding gravel drive toward her childhood home. She'd asked Liv to gather some of her personal items and fly in last night, after it was clear that, with her father's deteriorating condition, Rachel would need to extend her time in Arlington. Having Liv here would help maximize productivity over the next five days.

"It's a little shabby right now," Rachel said, noticing misshapen box shrubs and empty flower urns. "It looks better at Christmas."

It *used* to look wonderful all year long.

Liv leaned forward, peering out the window at the vast expanse of lawn and the picturesque barn that came into full view as Rachel turned onto the governor's drive. Liv's head whipped back around, and her brows rose until her glasses slid down an inch. "Do you have horses?" she asked, excitement in her voice.

"I think there are a few left." Actually, Rachel wasn't sure. Her Christmas visit had been cut short by work, and there'd been an awful lot of changes lately.

She'd loved to ride as a child, though. When the Reeds had moved here from Manhattan the year Rachel had started first grade, this place had felt boundless and magical. All the rooms, all the green space. Eventually the trade-off proved to be too steep, though, with Rachel's father spending the weekdays working in Manhattan while Rachel's mother drowned her loneliness in excessive domesticity. By the time Rachel had reached high school, she'd grown to resent her rural exile and crave the kind of excitement and freedom her father had.

"Could we stay here while we're in town?" Liv asked. "Please! Let's ditch the Uncomfortable Inn."

"No." Rachel appreciated Liv's enthusiasm, but … "There are already too many people and too much drama under this roof. You and I need to stay focused and get back to Philadelphia as soon as possible. The office won't run itself."

"That's why you left Richard in charge."

Rachel bristled. "And that pains me." She hated handing over the reins. It made her feel incompetent. She put the car in park at the top of the circle and leveled Liv with a serious look. "Failing my father, especially under these circumstances, is not an option."

"I know," Liv said. "Alzheimer's sucks." But it was spoken with the blithe tone of a twenty-five-year-old who might as well be complaining about spotty cell service in the middle of farm country.

Rachel nodded as she pushed out of the car and sunk her heels into the pea gravel. Regardless of what shape her father was in, today was bound to go much smoother than yesterday. At least her family knew she was coming. Not to mention Sam Sutter wouldn't pop up here to cause trouble.

She'd never expected to see him yesterday. Of all the trees in all the world, it just had to be the ones butt-ending Sam's property that she needed to cut down. From the dirty looks he'd given her, she could tell he wasn't so thrilled, either, which wasn't exactly a surprise. His mother had been a nature lover. Apparently, the apple didn't fall too far from the proverbial tree. What did surprise Rachel was the fact that a gangly, preteen gnat like Sam Sutter had grown up quite nicely, something that bothered her more than it should.

Back when she'd dated his brother, Sam was always coming around and wanting Luke to play catch or go fishing or watch a baseball game—anything to get his attention off her. He'd been annoying, rude, and a definite strain on the relationship. In the end, she'd let Sam have Luke because she'd set her sights on bigger things after high-school graduation: personal and professional progress. Breaking up with Luke had been the best thing for everybody.

Because the best thing for you is the best thing for everybody? She wrinkled her nose as Sam's words echoed in her head, and then she swatted at an imaginary gnat.

Up ahead, the double doors opened, and Rachel's mother swept onto the veranda like this homecoming was nothing more than a pleasure trip. Smile in place, she had a floral cardigan wrapped around her narrow waist and her arms open in welcome. The complete opposite of yesterday. "You're just in time for breakfast. When was the last time you lovely ladies had strawberry waffles with whipped cream?"

Strawberry waffles hadn't touched Rachel's lips in years—not since she'd turned thirty and her metabolism had shit the bed. She preferred to save her calories for wine. It was much better to end the day feeling warm and fuzzy than bloated.

"Thank you," Rachel said, giving her mother the requisite stiff hug, "but we don't have time for a full-on sit-down. We have to make up for the time we lost yesterday, and then we have to prep for a conference call with the Philadelphia acquisitions team. You remember my assistant, Liv."

"Of course," Jackie said, smiling at Liv. "Welcome to our home." Then she lowered her voice and spoke in a conspiratorial tone. "Don't let her work you too hard."

"Liv is every bit as hungry as I am," Rachel assured her mother.

"Then why won't you eat!"

"That's not the kind of hungry I'm talking about. Besides, I need to drink first. The hotel's coffee is terrible."

Her mother didn't have to be told twice. Jackie headed down the open entry hall toward the kitchen. "One coffee coming right up. Black, just like your father prefers." She tossed a smile over her shoulder and then asked Liv want she wanted.

Rachel walked along in silence, thinking about that statement—*just like your father*. If she'd heard it once, she'd heard it a thousand times. They shared the same tall, willowy build. The same sunny blond hair. The same tenacity to close a deal. The same ability to disconnect from anything that didn't result in a boost to the bottom line. It was a compliment really, but Rachel couldn't muster the usual pride.

"Good morning." Rachel's sister stood at the enormous kitchen island, backlit by sunlight streaming in from the windows overlooking the picturesque pool and patio. The rays accented the ribbons of red in Helen Anne's shiny brown hair. Her smile was welcoming, her hips generous, and she favored pastels and floral patterns right down to the apron. Helen Anne was just like Mom. Normally, Rachel didn't focus on the fact that the Reed family genes were clearly divided. But this Alzheimer's thing made her think.

A slight increase in risk was still an increase.

"Good morning," Rachel said in a calm voice that didn't divulge any of the unrest brewing beneath the surface. It wasn't hard to hide her true feelings from Helen Anne. They'd been too different to ever be inseparable, even as kids, and the occasional text messages, rare phone calls, and sporadic visits over the years did nothing but widen the gap between them.

Another spitting image of Jackie Reed appeared. Macy, Helen Anne's ten-year-old daughter, was wearing an apron, too, and flaunting floured palms. "Hi, Aunt Rachel. We made waffles from scratch."

"Yum." Rachel patted her niece on the arm as she passed, determined to get to the office, and said, "Save me some for later. Liv and I have work to do."

"There's no rush," Helen Anne said. "Dad's not even up yet."

Great. He must've forgotten again. Rachel glanced back at her mother who was busying herself at the coffeepot. "Can you wake him?"

"I would rather not. He tossed and turned last night."

"What else is new?" Her father had long been an insomniac, like Rachel herself. She'd always figured it was a sign of busy minds at work, but perhaps it was just another lovely genetic snafu she'd inherited. "That's why God made liquor ... and Ambien."

"This is different." Helen Anne poured cream into the cups her mother had filled—all except one, and then she handed that one to Rachel. "Sleep disturbances are common with Alzheimer's." She didn't seem to have any trouble saying the word.

"And Dr. Rictor wants us to try non-drug strategies first," Jackie said.

The mention of Dr. Rictor reminded Rachel of the conversation she'd had with her mother yesterday, and she felt frustrated all over again ... but not frustrated enough to lose sight of her business objectives for the day.

"Do you want a waffle?" Macy asked Liv, holding up a plate of food served with a heaping side of hopefulness, and Rachel's guilt multiplied.

"Yes, she wants a waffle." Rachel forced a smile for her niece's sake. "Liv is no good to me until she's fed. I, on the other hand, will take my coffee and get to work. Liv, I'll be in my dad's office when you're done. Mom, send him my way when he wakes up." Hopefully soon.

A few steps down the long hall that led to the office, a den, and a library in a dark and quiet corner of the house, Rachel heard Helen Anne call out her name.

Rachel stopped and turned slowly, not wanting to be waylaid.

"Are we ever going to talk?" Helen Anne asked, those brown eyes wounded. "*Really* talk? There's a lot going on around here."

A lot? Rachel could tell her sister about a lot. *A lot* was executing hundreds of millions of dollars in business decisions as the Senior Vice President and Broker for Reed Commercial Real Estate Services in Philadelphia at exactly the same time you needed to be available to the Pittsburgh office to give final approval when someone so much as sneezed. *A lot* was adding to that the preparation and sale of an indie pro baseball team. But Rachel dug down deep and tried to give her sister the personal attention she apparently needed—if only to cut this conversation short. "Is the divorce final?" she asked bluntly.

Helen Anne frowned, obviously taken aback at Rachel's briskness "Yes. I got the bookstore, and he got the house." Her nose wrinkled with what Rachel could only assume was disgust. "Somehow he was able to convince the judge it was a fair trade considering Macy and I have been living here for the past year and a half. I didn't argue because I didn't want to be forced to liquidate and sell the store just so he could get his marital share." Helen Anne paused for a breath, and her exhale was shaky. "Plus, considering Dad's diagnosis, it's a good thing I'm here. Mom needs more help than she's willing to admit." There it was, the reproach Rachel had assumed her sister would have.

Warranted or not, Rachel did not want to get dragged into a discussion that would no doubt end in an argument because she didn't have time to dote on her parents like Helen Anne did. Everyone had their place in the Reed family. Rachel's role had always been financial—just like their father's. "How's Macy holding up?" she asked instead.

Helen Anne's flawless brows pulled together at the top of her nose, and Rachel knew she wasn't happy to be detoured, but she said, "Macy is fine. She's happy here, and that's the most important thing to me—that the people I love are happy." She gave Rachel a pointed look that could've been saying a couple things. But before Rachel could decide if she was to be lumped into the collection of people Helen Anne loved, her sister added, "Please tell me you're going to spend some quality time with them this week. They need you to do more than lock yourself in Dad's office."

"That's arguable," Rachel said, despite the sinking feeling in her chest. "If you saw the list of things he's asked me to do, you would change your mind."

Helen Anne rolled her eyes. "Whatever, Rachel. Since you only seem to speak business these days, then how about this? Don't sell the team. Not yet. It's the only thing he has to look forward to. On good days, it's all he can think or talk about. And he's had way more good days than bad. I'm so afraid the tables will turn if he doesn't have the team to distract him."

Reeds didn't need distractions. They tackled things head on. That's what her father would say. That's what her father had done by marching into Rachel's office two months ago with a specific plan of attack.

"Dad told me to sell the team," she said. "He's written down every last detail of how I should do it. I'm legally obligated to sell this team on his behalf, and I'm morally obligated to do it the way he wants me to do it. I gave him my word when he gave me special power of attorney."

"Which means you have the power to delay the sale if you think that's best."

"Yes, but I don't. Risky doesn't begin to describe this investment. What happens if Dad gets worse while I'm sitting on the team? What if they need money for his treatment or care? Do you want Mom to sell other assets, like the house, or me to sell the team?"

Helen Anne frowned. "They have plenty of money, Rachel. They don't need millions of liquid assets right now. I'm not asking you to never sell it, I'm asking you to buy him some time. That's all."

"I don't have that kind of time. Commercial deals take several months to close in ideal situations. In these circumstances, God only knows. I'm expecting it to take the better part of a year. Plus, I've had two investors breathing down my neck ever since Dad told them he wasn't fit to carry out the five-year plan they agreed upon. Neither of those guys is interested in running the team. In fact, they want their money back as soon as possible. So, as much as I would *love* to buy some time for various reasons, I have to follow Dad's directives and do whatever it takes to secure a lucrative and timely sale. That's my only goal here."

"Your only goal? Nice, Rachel. Really nice." Helen Anne's eyes filled with tears, and she shook her head. "God, I don't know why I expected anything else from you. You're heartless."

Then why did Rachel feel the sting of those words deep beneath her breast? "Thank you for the compliment," she said softly.

She didn't expect her younger sister to understand what it took to thrive in the business world—under the watchful eye of their father. Helen Anne had the luxury of being the wanted daughter, while Rachel had been the daughter her father had never expected. Wasn't the firstborn of a powerful man supposed to be a son? Silly. Archaic even. But he'd told her exactly that over a few glasses of whiskey and a rare failed deal. She probably should've forgotten it by now. Surely, after forty years, she'd proven herself capable of achieving anything a son could have achieved. But it lingered, powering everything she did ... just in case he still wished she'd been someone else.

With Helen Anne retracing her steps down the hall, Rachel swung open the door to her father's office with renewed vengeance. To her surprise, the light was on in the wood-paneled room, and her father was sitting behind his regal desk wearing the same Pirates robe she'd seen him in yesterday. A cell phone was pressed to his ear. The flick of his wrist drew her attention to his leather folio and legal pad. He glanced up and nodded once. It was his usual acknowledgment and silent permission that she could stay as long as she didn't interrupt him—like she had as a child.

Rachel slipped into one of the leather club chairs to watch him work, struck by how much older he appeared since she'd seen him two months ago. Probably because he wasn't showered or dressed. A weak smile tipped her lips as she took in his frantic scribbling and noted the deep creases on his forehead. Complete concentration. She leaned forward, hoping to learn something about the call, but his handwriting had always been sloppy, and reading it upside down was an even greater struggle. Something about … trees.

"Can you repeat that?" More writing followed a frustrated sigh.

"Dad," she whispered, tapping her hand silently on the desk. "Put the call on speaker."

He looked at her and nodded, despite the tension on his face.

"I figured you would want to know Sutter came in here," said the voice on the phone.

Usually that last name conjured images of Luke Sutter in tears when Rachel had announced she had no plans of settling for a life in Arlington. With him. She hadn't said that last part, but it was clearly implied, and she had no regrets. Luke had been a good high-school boyfriend, but she'd been a confident eighteen-year-old with plans to take over the business world. Knowing he was back here waiting for her would've been nothing but a distraction to her grand plan. Just like his little brother was now.

But there was nothing little about Sam Sutter anymore.

Distant memories of Luke yielded to a stark image of Sam. Surely she'd seen him a time or two over the last twenty years, but if she had, he hadn't made an impression like this. Rough and rugged. Denim and flannel. A raw masculinity that was untempered by tailored suits and MBA-honed manners. She would have to be dead not to appreciate that. She would also have to be a teenager again to let it take up more than a passing thought.

Rachel spun the legal pad around and read the chicken scratch, putting the pieces together. Sam was complaining about the parking lot because he didn't want the trees cut down.

"He has no grounds for a protest," she said with certainty. "It isn't his property. I have the surveys committed to memory. I walked the grounds with Wes, and I've done the math. We'll be well within the fifteen-foot setback."

The voice on the other end of the phone stuttered with surprise.

"That's my daughter, Rachel. You're on speaker."

"Okay. Uh, the property line isn't the issue," the man said. "Sutter mentioned something about endangered balsam poplar trees and migratory bird patterns. We have to get an expert to look into those things."

Rachel swore under her breath. "How long will that take?"

"A couple weeks."

"No. A couple days. Tops. If there's nothing in the local ordinances to stop us from expanding on property we own, then we're moving forward as planned. We aren't going to go looking for obstacles."

"Suit yourself, but you might want to work it out with Sutter before you fire up those chainsaws. All he needs is a neighbor or two to back him up in filing a formal complaint. Then I'll have no choice but to halt the cutting until the experts have had their say."

Wonderful. Helen Anne might be getting more time after all.

"Okay. I'll talk to him," her father said, and it shocked the hell out of Rachel, because Reeds didn't pander to anyone. Where was his famous edge?

When he hung up, Rachel said, "We aren't really going to talk to Sam Sutter. Right? We don't owe him anything. It's our property. Once the two days pass, if the city gives us the go-ahead, we clear the lot and move on. Worst-case scenario, they fine us."

He steepled his hands and bounced them off his lips. "Give one, take one, Rachel. Remember?"

She did, and she was comforted he remembered, too. "The golden rule of closing a deal."

He nodded. "The success of this team is going to hinge on the people of Arlington getting behind it. And the sale of the team could very well hinge on the success of the team. We don't need bad blood between us and the Sutters and however many people Sam can get behind him."

It made sense. In fact, if not for the pajamas and the unorganized, written thoughts on the page in front of him, Rachel would've simply sat back and admired the cunning business prowess of the man she'd spent the last twenty-plus years emulating. Instead, she wondered how long before conversations like these were an impossibility. Could the doctors have been wrong? And if they weren't, was her father powerful enough to conquer the unconquerable?

A knock on the door saved Rachel from answering the gloomy questions.

When Danny called out, "Come in," Liv poked her head around the doorjamb. "Oh," she said to Rachel's father, "Mr. Reed, people are looking for you."

"What people?"

"These people." Rachel's mother walked in. "You scared the life out of me, Danny. I went to check on you in bed, but you were gone."

"I'm here."

"I see that." A smile replaced the worry. "Now, will you please get dressed? Liv doesn't want to see you in your pajamas." Under her breath she added something about eating and taking medication.

Rachel watched in surprise as her normally autonomous father followed his wife's lead.

"Everything okay?" Liv asked when the door closed.

"Fine," Rachel said, but the second she said it, she remembered Sam. "I hope. Apparently Sam Sutter has a problem with us cutting down trees to build a bigger parking lot."

"Who's Sam Sutter?"

"The brother of a guy I dated in high school. So, in other words, nobody important—except, he might be a credible threat to moving forward with this expansion, so we need to neutralize him."

"Ooh. Sounds exciting."

"Hopefully not."

Excitement with Sam Sutter was the last thing Rachel needed.

Chapter Two

Rachel's Tuesday had started off a lot like her Monday—drinking a lousy cup of something you couldn't call coffee while she sat on her bed at the Uncomfortable Inn looking over to-do lists and timelines for the upcoming baseball season. She gave up just a few sips in, dumped the bitter brew, and headed out to Starbucks with Liv in tow.

Big mistake.

"Maybe it would be faster to go inside?" Rachel stared, bleary-eyed, at the snaking line of cars and trucks in front of her.

"Maybe it would be faster to go to Buster's Bagels." Liv pointed across the street where the empty drive-thru lane beckoned.

"There's a reason everyone is in this line."

"Yeah. People are lemmings."

"No. Buster's coffee is mud water." She glanced into the rearview mirror and saw the line growing behind her. "They keep right on coming."

"Lemmings," Liv said again. "Don't forget we have a meeting with Arlington Staffing in twenty minutes."

Rachel growled a muddle of swear words as she overheard the boisterous driver of the car at the front placing his order for a triple-foam-no-fat-half-cap-latte whatever. "Straight coffee should be the only thing they serve in the drive-thru," she said, drumming her fingers on the wheel.

Edging the car closer to the bumper of the pickup in front of her, she debated her options. Wait and possibly be late, which was incredibly unprofessional and completely unlike her. Skip the coffee altogether, which meant the edge she was feeling now would carry through the meeting and bring along a headache that would last all day regardless of how much coffee she managed to drink later. Or … She watched one lonely car roll up to the drive-thru at Buster's Bagels. The driver received his coffee in record time. Maybe the mud water had gotten better over the years.

"Fine." She whipped the steering wheel to the right and pulled out of the line. "You said you wanted the Arlington experience while we were here. We're getting Buster's."

Liv laughed as Rachel wound erratically through the crowded plaza parking lot. "How bad can it be?"

"Remember you said— Shit!" Rachel slammed on the brakes, narrowly missing a huge black truck that cut across the empty spaces at the top of her aisle. "Idiot." An idiot who looked familiar, but she'd only had a split-second peek at his profile. "There are lines in this lot for a reason!"

"I think that truck said 'Sutter' on the door. Isn't that the name of …"

Of course it was! Rachel floored the gas and raced toward the exit.

Liv let out a terrified laugh. "What are you doing?"

"Exiting the right way and showing Mr. Sutter you don't have to cheat to get ahead."

"But you're speeding. Isn't that cheating?"

Rachel tuned Liv out and, while fully staying inside the lines, managed to cut off Sam at the exit. She looked into the rearview mirror and made smug eye contact with him. "Ladies first, asshole."

She shared a victorious laugh with Liv, but her satisfaction didn't last long. Sam sped past her at the light and then turned left through the intersection, leaving her staring at the massive Sutter & Sons Landscaping logo on the tailgate.

"So is *that* how you're going to neutralize him? By beating him out of the parking lot?" Liv asked.

"No, but …" *Ding, ding, ding.* Rachel's eyes widened. "We need a grounds crew, don't we?"

Liv looked momentarily confused. "Uh, yes."

"Sutter & Sons Landscaping." Rachel grinned. "That's an interesting coincidence, don't you think?"

"I suppose."

"It's kind of hard to bite the hand that's feeding you, isn't it?"

Liv nodded slowly. "I think I see where you're going with this."

Rachel, flushed with pure adrenaline, pulled into traffic and eyed up Buster's. "I'm going to get my mud water first, then I'm going to get the stadium staffed with ticket sellers and vendors, and then I'm going to make Sam Sutter's father an offer he can't refuse, thereby neutralizing his pain-in-the-ass son." She high-fived Liv.

• • •

Three hours later, Rachel strolled into the office of Sutter & Sons Landscaping with one eye on the lookout for her ex and the other eye watching for Sam. This meeting would go much smoother if their father, Paul, was the only one home.

"Can I help you?" The elder Sutter walked into the reception area from another room. His hair was thinning, and the skin around his eyes and mouth sagged, but he still managed to look soft and approachable like he had when she was in high school.

"Mr. Sutter, it's nice to see you again."

He looked at Rachel, looked at Liv, and then back to Rachel again. A slow smile balled his cheeks. "Well, I'll be …" He opened his arms to her as if she'd never left Arlington, never broken his oldest son's heart. "Rachel Reed. Get over here!"

Something about jovial Paul Sutter made hugging your ex's father completely normal, so she did, and then she introduced Liv, and he hugged her, too, like he'd known her all his life. "What brings you two beauties to my office today? Luckiest man in Arlington right here." He patted his chest and kept right on talking. "Can't remember the last time I saw you. Years."

"A long time," Rachel said.

"Seems like yesterday. You never age. Me, on the other hand." He rubbed his beer belly and smiled.

The door behind them opened, and Rachel turned to see Luke come to a screeching halt. His familiar blue eyes went wide, as if he hadn't seen her in the last twenty years. In actuality, he had. A handful of times. And while he was much worse at hiding his surprise than she hopefully was, she did feel a jolt each time she saw him. His eyes might be familiar, but the rest of him had changed. He was unmistakably middle-aged. Heavier, balder, and … happier, somehow. A lot like his father.

She smiled. "Hi, Luke."

"Hey." His expression turned from shock to curiosity. "I heard you were in town." Probably from Sam. She squared her shoulders at the thought of him.

Luke glanced at Liv, and Rachel introduced them.

"This is Ian Pratt." Luke gestured to a twenty-something, buff young guy behind him, who was obviously one of his landscaping staff. Pretty face, nice build, but probably short on IQ.

"Nice to meet you both," Ian said.

He had a firm handshake and made direct eye contact. Bonus points for the kid. Rachel watched him shake hands with Liv, who hadn't said anything since the guys walked in. And who was shaking the man's hand a little too vigorously while she breathed through parted lips. *Oh, brother.* Apparently Liv had a weak spot for the stereotypical landscaper type.

"What brings you here?" Luke asked carefully, giving them all some semblance of direction.

"Business, actually." Rachel happily turned to Paul and got things back on track. "Mr. Sutter, could I have a minute of your time?"

"Why certainly!" He pointed to the open door of the room behind him. "Make yourselves at home. Coffee on the counter is fresh. Give me five minutes to get these guys settled, and then you'll have my full attention."

"Excellent." Rachel glanced back at Luke, who—if she wasn't mistaken—looked a little worried. "Nice seeing you again." No hard feelings and all that.

Liv closed the door behind them and made a beeline for the coffeepot.

"Craving something other than mud water, aren't you?" Rachel sat at the table and pulled her iPad out of her leather tote. "I'll take a cup, too."

No response.

"Liv?"

She turned, leaned a hip against the counter, and looked at the door. "That Ian guy," she whispered. "He's kind of hot."

Rachel laughed. "We need to work on your transparency."

"Why?"

"I knew what you were thinking the minute you shook the man's hand."

"Great." Liv rolled her eyes and turned back to the coffeepot.

"Oh, big deal. It's not like you're ever going to see him again."

"True." Liv slid a foam cup across the table to Rachel as the door opened and Paul walked in.

"Okay, ladies," he said. "Let's talk business. You've got me plenty curious."

Rachel tapped the screen, bringing her iPad to life, and spun it in his direction. "Let me cut to the chase, Mr. Reed. My father needs a grounds crew for the new stadium, and we were wondering if you might be interested."

Paul's eyes widened like Luke's had. "Damn right I am."

Checkmate, Sam.

. . .

Sam navigated through the glare of the setting sun and pulled his quad-cab pickup truck toward the massive outbuilding where the landscaping equipment was stored at the end of every day. He was towing a tandem axle trailer weighed down with gas cans, commercial mowers, weed-whackers, leaf blowers—anything and everything a man needed to make sure the grass was greener on his side. And all of it had to be hosed down before it could be put away for the night. At least he had Randy to help him.

He glanced at the late-winter hire who was white-knuckling the overhead grip, apparently still not used to Sam's driving. "It's the ruts in the road, not me this time."

Randy nodded. "I thought that lady was going to kill us this morning. Road rage."

More like parking-lot rage. *Rachel freaking Reed.* "She doesn't want to kill us; she wants to kill my trees."

"What trees?"

"In my backyard. It's … never mind. It's not your problem. Besides, I think I have a handle on it. I spoke to someone at the municipal building and threw around my extensive dendrological knowledge," he teased.

"What the hell is that?"

"Knowledge about trees, man, and I have a lot of that." He grinned and puffed out his chest, then set his sights on his brother, Luke, who was up ahead already unloading his trailer with the help of Ian. Sam laid on the horn and laughed when the two men jumped.

Luke playfully flipped him the bird and went back to hosing off the underside of a mower. He waited for Sam to climb out of his truck to say, "Where the hell have you been?"

Sam made a face. "What do you mean where the hell have I been?" He gestured to his sweaty, grimy clothes. "Where does it look like I've been?"

"That's not what I meant. You're later than usual, and …" He cut the water and dropped the hose, looking suddenly serious. "We had a visitor today."

Sam glanced at Ian, who was smiling like the carefree goof he was. "You two had a visitor?"

"No, the office had a visitor," Luke said, and then he fake shuddered. "Rachel was here."

The hairs on the back of Sam's neck rose. "Why?"

"I don't know, but she wanted to talk business with Dad, which seemed weird—even weirder than seeing her in the office." Luke looked a little green around the gills when he hitched his head toward Ian. "We had to leave for an afternoon job, so I never got a chance to find out what happened. Now I'm not sure I want to know." Sam turned and made a beeline for the house. "Unload the truck, kid."

"Where are you going?" Luke asked.

"To find out why *that woman* was here."

By the time Sam reached the house, Luke had caught up with him, and when they walked into the office, their father was grinning from ear to ear.

"Why are you smiling like that?" Luke asked.

"Why do I sense impending doom?" Sam rubbed the hairs on the back of his neck and braced himself for a changeup.

He hated changeups. He'd struggled with the pitch from Little League on. There was something fundamentally evil about staring down what looked to be the perfect fastball, knowing you could blast it out of the stratosphere, only to realize too late it was taking too long to cross the plate.

"We have a new contract, boys. A big one!" Their father reached behind him and cracked open three beers as he announced, "You're looking at the official field crew for the Arlington Aces."

"Son of a bitch," Sam said.

"That's why Rachel was here?" Luke asked.

"Yep, and it's a good deal, a lucrative one."

"It's crazy," Luke said, which was exactly what Sam had been thinking.

"Are you worried what Mandy will think about you working with your ex-girlfriend and her family?" their father asked.

Luke scoffed. "No. I'm worried about how a staff of four—five, including you—can take on such a big project at the height of our work season without knowing what the hell we're doing. Field care is a science, Dad."

"I'm hiring more people. Already posted a couple ads. And we're going to learn all there is to learn about grounds keeping. So there. Problems solved. And just in case you're worried about Mandy, Sam is in charge over at the field."

"The hell I am," Sam said. "I don't want to be in charge."

"Why not? You know baseball fields better than any of us."

Exactly.

"Besides," their father added, "it might do you some good to get back out there."

"On a lawn mower?" Sam's neck heated until a thin bead of sweat slipped down his back. "You've got to be kidding me."

"Does all equipment provided and fifteen grand per season, plus additional hourly charges to consult with us on exterior stadium landscaping, sound like I'm kidding?"

Luke whistled. "That'll buy us those new Husqvarnas."

"Damn straight it will."

Sam shook his head wildly. "We don't need new equipment."

"Speak for yourself," Luke said. "That mower I'm using is on its last leg."

"What about Ian?" Sam suggested. "He knows his way around a ball field, and he's ready for more responsibility around here. Give it to him."

"Ian's not my son," Paul boomed. "How would it look for Ian to be managing our biggest account?"

Sam didn't really care how it looked. He just didn't want to be subjected to tooling around an infield on a mower while Rachel Reed looked on with those bright eyes and that smug smile.

"Your mother wanted this."

And just like that, all the breathable air was sucked out of the room. Heavy and stale. Sam tried not let his discomfort show.

"She used to bug me to go after commercial contracts all the time," their father continued. "She mentioned it more than once those last few weeks. 'Grow the business, Paul. Take care of the kids.' You know she meant grandkids, too." He looked at Luke and smiled. "At least you got that memo."

Because Luke had been there, at their mother's bedside, while she was making her wishes known. Sam, on the other hand, had been standing on first base in Eugene, Oregon, thinking the worst thing that could happen to him was being stuck in Short Season Single-A.

He'd been terribly wrong.

"You sure you don't want to head this up?" Sam asked Luke, one last-ditch effort to escape the inevitable.

Luke gave him a look. "I'm sure. I have no interest whatsoever in Rachel Reed, but Dad's right. This is Arlington. People will talk, and Mandy will hear it." He looked exhausted just at the thought of any drama. He'd always been a low-key kind of guy, one who'd thought Sam was crazy wanting a life of fame and fortune. "No, thanks."

Sam felt his back against the proverbial wall and momentarily thought about bringing up the trees. His mother wouldn't want business progress at the expense of nature, but … his father looked so damn proud. Maybe he could buy some time and figure out a way to make them both happy. "Fine. I'll do it," he said. "But only because it's important to you … and Mom."

"That a boy!" Paul pulled him into a hearty hug and then passed out beers. "A toast to our first commercial contract. May it be long and lead to many more."

Sam raised his beer even as he continued to think about what this meant for the trees. He'd planned to follow up tomorrow morning just to make sure his concerns were being taken seriously. But how could he go head-to-head with the family who'd just given his father the professional chance of a lifetime? He couldn't. At least not blatantly. He would need to try a different tactic. Maybe a little diplomacy. Or … an inside job. He had the access now. *Plus additional hourly charges to consult with us on exterior stadium landscaping.*

"I'll be the point of contact for the exterior stadium landscaping, right?" he asked.

His father nodded. "Of course."

"Excellent." Those trees could be lumped under the umbrella of exterior stadium landscaping. All Sam needed to do now was make them look like an asset rather than an obstacle.

He raised his beer again in silent toast.

Checkmate, Rachel.

Chapter Three

"What's next?" Rachel asked Liv as their heels click-clacked in unison down the cement hallway of a stadium that was looking less and less like a former community-college field and more and more worthy of a money-making baseball team.

"Well, with Mark Olean on board as general manager, we're ready to hire the rest of the coaching staff."

Rachel nodded confidently. "How hard can that be? My father has the pool whittled down and rankings assigned. I'll go over the applications to make sure he hasn't overlooked anything, and then we'll consult with Mark and set up some interviews. Let's see ..." She looked at her phone for the time and date. "It's Wednesday, which means we can try to schedule some Skype interviews for next week when we're back in Philly."

"Sounds good to me." Liv busied herself with her iPad. "Oh, wait."

Rachel kept on walking. "Wait for what?"

"You asked what was next. What's next on your schedule is a meeting with the new grounds crew. I didn't sync my calendars so I ..."

Sam. Liv's voice faded out, and Rachel picked up her pace. She was actually looking forward to seeing him again. Watching him squirm was going to be fun.

"Do me a favor, please," Rachel said. "Go up to the office and get a jump-start on going through those applications. I've printed out most of the top contenders. Make sure they all get printed so I can take a closer look at them and run things past my father."

"You don't want backup with Sam Sutter?" Liv teased.

"You're just hoping Ian is with him, aren't you?"

Liv's gasp turned into a laugh. "Absolutely not. In fact, I'm more than eager to go through those applications." She darted toward an exit to the stairs.

"Thank you," Rachel called out as she stepped into the bright sunshine and took a breath of crisp, early-March air. Up ahead, the new grounds crew waited, looking like a three-pack of frat boys turned loose on a baseball field. Two young men she'd never seen before sat in a row on the baseline railing while Ian tossed them what looked like a balled-up sock.

Suddenly her plan didn't seem so smart. Yes, this was indie pro ball and nobody was expecting the Yankees field crew, but a little professionalism, please. And where was Sam? She scanned the field. No sign of him. She'd been pretty clear about wanting him involved because of his history with baseball. Surely Paul didn't think this band of misfits could do the job unsupervised. That was not part of her plan.

A door opened to her right, narrowly missing her on the follow-through, and Sam appeared.

"Sorry. My bad." He stepped back and smiled, a charming expression that probably put most women at ease, but not Rachel. She got the feeling he was up to something, considering his not-so-charming parting shot to her in the woods. "I was using the facilities," he said.

She nodded, thankful to have years of experience with charismatic men who thought they could manipulate any situation. That gave her the upper hand. "I see you walk like you drive," she said evenly. "Hopefully you're better with a lawn mower."

That wiped the smile off his face. Good. Lest he forget who was in charge around here.

She walked on toward the field.

"Me? Jesus, you're the worst driver I've ever seen," he said, disintegrating into shades of the whiny kid he used to be. "How fast were you going?"

"Fast enough to beat you."

"Oh, I see how it is." He fell into step beside her.

She side-eyed him. "And how is it?"

"Same old Rachel. Always determined to win."

She huffed. "Please. I don't think being a better driver is something I can really count as a—"

"Not that," he sneered, cutting her off. "The trees. You want me to back off, so you can pave paradise and put up a parking lot, right? That's what giving us this contract was about."

Ooh. Perceptive. Maybe she'd underestimated little Sammy Sutter. Rachel stopped, giving them plenty of space before they were within earshot of the other men. Then she faced Sam and boldly lied. "This is not about the trees."

He grinned, and despite the devilish bent to the expression, he looked beautiful. "You thought by hiring my father's company to take care of this field, I'd be so grateful for the lucrative contract that I'd just roll over and let you have your way."

She exhaled, releasing a troubling sudden mental image of Sam in a compromising position. "You are here because my father's stadium needs a grounds crew, and I was given explicit directions to keep things local where applicable."

"No ulterior motives?"

"People always have ulterior motives, Sam."

He crossed his arms over his broad chest and narrowed his eyes. "You would know all about that, wouldn't you?"

She had a feeling he was referring to her relationship with his brother, but she wasn't sure how much Luke would've shared with a middle schooler. "What's that supposed to mean?"

"Nothing." Sam dropped his arms and looked away from her for a second before he sighed. "Fine, the contract isn't a bribe. Whatever. Are you still going to cut down those trees?"

"Yes. Are you still going to try to stop me?"

"Yes."

"Is that why you tried to run me over the other day—to get me out of the way?"

He laughed, a deep and alarmingly sexy laugh. "Come on now, Rachel. You can't be serious. I wouldn't kill someone over a few acres of trees. We would have to be talking about several hectares."

Whatever that meant. She rolled her eyes. "I'm not impressed."

He stepped forward, crowding her space. "I'm sure the only thing that impresses you is a big, fat bank account."

She narrowed her eyes at him and said, "Guilty," even as she admired the sheer size of him. Tall. Wide. Solid. And he had the most beautiful eyes. A soft brown with flecks of gold that flashed in the sun and hypnotized her. *What the hell?*

Sam Sutter wasn't even her type. For God's sake, she was forty. She didn't have a type. She had gentleman friends who took her to dinner, toasted her accomplishments with an expensive Bordeaux, and gave her utilitarian orgasms when she needed some stress relief. Sam Sutter was what? Mid-thirties now? In tired blue jeans with a good-ole-boy smile, driving a beat-up pickup truck. *Hell no.* She did not need to be impressed by him.

But that smile … Slow and low, it tipped the left corner of his mouth more than the right and supercharged the sparkle in his eyes.

"You've created a very interesting situation here." He tipped his head down toward hers.

She nearly flinched, unsettled by the proximity. "I don't know what you mean."

"I think you do. It's a little blast from the past. You and me bickering over the only thing we have in common. Back then it was Luke. Now it's the trees." He raised his brows. "I won the first battle. Remember?"

"Because I resigned."

"Maybe. Or maybe it was because you couldn't handle me."

Her neck heated, and her face flushed. Why was she getting such a charged heat from such a ridiculous conversation? Probably because time had honed Sam's rudeness into some semblance of wit and had turned his gangly body into what looked like something carved from pure granite. "Just cut the damn grass!" she said, unable to hide her exasperation.

This was not at all how she'd expected their interaction to go.

"I need to do a hell of a lot more than cut your grass," he said, a slight growl beneath his words as he leaned even closer for one long second that had her holding her breath. His smile turned wolfish then, and Rachel could tell he was fully aware that he'd rattled her cage. She almost growled herself, thinking that may have been his plan all along. But Sam backed off, sweeping the frayed ball cap off his head and running a hand through his hair as he surveyed the patchy infield. "I need to reseed it. From what I could tell, a couple million kernels of Kentucky blue. Do I have the budget for that?"

Rachel had no idea. She only hoped a couple million kernels was landscaper speak for a couple million seeds of grass, something that couldn't possibly cost too much. "Draft a proposal of everything the stadium needs to look impressive on opening day, and I'll let you know what can be done."

"Inside and out?" he asked.

She'd been talking mainly about the field, but ... "Yes, the landscaping around the entrance gates is a little shabby, too. Whatever you can do to spruce that up a bit and make a good first impression. But please, try to use some of what we already have." Her budget was already straining.

"Excellent," he said. And something in his tone made her straighten.

Sam was definitely sharper than she'd given him credit for, and he'd admitted to still wanting to block the tree cutting. She couldn't imagine him being selfish enough to do anything that would cost his father this contract, but then again, she didn't know him that well. She didn't know the adult version of him at all.

Boys!" he called behind her. "Get on over here and meet the woman in charge so we can get busy and cut some grass." He glanced at her, and then he lowered his voice. "I'm going to win this battle, too, Rachel. Mark my words. The trees are going to stay."

"Good luck with that," she said dryly.

"It's nice to know I have your blessing."

Then he smiled that knowing, wolfish grin again. Thank God she would be back in Philadelphia this time next week. She didn't need to be wasting time playing head games with Sam Sutter.

• • •

Wednesdays were normally Sam's light days in February and March. He spent those afternoons pruning Mrs. Deacon's extensive collection of wisteria, evergreens, and landscape trees. He took his time, because pruning was an art, something he'd learned in the depressing, confusing years following his exit from baseball. He also never topped off. Stub cuts and heading cuts shocked the hell out of a tree and made it vulnerable to everything from sunburn and insect invasion to death. Not on his watch. What had started out as a way to make a buck and fill his baseball-free time had turned into true passion. Sam took his trees seriously.

But on this last Wednesday in February, he was standing in the middle of center field with a clear blue sky overhead, trying to calm himself down. Sam Sutter was on a baseball field again. Something he'd sworn he would never do. Of course, it wasn't quite the same—not like he was picking up a bat or anything. Still, it was surreal.

Sensations bombarded him. The colliding smells of sun-dried grass and damp dirt in his nose. A warm, post-rain wind in his face. And the feeling of vast nothingness that somehow filled up every hollow space inside of him. The memories followed. A full count. Martinez, who'd been rehabbing in Double-A, on the mound. Sam could've sworn the imaginary crack of the bat had been audible. His muscles fired like he should be sprinting to first base, like he'd done that April day all those years ago, when he was so damn sure his big-league dreams were about to come true. Home run. Off Martinez. Sam was on his way. Only he wasn't. The changeup always seemed to get the best of him.

That's why you're standing in the middle of an old community-college outfield, idiot.

He took a deep breath, ignored the sensory overload, and pulled his hands out of his pockets so he could get to work.

"It's not in bad shape," Ian called from his perch atop the visitors' dugout.

It looked like hell. Clumps and divots. A drainage problem at third. A lip from the clay to the grass. Sam shook his head. "You're only saying that because you play on a sandlot. This condition"—Sam squatted to pick up and toss away a clump of clay that had somehow found its way to the outfield—"will not cut it in professional baseball." Even at a level lower than Single-A.

Ian met him at the pitcher's mound, which was scary looking.

"Okay, so this is dangerous," Ian said.

Sam knelt again and scraped a handful of earth off the hill. It came away much too easily. "Wrong kind of clay." He stood up and studied the area. "Wrong angle, too."

"I don't know. There's something else." Ian trotted backward toward home plate. "Let me get a good look." He squatted behind the plate, elbows to knees, and pumped a fist into his palm as if he were wearing mitt. "That's better."

Catchers. They were pieces of work. "And what does the expertise gained during four years of small college ball tell you?"

Ian popped back up in one fluid motion. "It tells me the distance is too damn short."

Sam stood atop the mound to make his own assessment. "I don't think so."

"You're not a pitcher, man. That's not your view. Take a look at it from here."

"What's that going to prove? I'm not a catcher, either."

"You're a batter. A damn good one, if I remember right."

He *was* a batter. Sam swallowed a wave of discomfort and walked slowly toward home plate.

"I'm telling you, it's short," Ian said.

Before Sam stepped on home and turned around to face the hill, he took a deep breath, hoping to clear his head. When he looked, he couldn't tell if it was short or not. He was too busy tryout to fight off the ghosts of pitchers he'd faced.

"What do you think?" Ian asked.

That, ex-girlfriend or not, Luke should be heading up this project. He was the oldest. The oldest son should get the shiny new contract. The youngest son had walked away from baseball and should be allowed to maintain his distance. But Luke wasn't here. Sam was. For better or for worse, and after that weirdly charged conversation with Rachel, he figured things could go either way. So, he exhaled and focused on the worn grass between home and the hill. His eyes narrowed. His hands twitched. Even his feet responded as if they were on autopilot, widening his stance and shifting his weight. Sam Sutter was standing at home again.

Home.

"Do you think it's too short?" Ian asked.

"Maybe." Sam's voice sounded rough in his ears, so he cleared his throat, stood a little straighter, and shoved his hands into his pockets. "But we shouldn't be worrying about it now. Let's make a list of the materials we need first. We can take official measurements later."

Over the next hour, they developed a decent plan of attack and fairly accurate figures for rehabbing the field. The longer they lingered, the more comfortable Sam felt in his skin. Being here. Fielding the memories. It was all good, because now came the part where he would save those trees.

"I'm going to take a quick walk around the outside of the stadium and look at what can be salvaged." Rachel had given him the perfect jumping-off point when she'd asked him to keep whatever he could. Why not keep those trees? That would save the Reeds a bundle.

Ian, who'd gone back to worrying about the distance between home plate and the pitcher's mound, nodded. "Text if you need me. I'm going to measure this once and for all."

Outside the stadium, Sam strolled the sidewalk with his eyes on the thick patch of trees that shielded his backyard from the ball field. There had to be a good three acres between where he was standing and the tree line, with about an acre already covered in cement and lined for parking. How many people could they cram into this stadium? 4K? 5? How many cars did that mean? Off the top of his head, he had no clue. He needed a piece of paper, a pen, and some time to work it out. Some days his biggest regret was not having a college degree, but then he remembered all he really needed was a calculator.

He kept walking around the backside of the stadium, where undeveloped land stretched out for miles. Why couldn't the Reeds use this? Add a right-field entrance? Or hell, just make people use the legs God had given them to walk to the nearest gate. That sounded reasonable. Cutting down half an acre of trees so you could lay another two acres of parking lot, which may or may not be used on a regular basis, didn't.

Buoyed, Sam headed back into the stadium to tell Ian to pack it up. They could work on parking lot-focused word problems over a beer at Foley's. But when he reached the field, Ian wasn't there. Maybe he'd gone back to the truck.

Sam pulled his phone from his pocket and was about to text Ian when he was startled by a distinctive crack. He spun around in time to see a ground ball racing toward him in an erratic pattern over the shitty grass.

"Fielder's choice!" Ian yelled, and that's when Sam saw him down the third-base line almost in the dugout.

Sam locked eyes on the ball again, and despite his body's natural inclination to scoop it, he hesitated and wound up trapping it with his foot instead.

"What the hell was that?" Ian asked. "Garbage." Then he looked behind him into the dugout and added, "I would give you another shot, but that's the only ball I could find."

"Forget about it. We have things to do."

"Oh, come on! One time. Give it here." He held up his outstretched left hand.

Sam froze. *Go on. Humor the man. It's not a big deal.* At least it wasn't supposed to be a big deal. But he stood there, looking at the ball as if it were a foreign object. Finally, slowly, he bent over and grabbed it. Soft and gritty. Maybe a little waterlogged, too. Nothing like the snow-white, silky smooth baseballs from his past. God, how he'd loved to scuff the hell out of those with one swing. He squeezed the ball over and over again as he wandered a few steps forward.

"Are you going to throw it or kiss it?" Ian asked, and that's when Sam realized he was standing at first base. There was no bag, but the angle was spot-on. A first baseman never forgot this view.

Sam's breathing shuttered. How big of a mistake would it be to finally admit how much he missed this game?

A noisy flock of birds attracted attention overhead.

"They'd better not unload!" Ian yelled with a laugh. And all Sam could do was look skyward, remembering how his mother had encouraged him to race flocks just like that when he'd been a kid. He'd never had a chance of beating them, but there'd been no better early training for the sixty-yard dash. So long ago. Another lifetime.

He dropped the ball, motioned for Ian, and walked off the field. The only thing he was going to admit was what he'd been admitting for the last ten years: he'd let his mother down because he'd put baseball first. He wasn't going to let her down again.

When Ian caught up with him, Sam said, "You up for a beer?"

"Hell yeah. And can I add you're a lot more fun to work with than your brother—even if you won't pick up a ball."

"I picked up a ball."

"Okay. Then maybe next time we can get you to throw it."

Fat chance. "No time to be messing around, man. We need to put our thick heads together and hash out some numbers."

"There's way too much math involved in landscaping," Ian said, laughing. "Who knew?"

Sam would've laughed, too, if he wasn't staring at those damn trees again. They needed to be his driving purpose, now. He couldn't afford to let baseball distract him.

Chapter Four

At eight o'clock on Friday morning, Rachel's last day in Arlington—*thank God*—Mark Olean called her mobile phone, which connected through her BMW's hands-free calling.

"I've been trying to get a hold of your father," he said. "I've left multiple voicemails with no response. Today, I called his office, and they referred me to you."

Rachel suppressed the alarm that came with the knowledge that her father either wasn't getting or was forgetting important voicemails and asked, "What can I do for you?"

"Well, I know I said I'd be in town this weekend and ready to start, but something urgent has come up, and I need until next month to get things settled here. I plan to work remotely as much as possible as long as it's okay with your father."

Rachel closed her eyes briefly. "Mark, we really need you here."

"I know, but I really need to be here right now. If I could tell you more, I would. I just … I understand if you want to cut ties and hire someone else."

"No." That was the last thing she wanted to explain to her father. Securing Mark Olean had been his top objective. "We'll manage." Somehow.

When Rachel disconnected the call, she swore under her breath.

"That sucks," Liv said. "Olean was supposed to take over for us and act as point for hiring the rest of the front-office staff. Now what? Can he do that from a distance?"

"Not easily," Rachel said, and she zipped around a loudly painted plumbing van doing 20 in a 35-miles-per-hour zone. "What choice do we have but to let him try? We have other responsibilities." Despite lengthy, nightly phone calls with Richard,

Rachel still felt out of the loop when it came to their business dealings in Philadelphia, and she still had to find some time to get to Pittsburgh for some face time with the senior management team.

"Right, so you and I leave today as planned. And the people from the temp agency, who are starting on Monday will just … wing it?"

Not to mention the cowboy grounds crew Rachel had hired. They would definitely need to be corralled now and then, especially once Sam got word local government officials had given the green light for the tree cutting. Something about those dirty jeans and that cocky smile made her think he would rebel.

Rachel hated the fact that a tiny piece of her wanted to be around to see that.

She exhaled loudly. "Maybe my father can hold it together long enough to get us through until Mark gets here."

"Maybe," Liv said, but when Rachel glanced at her, she saw the look of doubt.

"Damn it." But even as she tightened her grip on the steering wheel, she refused to unleash her panic. "Let's think this through, shall we? Technically, the only people from the temp agency we need to worry about right now are the ones manning the telephones and preseason ticket sales. They start on Monday, and we have a software rep scheduled to train them. He confirmed, right?"

"Yes," Liv said. "His flight arrives tonight, and I set him up with a rental car and a room at the Uncomfortable Inn. Mark was supposed to meet him for breakfast, but since Mark's not coming in now, I'll have to make sure those plans get changed."

"We can hang back tonight and take him to dinner, explain the situation. I'll see if my father is able to come. That will buy us some time. In the meantime, see if you can set up a meeting with the sales lead. What was her name?"

"Um ..." Liv's fingers raced over the screen of her iPad. "Chelsea Gross."

"Yes, her. Get me a meeting with her. I'll decide whether or not I think she can handle a little more responsibility than originally planned." Rachel lifted her cup from the console and pressed it to her lips. "I can always come back next week sometime and check in on the ticket office to make sure things are running smoothly."

"So Chelsea will be the only on-site person in charge ... of everything?"

Rachel swallowed her tasteless coffee and thought of some local girl who'd been hired to sell season tickets landing in what could be perceived as a remote power position over the likes of a motley janitorial crew and Sam Sutter with his trusty frat-boy sidekicks. The words "potential disaster" came to mind. If a half-assed staff flubbed up this season, she would never sell the team.

It's probably the last thing I'm ever going to ask of you.

"I have to stay," she said, almost silently.

"What?"

"You know how crazy I get when a deal is in jeopardy."

Liv nodded. "Certifiable."

"Well, Mark not being here puts the deal in jeopardy, and this deal is like no other. So much is riding on it." She exhaled. "Turns out my father used the house as collateral in the stadium purchase."

"Yikes," Liv said.

"Tell me about it. I know it's a pipe dream to sell this team before the season starts in three months, which is why I've given myself until the end of the season before I panic, but the pressure is on, Liv. If I fail, my father's not only going to lose his net worth, my family is going to lose their home." Helen Anne and Macy included.

Once again, the fact that her brilliant father made such an irrational business decision set her teeth on edge.

"That's a lot of pressure," Liv said.

"I can handle it. And to handle it, I need to stay."

"Okay. So we stay." Liv smacked her lips around another mouthful of Buster's infamous coffee. "Richard will love playing king a little while longer."

Rachel shook her head. "I stay. You go. We'll rent a car for you right now, and you can fly out of Pittsburgh."

"But …" Liv frowned.

"I won't be far behind. Maybe I can convince Mark to make it into town sooner. And if not, I'll simply concentrate on helping him hire the rest of the front office, and then I'll be off the hook and can focus on selling this beast." Liv still didn't look sold on the plan, so Rachel added, "I need one of us to be in Philadelphia to keep an eye on things."

Liv sat a little bit straighter. "Can I use your desk while you're gone?"

Rachel chuckled. "Yes. As long as you keep it clean. I don't want to find one single sticky Frappuccino ring on the enamel."

"Aye, aye, captain." Then Liv drank her mud water and got quiet, which gave Rachel way too much time to ponder the predicament she was in.

She sold commercial real estate. She developed commercial real estate. She wasn't a human resource professional. RCRE's Philadelphia division had its very own personnel department, which she occasionally interacted with. It was by no means an alternative to formal training. But that, along with common sense, would probably enable her to do a respectable job here. Too bad she didn't know a little more about the business of baseball. Hopefully her father would continue to be a resource. If not, Mark was going to have to be brought into the Alzheimer's loop sooner than her father wanted, because Rachel wasn't sure she could do this on her own.

Ugh. She hated being in this position. She rarely lost her footing. The steps to success were clear. At least they had been. Now, everything looked hazy.

As she drove, she stared out the windshield, watching the Hobby Mart, the super-sized Sheetz, and the high school fly by. Another week in Arlington. This was about to be her longest stay since the summer before her freshman year in college. She could handle it.

She could handle anything.

• • •

With some input from his father, Sam finished the stadium landscaping proposal Wednesday evening, but he waited until Friday afternoon to take it to the stadium. He'd heard Rachel was leaving town this morning. By now, she would be gone and her father would be back at the helm, which meant Sam could stroll into the office and have a man-to-man discussion about what made the most sense when it came to those trees.

He felt calm and confident and … kicked in the balls when he walked into the office and saw Rachel behind the desk.

"Surprise," she said, sounding about as pleased as he must've looked.

"Uh, yeah. I was expecting your father."

"I figured from the way your eyebrows tried to climb off your scalp. Sorry to disappoint you." She stood up and walked across the room on a pair of teetering tan heels to pull open the bottom drawer of a filing cabinet. Her skirt revealed acres of legs. Miles really. And he had no doubt those legs felt as good as they looked. *Damn.* Why couldn't she have gone back to Philadelphia? It would've saved him a hell of a lot of aggravation.

"Listen," he said, sounding gruffer than usual. "I have the proposal you asked for, but I'd really like your father to see it, too. He owns the team, after all."

She glared up at him from her seductive crouch. "My father is busy. This baseball team is one of a dozen business dealings for Reed Commercial Real Estate Services. And while he's busy, I'm his eyes and ears. If you have a problem with that, then I can always find another grounds crew." She stood and kicked the drawer shut. "Believe me, I'm a personnel pro these days."

She was plenty pissed, but he got another vibe from her, too. Frustration, maybe? He didn't know. He shouldn't care. She'd basically threatened to fire Sutter & Sons. Without any of the flirty tension that had simmered between them the other day, he imagined she was capable of following through, especially in her current mood.

"Is everything okay?" he asked, trying to strike the right chord, one that wouldn't piss her off even more.

"Everything is fine." She sounded annoyed, but when she looked at him she actually smiled. "Now, I can only give you twenty minutes, because I have a conference call." She sat and didn't bother to roll her chair closer to the desk. Instead, she crossed her bare legs and stared at him expectantly.

He dropped his gaze to her knees, let it travel momentarily to the shadow between her thighs, and then fought a rush of heat to make eye contact. "The details are all in here," he said, losing his head for a moment and offering her the folder.

She hit him with a melodramatic frown. "You mean there's no presentation? What a disappointment. I was expecting to sit back and watch someone else do all the work for a change."

Again, his gaze dropped to her legs, and for a minute, he imagined sinking to his knees right there, so she could sit back and really watch him work … But then, she cleared her throat, bringing his attention back to her face and an expression that was laced with superiority on top of amusement.

"Just give me the gist of what's in that folder, and I'll take a closer look later," she said. "Although, I'm sure we both know what you're ultimately trying to achieve here."

Why did it feel like she was always one step ahead of him?

"I wouldn't be doing the job you hired me for if I didn't give you the most cost-effective options to make these grounds beautiful. Keeping those trees is by far the best way to save money and preserve the visual integrity of the land."

She stood, walked over to the windows lining the exterior wall of the stadium, and with the flip of a switch, opened the blinds. Sunlight poured in, washing out everything in its path, leaving him with a view of his trees that would make a photographer weep. Ethereal branches mixed with lush pines. The shadow of buds hinted at spring. The gradient of colors, greens and browns, were bright where the sun could reach, but too dark to be differentiated near the ground.

"They are definitely pretty," she said.

It felt like a fastball, even looked like one coming off the grip, but his gut told him *changeup*, and he tensed.

"Why are those trees so important to you?" she asked. The sincerity on her face surprised him more than the words did.

"Balsam poplar trees are—"

"Not the reason you're going through all this trouble. I've Googled you, Sam. I haven't come across a single picture of you chained to balsam poplar trees anywhere else in the state. So does that mean you only care about the ones in your backyard?"

"I care about all trees everywhere."

"Good. Then this should be easy to resolve. I'll find a nearby location and plant twice as many trees as we cut down here. I'll even make a sizable donation to your favorite environmentalist charity. Sound good?"

"No. That's not an acceptable alternative."

She studied him closely, letting her intense gaze linger on his face as she tried to figure him out. *Good luck with that, sweetheart.*

"Why, Sam?" she asked. "Why isn't it good enough?"

"Because those are mature trees. You can't pacify me with saplings after you've slaughtered century-old trees. Do you know how long it will take for the trees you plant to bring joy to anyone? Kids will be grown before they can climb a single tree. Parents will be gone before they ..."

He tripped over his words, giving her enough time to jump in with, "This is about your mom. Isn't it?" Her gaze softened. "She was always a big wildlife advocate."

Vulnerability coursed through his veins followed by a tidal wave of annoyance, and still he figured it best to shoot straight. "That's part of it. She loved those woods. Hiked them every Sunday for most of her life. It was a part of her." He shrugged away the pain. "It's a part of me."

Rachel closed her eyes briefly, and he hoped he'd struck a nerve. It felt like he had. "I'm sorry, Sam. I didn't know there was such a deep personal connection. I'm even sorrier about your mom's passing. She was a great lady. I remember when she took riding lessons from my mom. Did you know the horses wouldn't eat apples unless they were from her?" Rachel chuckled at the memory. "It was so strange. She just had a way about her."

A smile warmed his face, and he said, "That sounds like my mom."

Rachel nodded, but then her expression changed. She cleared her throat and her face suddenly seemed sadder, but also colder. "Unfortunately, according to the research my father has compiled over the last eighteen months, to accommodate the type of car traffic this stadium needs to keep ticket sales in the black, those trees must come down. I have a plan to follow and deadlines to keep."

Unbelievable. "Why did you waste my time asking those questions if there wasn't a shot in hell that the answers would change anything?"

Her face twisted with bewilderment. "I don't know. I guess curiosity finally got the better of me. Maybe I was even hopeful there was a way we could both walk away from this with what we need. I'm sorry, Sam. I really am."

He was sorry, too, because no matter how important this commercial contract was to his father, Rachel was forcing his hand. He needed to consider his next step very carefully. All it would take was the support of one neighbor to file a formal complaint, which would force the municipality to call in environmental experts. That would give the trees a two-week reprieve.

Sam could have that kind of support by Monday morning. He wasn't sure what a two-week reprieve would do, except maybe give him time to get through to Rachel's father.

"Look, if I could just talk to your dad …"

Her lips tightened into a thin, flat line, and any sadness he thought he'd seen lingering there was gone immediately.

"The municipality has given us the green light, and Wes Allen is scheduled to start next week. That's the bottom line, Sam."

His fists balled at his sides. "Of course. And the bottom line's all that matters to you, isn't it, Rachel?"

He stormed out of the office before she could even respond. As he headed to his truck, Sam's brain went into overdrive. There had to be a way to salvage the trees; there just had to be. The question was, how far was he willing to go to honor his mother's memory? Far enough to sabotage his father's business?

Chapter Five

Rachel never understood the concept of a weekend. If you wanted to be on top, you only had seven days each week to get there. Just because she'd been stuck in Arlington for almost two weeks now didn't mean she was going to change her ways.

"If you're going to be in this tent, you have to wear one of these," Helen Anne said.

Rachel looked up from the pile of used books she was sifting through to find her sister standing over her holding up a black apron with the Reed's Re-Readables logo ironed on the bib. "I'm not wearing an apron over a fleece jacket. Besides, I'm not here to talk books. I'm here to sell tickets," Rachel said, pointing at her royal-blue baseball cap. The newly assembled sales team needed all the help they could get.

"Well, you're crashing a festival tent that was paid for by me on behalf of my bookstore, so if you're staying, then you're wearing this."

Rachel looked at the matronly apron again. "Fine. Then I won't stay in the tent. I'll stand outside."

"Then you're going to annoy the festival committee because you didn't pay to be a legitimate vendor, and"—she crossed her arms and lifted her chin—"you're going to disappoint your niece when she gets here. She helped Mom make these, and she made one for you."

Ooh. There was no graceful way out of that, so Rachel stood and accepted the apron from a smug Helen Anne. In the process, she spied a stack of baseball hats on the table. Never one to miss an opportunity to further her own agenda, Rachel said, "You should advertise both, too." She fit a cap onto her sister's head.

Helen Anne swatted at her. "You're going to mess up my hair. Besides, I look terrible in hats. Jeremy said so all the time. Trust me, if I looked like you ..." Her voice trailed off, her lack of self-confidence pitiful to Rachel's ears. Helen Anne's egotistic ex had always required way too much care and feeding and ego stroking. What an awful way to waste a minute of your time, let alone eleven years.

"You're better off without him," Rachel said sincerely.

But it must not have been what Helen Anne wanted to hear, because she made a face and walked away. So much for being sisterly.

Rachel squatted and picked up a copy of *Little House in the Big Woods*. A simple flip through the yellowed pages reminded her they actually had been sisterly once. Reading books, riding horses, talking about boys. A long time ago. Before Rachel had left for UPenn and no longer had time for the horses. Before Helen Anne had gotten wrapped up in Jeremy and no longer had time for Rachel. People changed. Whether you wanted them to or not.

Thoughts of the Alzheimer's diagnosis reared their ugly heads again, and Rachel dropped the book, preferring to focus on ticket sales rather than her family drama.

Over the next couple hours, people streamed in and out, talking books and authors with Helen Anne, and occasionally—rarely—baseball with Rachel. A lot of people didn't seem to recognize her. Not that she could blame them. She'd been a willing stranger in these parts. Maybe that's why when she saw a familiar face, she pounced.

"Could I interest you in a limited-time deal on Arlington Aces season tickets, Mr. Jackson?" Rachel's former high-school health instructor was milling around at the mouth of the tent while his wife went through boxes of paperback thrillers. He still dyed his hair jet black and wore track pants pulled above his navel.

"Rachel? My goodness! It's been a long time."

"Years," she said, nodding. "Now, let me tell you about these tickets. Opening Day is May 11. That's only a little over two months away."

He shook his head before she could go on. "I don't think so. Can't justify it. The Sandlot League's not half bad, and it's free. Besides, my son takes me to Pittsburgh to see the Pirates a couple times a year. That's enough baseball for me."

Rachel didn't like the sound of that, and she certainly didn't want the competition. "I don't know anything about The Sandlot League. You'll have to fill me in."

He told her about the six-team recreational league comprised of local men who used the high-school field during the summer months. It sounded homey. Picnic lunches. Coolers of beer on the tailgates. Kids digging in dirt piles while their moms watched their dads play.

"Got a couple college-level athletes on those teams," he said. "It's entertaining."

"With all due respect, Mr. Jackson, the Aces will be better, an entire team of college-level and above athletes. We'll have former minor leaguers, too. Guys from all over the U.S. And while we can't give away the entire season, if you buy a season-ticket package today, you'll get it for 50 percent off. That's like getting twenty-five games free. Plus, you get this hat." She tapped the brim and shot him her shiniest smile. "You would look great in this hat."

He thought about it and then took the bait. "How much are we talking here?"

"A little help, please!" The shrill voice interrupted them, and when Rachel turned to see where it had come from, she saw Mrs. Jackson dragging a full box of books toward the register.

Mr. Jackson sighed. "Sorry, Rachel. Another time maybe."

"But the discount won't be available another time. It's one day only."

He shrugged. "Then there's nothing I can do. Somebody has to support my wife's reading habit."

If Rachel hadn't been so surprised and disappointed at not closing the sale, she would've given him props for being the kind of man who put reading ahead of sports—or at least a happy wife ahead of sports. But she *was* disappointed. One hour down, and she hadn't sold a single thing. How could she be so adept at selling multimillion-dollar properties and so inept at peddling baseball tickets? Fifty percent off was a huge price break! Twenty-five tickets free? That was crazy. People had to recognize the opportunity. Obviously, she needed to do a better job getting that point across.

The next sale closes no matter what.

Rachel grabbed a stack of hats and stepped out of the tent into the sunshine, where a throng of people was browsing booths during Arlington's Annual "March Spring Madness" Festival, which was billed as a way to shake off the winter blues and support your neighborhood businesses. She only cared about that last part. Someone in this crowd was willing and able to support the Aces. All she needed was a split second of eye contact to find her mark.

Bam! She connected with someone all right—Luke and his pregnant wife. He acknowledged Rachel with a nod and then spun his wife in the other direction. Another strikeout.

Frustrated and more determined than ever, she scanned the crowd for another mark and picked a young family she'd never seen before. Two little boys. *Perfect.* She could sell four tickets in one fell swoop. "Excuse me. You're just the people I've been looking for! Have you heard about the Arlington Aces baseball team?"

Skepticism wrinkled the woman's face, while the man nodded. "That's the team moving into the old community-college field, right?"

"Yes! And today only we're giving away tickets to twenty-five home games when you purchase a full season-ticket package." It sounded much more impressive when you said it that way.

"We're not interested," the woman said as she took her boys by the hands and started walking away, but the man hung back.

"How much?" he asked.

Rachel smiled and reeled in the line ever so slightly, handing him a full-color pamphlet. "Those are the regular prices, but if you come with me to the Reed's Re-Readables tent, I'll ring you up for 50 percent off."

He whistled.

"I know. It's a great deal," she said. "For a very limited time. Today only."

He gave back the pamphlet. "It's a little steep for me. I'm not even sure my kids will sit still for nine innings. Maybe next year."

No! Not two in a row. "Sir …"

"Rachel!" It had only been a week, but she recognized the rasp in the distant voice before she even looked up. *Sam.* She ignored him.

"This is the cheapest you'll ever see these tickets. Next year, they'll be the hottest tickets in town. What if you only bought two … and I gave you a hat for each boy?" She shoved two hats toward him. "Do we have a deal?"

"Rachel!" It was Sam. Again. Only closer.

The man took the hats, studied them, and then said, "I don't think so."

"Rachel!" She was going to have to face him eventually.

The man held the hats out to her, and she shook her head. "Keep them. Give them to your boys."

"Thanks. Have a nice day."

Deflated, she watched him take a few steps away from her before she turned to rip into Sam, but the harsh words died when she saw him making his way through the crowd with her father in tow.

"Dad?" His eyes were rimmed in red, and his expression was fearful. "Is everything okay?" She looked beyond him. "Where's Mom?"

"She's, uh …" Danny looked at Sam. "You know my wife, right? Where's my wife?"

Rachel attempted to hide her alarm by rushing a smile and taking her father's arm before Sam could get a word in edgewise. "Oh, she's probably back at the tent with Helen Anne or buying Macy a treat. Let's go find them." She tugged once, fully intending on escaping without addressing Sam directly, but her father didn't move.

"I didn't know where I was," he said. "Nothing looked familiar."

This was going from bad to worse. As far as she knew, he wanted to keep the diagnosis hush-hush for as long as possible. For the sake of privacy, integrity, and all those things. She needed to get him out of here before Sam caught on.

"Dad …" She tugged again.

"But then I saw Sam beside me," he said. "Thank you for helping me get my bearings. How's baseball? Cubbies, right?"

Sam's face twisted a little, and his eyes shot to Rachel. "I, uh, don't play anymore, Mr. Reed. It's been a long time actually."

"Oh," her father said, looking confused. "I'm sorry to hear that."

"That's alright."

For one blissful second, Rachel thought that would be the end of it, and she could finally get her father out of there, but then Sam took advantage of the situation and added, "I'm glad I ran into you, Mr. Reed. I've been wanting to talk to you about something baseball related."

"It will have to wait," Rachel said, cutting Sam off and tugging on her father's arm. "I bet Mom is looking for us too, Dad. You guys are always getting your wires crossed." Rachel played it off by giving Sam a quick smile. She hoped it conveyed this was all perfectly normal and her parents were a little crazy.

Thank God her father followed her. When she was sure Sam wasn't going to come after them just to plead his case on behalf of the trees

Rachel took a deep breath and prayed she'd covered well enough. The last thing they needed was for this to get around town and somehow tarnish the baseball team. She'd have to do damage control on top of everything else. With any luck, Sam had been so focused on trying to bend her father's ear about those damned trees that he hadn't noticed exactly how out of sorts her father had been. Yes, that seemed highly possible. By now, Sam had probably forgotten about anything other than winning the battle for the trees. Except …

Rachel could've sworn she'd felt his eyes on her back all the way to the tent.

...

Sam watched Rachel walk away arm in arm with her father. What the hell had just happened here? One minute he'd been helping his family at the Sutter & Sons Landscaping tent, and the next he was pulling Rachel's father out of the middle of the crowd, where he looked ready to pass out. There was also that whole awkward baseball conversation. Something wasn't right with the man, and Rachel had sure been acting weird.

When Sam got back to the tent, Luke asked, "Is everything okay?"

"I don't know," Sam said honestly.

He kept glancing in the direction of the Reeds' tent, wondering if maybe the man had suffered a stroke or an aneurysm. Maybe none of those things were a possibility, but his gut told him whatever was going on, it was serious. Once the crowd died down around here, he would take a walk. It wouldn't hurt to make sure Mr. Reed was okay. It also wouldn't hurt if Sam was able to get the man alone for a moment so he could plug for those trees—as soon as he knew nothing terrible had happened, of course.

For the rest of the afternoon, the Sutters took turns fielding questions from potential customers and trying to attract more people to their tent. It wasn't hard. Sam's father was an attraction in and of himself—calling out to people in funny accents and offering kids candy as they passed. It helped take Sam's mind off the one thing he hated thinking about more than his mother's death: his reaction when people wanted to talk about his baseball career.

Eventually, things died down. The crowd thinned out. A lot of people had headed off toward the pavilion for the barn dance, and the rest were probably claiming their spots for the fireworks. Still, there were enough people lingering around that Sam's dad could be heard bragging about taking care of the baseball field while trying to convince some guy who owned several rental properties to use Sutter & Sons for his landscaping and snow-removal needs. Nearby, Luke was explaining overseeding to Mrs. Jennings, who was already their client but never satisfied with the plan she was paying for. And Mandy was FaceTiming with their two little ones, who were at home with a sitter and refusing to get ready for bed. That left Sam unoccupied when his neighbor, Dave Little, walked up wearing an Arlington Aces cap.

Sam glanced toward the Reeds' tent again. "What's going on, Dave?"

"Nothing much." He reached over the wood-plank counter to shake Sam's hand. "Amy has the boys at the snack tent, so I thought I would hit some of the non-crafty tents while I have the chance."

"Nice." Sam glanced at the hat again.

Dave must've recognized the target of Sam's attention because he asked, "Like it?" and adjusted the brim. "Some woman tried to sell me season tickets. Seemed a little desperate." He laughed.

"Rachel Reed," Sam said mindlessly.

"You know her?"

"I do. She dated my brother back in high school. Now I deal with her over at the field." At least until he finagled it so Ian could take his place … or she fired them after he filed a formal complaint about those trees. Dave just might be the neighbor he needed to get that ball rolling. Standing three feet away from his father wasn't the best place to discuss an act of treason, though, and Sam still wasn't sure he could pull the trigger on something so underhanded.

He'd thought about appealing to his father on behalf of his mother's love for those trees, but that could create an entirely different mess—one that started with his father agreeing that Rachel planting trees and making a donation in Mary Sutter's name was a nice compromise and ended with Sam admitting how uncomfortable he was with the idea of staring down a baseball field for the rest of his life. "We've been contracted to act as grounds crew," he added, less than happily.

"You don't say. So when it rains, you'll be one of the guys rolling out the tarp?"

Hell no. Sam wasn't going to be around long enough for that.

Dave kept right on talking. "Maybe I'll have to rethink those season tickets. I couldn't authorize something that pricy without talking to Amy first. Of course, she thinks it's a racket. She says we can drive to Pittsburgh and see real baseball a couple Saturdays during the season for less money and have a better time. I think she just likes the idea of staying in a hotel and having someone else clean up after us. You know?"

Real baseball? That hurt. Sam knew what it felt like to be clawing your way up from the depths of a farm system. The odds stacked against guys in unaffiliated organizations were even worse. They deserved better than some offhanded comment by some guy who probably hadn't played the game past middle school.

"This *will* be real baseball, Dave, with real guys taking the field. Only these guys will be playing like there's no tomorrow, because for them, there's not. No long-term DL. No minor-league rehab. Just a bunch of men who love the game and are willing to play their hearts out for less than minimum wage and a chance at something."

"Sounds miserable."

Sam stared off into space. "Not if it's the air you breathe." He'd been that way once, willing to play through anything. "For guys like that, it's one step away from heaven."

"Really? So you think I should spring for those tickets?"

Sam looked at the man. "I can't tell you what to do with your money, but I can tell you those guys would be grateful to have a full house. And your boys will go nuts. If this league is anything like the minors, you'll have more than pierogi races and trivia contests between innings. Hell, out here you might have cows on the field." Which added to his dislike for the grounds-keeping gig. "It will be a real father-son bonding experience. Talk about memories."

"Hey, man, thanks." Dave extended his hand. "I'm going to see if I can find your friend. What was her name again?"

"Rachel." Sam stopped short of telling Dave she wasn't a friend, just a nuisance. Why bother going into details? Besides, a crack like that would seem unnecessarily cruel, considering something worrisome had definitely been going on with her father.

Again, Sam looked toward the Reed tent, where Dave was headed. A clear image of Rachel's troubled expression remained forefront in his mind.

Eventually, Luke asked, "Are we ready to pack it up?"

Mandy nodded enthusiastically and added something about getting home in time to kiss the kids. Paul agreed for the sake of snagging some of those food-truck tacos he suspected would sell out before sundown. And Sam had somewhere else he wanted to be, too.

After what had happened, any decent human being would check on Danny Reed ... and his daughter.

Chapter Six

Rachel sat on a box of books with her head in her hands. For the hour since her mother had swept her father away from the festival so he could rest, Rachel and her sister had lamented Danny's obvious decline until it came down to Helen Anne saying, "He's never gotten lost before."

"So does that mean it's going to start happening more often?"

Helen Anne shrugged. "I don't know. If I didn't have the store and Macy, I would insist on being at the next appointment with them. Sometimes I think they don't tell us everything because they don't want us to worry."

"Too late for that."

Macy came bounding into the tent with a bag of cotton candy, which stopped the conversation and left Rachel on the box with her thoughts. How long before he really didn't remember anything—including them? *Long.* She sat a little straighter and told herself it wasn't anything a little medication adjustment couldn't fix. But she didn't know that for sure, so there was no real comfort there. One thing she did know, they couldn't keep the diagnosis quiet much longer. Other people had probably begun to notice something was strange. Sam sure had.

She slumped again, recalling the torturous look on Sam's face when her father had asked him about baseball. What had happened to his career? When she'd Googled him the other night just to make sure he wasn't some radical environmentalist with the likes of Greenpeace behind him, all she could find were a handful of statistical mentions about his time in the minor leagues. Nothing overly impressive. Nothing dramatic by any means. Now, she really wondered.

"Excuse me."

Rachel looked up to see one of the men she'd tried to sell season tickets to. He was wearing an Arlington Aces hat.

"I'll take four," he said.

A silver lining in the storm clouds.

She used her laptop to complete the purchase through the team's website and sent the man on his way with a confirmation emailed to his phone. The success of the sale went a long way in calming her frayed nerves, because closing a deal was the best medicine. She needed to focus on that bottom line.

"I'll be back," she told Helen Anne, and then she hit the pavement looking for another sale. Four was better than none, but she wanted to go home with at least a dozen sold.

Since the twenty-five-tickets-free wording seemed to have worked for the last guy, Rachel stuck with that. Only to have two people wave her off and walk away before she could even start her spiel. How frustrating! If she had a PowerPoint presentation and her iPad, she'd be golden.

"Excuse me," she called out to a couple pushing a baby stroller. The woman turned, and Rachel recognized her immediately as a former classmate, but she couldn't remember her name.

"Rachel Reed? Holy cow! Is that you?" The woman left the stroller in her husband's care and walked closer.

"It's me. How are you?" What the heck was her name?

"Great! I had a baby. Finally. Can you believe that?"

Rachel's eyes went wide as she shook her head with a disbelief she didn't feel. "That's wonderful! Good for you." And then she braced herself for the inevitable questions about her family, her husband, her little ones. The whole damn world seemed hell-bent on tying happiness to the nuclear family. It used to make her mad; now it just made her feel sorry for them and their myopic view.

The woman eyed Rachel's baseball cap. "Are you back in Arlington full-time?"

"Not full-time. I'm actually selling season tickets for the Arlington Aces, helping my family out. If you buy a full season-ticket package today, you'll get twenty-five tickets free. Fifty percent off! That's crazy."

Rachel smiled brightly, hoping to seal the deal, but the unnamed woman just stared at her for a moment before she said, "That is definitely crazy. I'll have to pass, though. Not much of a baseball fan. Take care." She backed away, rejoined her husband and baby, and left Rachel without a sale once again.

Rachel threw her arms up, looked at the darkening sky, and said, "What am I doing wrong?"

"Well, you *did* just try to sell baseball tickets to a woman whose family fought the district to defund the athletic program in favor of the arts back when we were in high school."

Oh my God! But it wasn't. It was Sam Sutter. Again. She would've lamented his impeccable timing a bit longer had she not realized the faux pas she'd committed a few seconds ago. "That was Penelope Rollins?"

"Penelope Rollins-Sullivan. She's married now. Her husband is some big-time orchestra director in Pittsburgh."

Well, that explained the strange look Penelope had given her.

Rachel slapped a hand to her forehead. "I didn't know."

Sam shoved his hands into his pockets and nodded. "It happens. You miss a lot when you're gone."

"Yeah, but that? That was kind of big." And it was coming back to her in big chunks of distant memory now.

Helen Anne had been on the cheerleading squad the year Penelope's family had sued the school. The story had been all over the news because Arlington Area High School had been forced to cancel the entire football season due to the litigation. Rachel had heard about the endless drama from her very aggrieved sister, who, along with the cheer squad, had hand-washed every car this side of the Allegheny Mountains in order to pay for new uniforms they weren't even going to get to wear. "I just can't believe I missed something that big," Rachel said, reflection in her tone. God, was she starting to lose her edge, too?

"Don't beat yourself up. I've missed bigger."

She didn't know what he was talking about, but his face twisted like it had the moment her father had asked him about baseball. "Sam—"

"Yoo-hoo!"

They both turned at the same time to see Ruby Post waddling toward them. She wore a big button on her floral blouse that said, "Festival Committee," and she carried a neon-pink clipboard. Ruby had taught Rachel in Sunday school once upon a time.

"Hello, Mrs. Post."

"Rachel." She smiled, revealing teeth smudged with pink lipstick. "Samuel." And then she looked back at Rachel again without the smile. "I'm sorry, but I don't have you listed as a vendor, and the committee is very strict about keeping the pool pure. I'm going to have to ask you to stop peddling your wares."

Why did that make it sound like Rachel was a hooker? Sam must've thought so, too, because he turned his head to hide his smile.

Rachel stood a little straighter and smiled confidently at Mrs. Post. "May I see that list?"

Mrs. Post pressed the clipboard to her massive breasts. "It's confidential. Committee members and vendors only."

Rachel didn't flinch. "I'm a Reed, Mrs. Post, and the Reeds are on that list."

"Reed's Re-Readables is on this list, and no one has complained about *them* selling outside their tent."

"Someone complained?" *Penelope.* Boy, that was fast. "You've got to be kidding—"

"Thank you, Mrs. Post," Sam interrupted. "We were just heading to the dance, anyway." He slid his hand beneath Rachel's elbow and gripped it softly but snuggly. A warm tingle heated her skin, and it distracted her enough to let Sam start leading her away from the confrontation. "Have a great night," he added.

She was letting him lead her. The minute Rachel realized that, she stopped in her tracks. "I didn't need to be rescued from Mrs. Post."

"No, but you needed to be rescued from yourself."

She scoffed. "Hardly. I was just trying to sell some season tickets for God's sake. It wasn't like I was offering cocaine and a hand job in the backseat of my car."

His right eyebrow raised, followed by a twitch of his lips. "Maybe you would've been more successful with that."

She socked him in the right arm and was surprised by just how solid he felt beneath the Sutter & Sons sweatshirt he was wearing. Not that she should be surprised. He'd been a professional athlete who did manual labor for a living. Muscles were part of the package. *His package.* From there, it was a one-way ride to inappropriate thoughts.

"Next time, save the rescue for someone who needs it," she said gruffly, simultaneously stepping backward. She may have been off her game not remembering the Rollins lawsuit, but attending a barn dance? No flipping way.

But he caught her by the hand, gently this time, and some part of her melted at the sensation. When was the last time she'd held hands with anyone?

"Not so fast," he said. "You owe me a dance."

"I don't owe you anything." She didn't sound as convincing as she'd hoped to. "And you're up to something. You're always up to something."

He grinned. "Nah. It just seems like the least you could do for the man who sold four season-ticket packages for you."

"You did nothing of the sort."

"Does the name Dave Little ring a bell?"

Her jaw dropped, but she closed it with as much grace as possible, considering Sam was flashing a high-wattage smile that did ridiculously immature things to her insides.

"I see it does," he said.

"How? What did you say to him? What could have possibly been more compelling than telling him they'd get twenty-five free tickets if they purchased today?"

"I just told him the truth about the kind of baseball he would see. I told him his kids would have a great time."

"You took the emotional route," she said, unimpressed.

"I took the personal route, because the bottom line isn't always the only thing that matters." He didn't say it unkindly, and Rachel shrugged.

"We're going to have to agree to disagree on that." As far as life went, she'd done pretty well for forty years focused solely on the bottom line.

"I have faith you'll see it my way one of these days."

"And why is that? Because all this fresh air and time on your hands makes you enlightened beyond the likes of a big-city, career-obsessed woman like me?"

He chuckled, brushed his thumb along her knuckles, and said, "Not at all. I just know that life eventually knocks everyone down, and when we stand back up, we finally see the little things were the big things all along."

The little things. Like holding hands. And staring into a familiar face long enough to see it in a whole different way. They were dangerous thoughts that on any other day and in any other place she never would've entertained.

Rachel pulled her hand away. "So what sort of baseball will Dave Little and his family see here?" she asked, steering the conversation away from those bothersome little things.

A wistful look flashed across Sam's face as he said, "The best kind. The kind that isn't weighed down by big money and league politics. The simple, beautiful game."

It was another little thing, but one that echoed loudly in her ears until she realized Sam Sutter and his poetic take on baseball might be just what she needed to sell this team.

•••

Sam caught himself before he dove in and drowned amid the sentimentality. "Now, about that dance." He still wanted more information about Rachel's father than he'd been able to get from Helen Anne back at the tent, and so far, softening his interactions with Rachel certainly had things looking promising. Maybe he could find out exactly what Helen Anne had meant when she'd said her father was "just under a lot of stress lately." Maybe that would be something he could use to keep Wes Allen's chainsaws away.

"I don't dance," Rachel protested as he took her by the hand and led her to the old, rustic outbuilding bedecked with twinkling lights at the park's far end.

But she didn't protest enough to pull her hand away, and he liked that, even though he wasn't sure why. Maybe it was because the tables had turned, and Ms. All-Powerful was finally following someone else's lead. Or maybe it was because her hand fit inside his so perfectly, warming him from the outside in.

Since that last thought presented way more trouble than he wanted right now, he pushed it aside and faced her. "I don't dance, either, but how hard can it be?" He lifted her free hand and deposited it on his shoulder. "You put a hand here." He slid his hand to the curve of her waist. "I put my hand here, and then we sway." He twisted the hand he was holding, tucked it against his chest, and started moving to the beat of some semi-upbeat country song the DJ was playing.

Rachel barely moved. In fact, her eyes were the most expressive part of her body as she watched him wriggle. "Aren't you embarrassed?"

He laughed and exaggerated his sways even more, pulling her along for the ride. "Hell, no. I'm dancing with the prettiest girl out here."

The look on her face … Wide eyes. Open mouth. Complete shock. He sort of felt that way in his gut, too. Calling her the prettiest girl probably wasn't the smartest thing, considering he was only trying to soften her up so she would see things his way. And yet, a part of him wondered if he wasn't kidding himself. He certainly wasn't joking about her being pretty, and he was starting to realize there was more to her than the haughty personality and sharp barbs she threw his way. He'd seen something softer in the office when she'd talked about his mom. He'd seen it again mixed with worry for her dad. It made him curious about her, made him think he may have misjudged her all of these years. One thing he knew for sure, though … there'd always been something about Rachel Reed that had gotten under his skin.

"I'm not a girl, Sam," she said, straightening.

He stretched his fingers to grip more of her waist. "No, you're not." She was soft and warm at the very same time she was strong and cool. A girl couldn't pull that off.

"I'm as old as your brother, which makes me considerably older than you."

Sam shrugged and spun her around. "Doesn't bother me." When her brow quirked, he added, "I was taught to respect my elders."

Finally, she smiled. Small at first, but when it reached her eyes the spark was pure magic.

"I'm thirty-five," he said. "That doesn't count as considerably anything to me. Besides, I have a lot of hard life experience on me." He rolled her fingers around in his hand. "Feel those callouses? Those are at least the callouses of a forty-five-year-old man."

Her smile turned into a smirk. "Nice try, buddy. I still have seniority here."

He spun her around a couple more times, touched his cheek to her temple, and whispered, "Then why am I leading?"

She surprised him with a laugh, and when he saw it light up her face all he could think was, *How beautiful ... and how inconvenient*. This was not a woman he should be interested in. He'd already drawn the battle lines—at least in his head. Besides, she was his brother's ex. Twenty years didn't erase that sort of bro code. Did it?

"Thank you for speaking up on behalf of the team today," she said. The thoughtful way she was looking at him reminded him of the way she'd looked at him in her office when she'd questioned him about the trees.

Expect the changeup. That had certainly become his MO when dealing with Rachel Reed.

"You're welcome," he said.

"Apparently, I ..." She cleared her throat and squirmed a little. "I need the help, which is not something I like to admit."

She looked pained, so he smiled and said, "Your secret's safe with me."

The second he said the words, the music slowed, and her face read complete confusion—*Should I stay or go?* The latter seemed like a waste of a perfectly good song, so instead of letting her end it, he pulled her in. Closer. Sliding his hand from her hip to the small of her back.

To his surprise, she stayed in his arms, and a few beats later, she surrendered completely, laying her head on his shoulder, where he could smell the sweet, citrus scent of her hair.

"What's going on with your father?" he asked, thinking it best to get back to the main reason he'd brought her out here.

Her body stiffened, and then she lifted her head from his shoulder and glanced around.

The dance floor was packed, but the dancers must've been preoccupied enough to satisfy her need for privacy, because she simply said, "He has Alzheimer's."

"I'm sorry to hear that."

She nodded. "He's only told the family and a few very close friends at this point, but after what happened today, that's going to have to change."

It made a world of sense. "So that's why you're here?"

"Exactly. He can't consistently and competently take care of business, including the team. And, because he's such a control freak"—she offered a small smile—"like me, he didn't ask for help until it was almost too late. I'm here for the short-term to ..." She hesitated. "Get things stabilized until the new GM can get here."

"What about Philly?"

"It's still there, going on without me for the next week or two. Believe me. He has plenty for me to do when I get back there. He gave me a grand plan in the form of a seventy-five-page, single-spaced document."

"Wow," Sam said.

"I can handle it." There was that hard, capable edge.

"I don't doubt that for a minute." He pulled her closer, letting the warmth of her body sink in, and considered how this news about her father's illness changed things.

Talk about a changeup.

Rachel's hardheaded inconsideration of his trees was because she was under a lot of stress and following someone else's plan. *Seventy-five, single-spaced pages.* He didn't even know what that looked like. And as much as his mother had loved those trees, hadn't she also taught him not to add to another person's pain?

His mother, of all people, would've given more credence to the story than the bottom line. People came before trees. Just like people came before baseball—*should've* come before baseball.

Sam had made his mistakes. And while he desperately wanted to make up for those mistakes, it didn't seem right to back Rachel into a corner where she might have to choose between her father's instructions and those trees. And speaking of fathers … Sam's had been as proud as a puffed-up peacock today, telling passersby about their involvement with the baseball field. How could Sam mess with that? He couldn't. He would rather live with a baseball stadium lurking outside his kitchen window.

All signs seemed to be pointing to a concession here.

When the song ended and the DJ took a break, Rachel slipped out of Sam's arms. "I have to go," she said. "Thanks for the dance."

And with one look, he knew something had changed between them. He could see it in her gentle expression and the way she didn't flee.

"Thanks for the *dances*," he said with a smile. "There was more than one."

"True. There were two, and I only owed you one."

"Well, you owed me four if you count each individual season-ticket package I sold."

She rolled her eyes. "I don't, so that means you owe *me* one."

He raised his brows suggestively. "One dance?"

"If you're offering something else, then let me think about it." She grinned. "I may have something in mind. I'll be in touch."

He didn't know what had gotten into him, but he wouldn't mind if she followed through.

Chapter Seven

In the middle of the week, Rachel took a break from staffing the stadium, hiring coaches and trainers, and dealing with equipment companies, so she could accompany her mother and father to a doctor's appointment. Helen Anne had been right—one of them needed to be there to get the whole truth and nothing but the truth, especially after their father had gotten lost at the festival.

Unfortunately, Rachel couldn't think about the festival without thinking about Sam. Dancing. Divulging. She really should've passed on the dance and kept her mouth shut. But she couldn't shake the feeling that she needed him—in some capacity—to help her successfully launch this baseball team. Unfortunately, he was way past the league's twenty-seven-year-old age limit to play. Maybe he would be willing to coach? Except her father already had a list of candidates for that. Maybe operations? Administration of some kind? How to use Sam to benefit the team should've been the extent of her interest in him. *Truly.* And it would've been, had she not felt such a rush in his arms.

So now what? She, of all people, could work with an attractive man and not get sucked into something personal. She wasn't one to mix business and pleasure usually, although she'd had the occasional *arrangement* with a like-minded colleague here or there. Always short-lived, always explicitly clear on what the boundaries were.

It had been a while since she'd indulged in something like that. Rachel's mind quickened. It wasn't as though she'd be working with Sam long-term. She'd be back in Philadelphia as soon as she could stabilize the team enough to babysit it from afar. Maybe a temporary *arrangement* could be … mutually beneficial. She wondered how Sam would feel about that—should the opportunity arise.

Talk about a change of plans.

"Ms. Reed? You can follow me."

Rachel blinked once to clear her head and then fell into step behind the nurse who led her down a long, sterile hallway to an office, where her parents were waiting after completing routine cognitive testing.

Before she could ask how it went, the doctor entered the room. He wasn't much younger than her father. Gray. Distinguished. And, like Danny—and Rachel—he cut right to the chase.

"What your father experienced at the festival is called motion blindness," he said. "Think of it like snowflakes falling on your windshield, but your wipers aren't working. Your vision gets more and more obstructed until you can't make out the details, and you end up lost. As soon as your wipers start working again, it's clear and you can find your way."

"Is that what happened, Danny?" Jackie spoke to her husband as if he were a child.

"I guess," he said, clearly not remembering the event as well as everyone else did.

Meanwhile, the same storm of emotions that had been brewing inside Rachel since the festival kicked into high gear. She literally vibrated with helplessness. "So what's next, Doctor?"

The man blinked. "Next?"

"Yes. How do we go about fixing this?"

"Perhaps you don't understand, Ms. Reed, but Alzheimer's is, unfortunately, a chronic condition, not a curable one."

"Of course, I'm aware of that. But there has to be something more you can do. Some ... oh, I don't know ... mental exercises, therapy, something ... *anything* but sitting around twiddling our thumbs and waiting for the inevitable while you pretend you're actually helping him!"

"Rachel!" her mother exclaimed, clearly appalled. "Dr. Rictor is doing his best."

"I'm sure he is, but sometimes our best isn't good enough … and someone else's is." She glanced at the good doctor, whose cheeks were flushed and face looked pinched, and added, "It's nothing personal, beyond the fact that this is my father, and it's unacceptable to me that he's declining so quickly."

Dr. Rictor opened her father's chart for a quick look. "I understand your frustration and concern, but I have to tell you, the two-year mark isn't excessively early to be experiencing middle-stage symptoms, including things like wandering, changes in sleep patterns, and the forgetfulness you've described. It simply means he's progressed from mild to moderate Alzheimer's, which is to be expected, and we need to rethink some things."

The two-year mark? Two months ago, her parents had walked into her office and dropped this bomb. They'd known for *two years*?

Rachel glared at her parents.

Her mother broke eye contact. Her father looked vacant.

"Has Helen Anne known this whole time?"

Her mother nodded.

Of course. The room quieted for a few seconds while Rachel seethed. No doubt they'd lost valuable time treating this disease by keeping it from her. Had she known two years ago, she would've made it her primary goal to find him the most revolutionary care.

"What about clinical trials?" she asked. "Somebody out there has to be doing something that will help more than this."

"There are some," Dr. Rictor said. "But I have to warn you it's not a decision to be made lightly for various reasons. There are no guarantees. There's also nothing local at the moment, which means you'll have travel and lodging expenses beyond what the trial's host will cover. Some of these studies are fully funded and work with your insurance company to ensure minimal out-of-pocket expenses. Others aren't. The price can be astronomical."

And with a huge portion of her father's assets wrapped up in an unproven baseball team, not even Danny Reed could afford astronomical.

"Let me do some research," the doctor said. "I'll see what's available, and then we can go from there. But please, keep in mind trials aren't always the home run you're hoping for."

"Hank Aaron was the home-run king," her father said, chuckling. It was a jarring sound considering the mood in the room.

But Dr. Rictor didn't seem fazed. He smiled and said, "Yes, he was. Between you and me, he still is. Bonds doesn't count."

Her father laughed again. "Are you a baseball man?"

"I am. I played third base throughout high school and some summer ball in college, but there weren't many opportunities in medical school."

"I own a baseball team," Danny said proudly, and this time it got to Rachel, pinched her heart, and made her almost sadder than she was angry. "The Arlington Aces."

"Sounds like every little boy's dream," Dr. Rictor said.

"I always wanted a little boy. I wanted to pass down my love of the game."

Rachel looked away. The successes of the past forty years should've be enough to dull the sting of those words, but they weren't. *Why?* What did it matter in the face of all this?

"We have two beautiful, talented daughters, Danny," her mother said.

"Seems like an excessively fair trade," added Dr. Rictor, but then he side-eyed Rachel, and she expected payback for her earlier outburst. "If your other daughter is as … passionate as this one, then you're a lucky man, Mr. Reed. At least you're lucky to be on her good side," he added pointedly.

She supposed she deserved that, but she refused to apologize.

"I am very lucky," her father said, as if he hadn't said anything even remotely disheartening.

As Dr. Rictor launched into a discussion about medications and expectations, Rachel got lost in thought. Things were much worse than she'd thought, because her father had already been dealing with Alzheimer's for *two years*. How could she not have known? She'd seen him regularly during that time period. Well, *regularly* was a relative term. She hadn't seen him as regularly as Helen Anne had, but Rachel had spoken with him almost weekly. Nothing on those calls had made her think anything was amiss. She'd seen him every three months for the last two years. Again, nothing had caught her eye.

"It's the little things," Dr. Rictor said, yanking Rachel out of her head and back to the conversation. "They will make the biggest difference."

The little things. You mean the things she'd missed that would've tipped her off to her father having Alzheimer's? She'd made it easy for her family not to tell her. She'd been clearly focused on something else. But how could she fault herself for that? Her father had always relied on her to have everything under control.

She'd made a promise to him two months ago, and she was going to follow through. Nothing that had happened here changed that—except maybe it increased her sense of urgency. The faster she sold this team, the faster her parents would have the liquid assets they needed to pursue all angles of care, including the potentially astronomical clinical trials Dr. Rictor had mentioned. And who knew? Maybe in the process she could prove to her father, once and for all, that she was better than a whole team of sons. Although, this time, she wasn't quite sure she could do it alone.

Maybe, just maybe, she wouldn't have to.

• • •

Another day. Another step closer to getting this field in playable condition. Sam hosed a patch of right-field sod and squinted overhead at a flock of birds. *Move along*, he thought. *Nothing to see here*. He'd been informed via email they were on an even tighter timeline than he'd expected. Tryouts were coming up in four weeks. The field needed to be ready. He didn't need a bunch of birds dive-bombing the feed and seed.

Two new crewmembers carted in bags of clay with Ian, and Sam had to admit the extra hands were a big help, not to mention a point of pride. Sutter & Sons Landscaping was growing leaps and bounds thanks to this stadium job. He tried to keep that in mind every time he thought about those trees, which, to his surprise, were still standing. But any day now …

Opening Day would be here before they knew it.

Looking around the grandstand, which had undergone a transformation long before Sam had stepped foot in this place, he tried to imagine the stadium filled. The Reeds were definitely ambitious, growing the capacity from 1,500 to 5,000 seats. Sure, 15,000 people called Arlington home, but most of these seats would probably remain unfilled. He couldn't imagine 5,000 Arlingtonians gathered together for anything besides the county fair. To get 5,000 locals to a baseball game, the Reeds were going to need one hell of a draw.

"Sam?"

He turned, taking the hose with him, and the errant spray of water targeted Rachel, who was standing in the dirt near first base.

She jumped back and leveled him with a face full of serious accusation.

"It was an accident," he said, stifling a laugh and admiring her ivory pantsuit.

Since the festival, he'd thought of her every night when he drifted off to sleep. How she smelled. How she felt. How she looked at him when her walls came down. Was it possible she'd gotten even prettier since then?

She shifted her shiny black tote bag to the other shoulder and brushed at the watermarks on her lapel. Then she turned to the side to check the farther reaches of her outfit, which gave him a great view of her rear assets.

"As lovely as those pants are," he said, "you probably shouldn't be hanging around a baseball field in them."

"There wouldn't be any problem with wearing these pants around a baseball field if you could learn to control your hose."

Her eyes widened simultaneously with his.

"Nice," he said.

"You know what I meant," she said, chuckling.

"For the record, I have excellent control of my hose when you're not around." *Or on my mind.* "You ..." He reached for the right word. "Fluster me."

She made a face. "This does not sound like an appropriate conversation."

"Oh, come on. You're a beautiful, powerful woman in a kick-ass pantsuit. I'm allowed to openly admire that."

"Fine, then I'm allowed to meet that admiration with open cynicism, because frankly I'm conditioned to wonder what you're hoping to gain from it."

Damn. She was direct, and not in a four-beers-overheated-take-me-now kind of way. *That* way was easy to handle. You called the girl a cab and sent her home safely. But Sam wasn't sure how to handle a woman who talked like this. No lines, that was for sure. Rachel would call him on every one.

"Would you believe I have no idea what I'm hoping to gain," he said sincerely. "I'm just working on impulse here." Kind of like he'd been when he'd asked her to dance.

She looked him over, up and down, and then shook her head until she smiled. "Yes. I would believe that."

"It's the ripped jeans, isn't it? They give me away as a guy with no real plans."

She stared at him for a beat too long, and the air crackled between them. "I like the jeans. Anybody can make plans, but not just anybody can wear those jeans … and look good."

He grinned. "And what are you hoping to gain from saying that? Because I'm starting to have a few ideas."

She stepped closer, maintaining eye contact, and he started worrying about his wayward hose. "Well, I've been thinking about those dances." *That made two of them.* "And how you owe me one, since I got suckered into two." She grinned. "I'm ready to cash in."

"Excellent," he said.

"What makes a good baseball coach? I need a list of traits."

He blinked as his brain reset and his heated and primed body realized it had just been played like an expert no-hitter. "You're asking me for advice on who to hire to coach this team?"

"I am. Did you think I was asking you for something else?"

He chuckled. "You are a piece of work, Rachel Reed."

"I have no idea what you mean," she said innocently. "But, seriously, will you help me? My father created a ranked list for coaching prospects, but I'm finding some of the top choices have already taken jobs elsewhere, which has made a real mess of my list, and … well, my father isn't exactly up to creating a new one at the moment."

It seemed innocent enough. "I don't know," Sam said. "This feels like another changeup."

"A what?"

"A pitch that looks like a fastball, right down the pipe, but ends up being off-speed and devastating." *At least for me.*

"I'm not sure exactly how that relates to this," she said. "I just want to know how to read these guys. I want to make sure their resumes don't get the best of me. I want to get a handle on who a baseball player would really want to play for so I can recognize it when I see it."

Sam appreciated the approach. Experience wasn't always the best predictor of personality. Some of his worst coaches had been veterans—jaded, set in their ways. Honestly, he had a lot to say on the topic, but the churning in his gut felt like a longing he didn't want to explore.

"I'm not a baseball player," he said. "I'm a landscaper."

"Oh, please." Rachel gave him a look that said he was full of it, and that simple look rattled him.

"It was a long time ago," he said, trying to get his bearings.

This time, when she stared into his eyes, it felt like she was seeing everything. The highs. The lows. The pleasure. The pain.

He looked away.

"It wasn't long enough to make you forget everything, Sam. We both know you still think about baseball. Surely, you can tell me what makes a good coach. It would be a big help. And you owe me."

When he looked at her again, she was smiling, and somehow that went a long way toward soothing his anxiousness.

Fine. If Rachel wanted something out of him, he was going to get something out of her. "We can talk about it tonight over a beer."

"I'm booked solid," she said.

"Of course you are." Despite the sarcasm in his voice, he knew she was telling the truth. He couldn't imagine what it would take to start a baseball team from scratch. And to be doing it in the face of your parent's serious health issues?

Actually, that gave them a few things in common. Ten years ago he'd been building a career in the face of his mother's illness. For him, it proved to be an impossible situation. Eventually he'd had to choose ... Something more than a few coaches had encouraged him to do. *What would your mother want you to do?* Amazingly the answer had been play baseball. Make her proud. Achieve his major-league dreams. Only one coach had ever tried to get him to go home. *Benny Bryant.* "Your mother's going to tell you to focus on your career, because that's what mothers do," he'd said. "They put their kids first. You ought to put her first." It had given Sam a lot to think about, and he'd stayed up most of the night doing so. But come morning, when he'd pretty much made up his mind to take a few days off and go home, he'd been called up. Triple-A. One flash in the pan away from playing on the big-league stage.

Damn it. Sam should've listened to Coach Bryant, because his career had gone downhill from there, and in a frantic attempt to save it, he never did get home—until it was too late.

He clenched his teeth and weathered the memories. "You want to know what makes a good coach?" he asked, letting his gaze land on the white plate behind Rachel. "I'll tell you. It's a man who sees the bigger picture, even while he's studying your micromechanics. It's a man who teaches his guys to play hard and play to win, but not to hold on so tight you squeeze the life out of it. It's a man who knows, in the grand scheme of things, baseball is just a game."

Rachel was quiet for a minute, looking him over with concern in her eyes, and then she asked, "Do men like that really exist in professional sports?"

Sam nodded. "I've met a few. A guy named Benny Bryant comes to mind."

"Think you could pick out a man like Benny Bryant from my father's lineup?" She reached into her big, black bag and pulled out a stack of folders held together by a thick rubber band.

Boy, you gave her an inch, and she took an acre. "That's a little more than I agreed to."

She smiled, and he felt his mood lift again. "That extra dance was bound to be costly." Then she glanced at his feet but not before she seemed to target the button-fly of his jeans. "Not to mention the little incident with the hose."

He chuckled. "Couldn't I just pay for your dry cleaning?"

"You could, but this would be a lot more fun."

"For who?" he asked, even as he reached for the papers.

To his surprise, she placed her hand in his and squeezed. "Thank you. I mean it. You're helping me out more than you'll ever know." Then she passed him the folders and glanced down at her feet, where the tips of her shiny black heels were speckled with droplets of water. "Your hose is leaking," she said, pointing to a miniscule spray of water shooting out of a pinhole a foot or so away. "Might want to have someone take a look at that."

It was difficult, but he managed to refrain from suggesting she take a good, long, close-up look herself … any time she wanted. He had a crew in the outfield watching his every move.

Still, she was tempting. And no matter what she said or how she deflected, she was interested in him, too. He could tell. He'd been flirted with as a means to an end before, and while he was certain some of that was going on here, there was something else too. Something more. Something he couldn't wait to explore.

The question was: When and where?

Chapter Eight

"Boss man, we're loading up!" Ian yelled.

Rachel stepped away from Sam, who was dishing out the most intense eye contact she'd ever received, before she blurted out the proposition she'd been contemplating these last few days. The one that had nothing to do with baseball.

"You're being paged," she said.

Sam nodded and waved at Ian without taking his eyes off Rachel. "I'll be right there."

Which was probably a good thing, because the middle of a workday was not the best place to proposition someone who worked for you. *Temporarily*, she reminded herself. Indulging in a little fling with Sam wasn't going to cross any ethical lines as far as she was concerned. Still, she could be patient. Although, it would be a lot easier if he didn't look so good in those jeans.

He left her for a minute, placing the folder full of resumes on the seat of a utility vehicle otherwise weighed down with various field supplies, and then he walked back and said, "How's your dad? You mentioned he wasn't up to helping you make a new list. That doesn't sound good."

Talk about a change in topic. "He's, uh, good." But he wasn't.

Sam held her gaze with a tilt of his head and an "I'm not buying it" look. Just like she had when they'd been dancing, she opened her mouth and spilled her guts. "He's not good. I went to a doctor's appointment with my parents and learned he's had Alzheimer's for two years. Can you believe that? I just found out two months ago. It's infuriating."

"I bet," he said.

"If I'd known two years ago, things would be different now."

"How so?"

"Better doctors. Better medicine. Anything and everything. I wouldn't have sat around and accepted things the way they were."

"You still won't. You're not that kind of person. And the way I look at it, it's better late than never. The bottom line is"—the most beautiful smile punctuated his words—"you being here is a good thing. A great thing, actually."

She thought about that for a minute, thought about him, standing there, looking at her like she was the only woman in the world, and the heat was undeniable. The attraction unmistakable. Sam Sutter was a mouth-wateringly beautiful man. Five years younger and without a discernible life plan, but, damn it, libidos didn't care about those things. And honestly, the only thing holding her back from taking out all her recent frustrations on his blessed body right now was the fact that his crew was just outside the left-field wall.

To neutralize the lust bubbling in her veins, she asked, "Do you miss baseball?"

He looked blindsided by the random question and didn't rush to answer.

"I know that came out of left field"—she grinned at her cleverness—"but I've been wondering about it ever since the festival. When my dad was asking you about baseball, you looked very uncomfortable."

His gaze shifted away from her and anchored onto something in the grandstand, but then he shrugged like she hadn't hit a nerve. "I was uncomfortable because I was worried about your father. I wasn't sure what was going on. That's all." But his jaw pulsed, and she knew better.

"Sam ..." She stepped closer, narrowing the space between them. "I saw that same look a minute ago when I asked you to help me out with the coaching prospects. You miss baseball. It's okay to admit it. If you didn't, you wouldn't be human. God, you played every year of your life until you were how old? Just because you were ready to hang it up professionally doesn't mean you don't miss the game personally." He looked at her then with a hurt in his eyes that seemed to be saying maybe he wasn't as ready to hang it up as he pretended to be.

"I miss some things more than others," he said. "There's a rush you get from playing the game." Silence stretched out between them as the warm wind wrapped them in the sun-dried fragrances of spring. All the while, his eyes roamed her face until they focused on her lips. "Fortunately, you can get that rush from other things."

"Like?" she asked breathlessly, knowing damned well she was encouraging him.

"This," he whispered before he leaned in and kissed her, a brush of his lips, soft as the breeze that carried the heated scent of his skin to her nose and then to her brain.

Not enough, it said. *More.*

She grabbed his shirt, pulled him closer, and touched her tongue to the seam of his lips.

He opened, tangled his tongue with hers, slipped his free hand to the small of her back like he had when they were dancing, and held her body tight.

More, she thought, even as the blood pulsed in her ears and her skin buzzed with pleasure. And the minute she felt him hard against the soft of her belly, she knew exactly what it would take to satisfy her. All of him. Too bad she wasn't naïve enough to think this was the time or place.

Rachel took one last lick of his lips and pulled away. The world was spinning. She took a deep breath and blinked a few times to steady herself. Maybe she'd forgotten to eat. Maybe she'd been so wrapped up in selling this team and, before that, selling whatever she could get her hands on in Philadelphia, that she'd neglected her physical needs. Because this was a bit melodramatic as far as post-kiss reactions went. *Spinning?*

"Damn," he said in a raspy voice that made her world teeter again. "I was curious. I'm even more curious now." He reached for her.

"Sam."

"Don't Sam me," he said with a grin. "You felt it, too."

"Of course I did. I'm not dead." She tried to make light of the situation, but her face burned from the body heat, and her lips ached for one more taste.

"Then why don't you satisfy my curiosity?"

"Because your crew could walk back in here any minute."

"Then let's find someplace else."

Now *that* was a dangerously attractive invitation. But over Sam's shoulder, Rachel saw Ian coming through the left-field gate. Perfect timing. Mostly. She stepped back and shook her head. "Not today, Romeo. You're holding up your crew, and I'm booked solid. Remember?"

"Dude, should we leave without you?" Ian asked.

"Yes," Sam mouthed at her.

"No!" she yelled to Ian. "He'll be right there."

Sam looked frustratingly sexy when he asked, "Are you busy tomorrow?"

"I am."

He bent down, picked up the hose at his feet, and pulled it back toward the dugout. "You can't be busy forever, Rachel."

"You don't know me very well."

"You should let me get to know you."

Meaningful conversation was an unnecessary step when it came to the casual sexual relationships she was used to, and come to think of it, that kiss was anything but casual. She glanced at the stack of folders sitting on the seat of the utility vehicle and knew there was a lot to lose if she made a misstep here. Yes, she was a grown woman who could handle a work-related fling, but something was telling her this time, she shouldn't let it go that far. "You know, maybe we should forget this ever happened."

He looked at her pointedly. "That's not possible."

Exactly. Her hands were still shaking.

"In fact," he added, "I'm going to remind you about it every day for the rest of the time you're here, and by the time you leave, you won't be able to forget me if you tried." He wiped his hands on his glorious jeans and gave her a wink and a smile before he walked off to join Ian.

She admired him all the way around the warning track.

Great. Another challenge. One more thing she could add to her to-do list while she was in Arlington: don't get sucked in by Sam Sutter.

• • •

Sam didn't feel like entertaining tonight. He had a stack of applications to go through on his kitchen counter and some serious rehashing of the hottest kiss he'd ever laid lips on to do. Not to mention brainstorming a plan to get Rachel to let that damned guard of hers down so next time they could take things a little further.

So much for being a man without a plan. He touched his beer bottle to his bottom lip and smiled.

"What are you grinning at?" his father asked.

"Just thinking about something Ian said at work." He knew that would be enough to squash the line of questioning.

"Speaking of work …" His father leaned forward in his Adirondack chair and poked a stick into the fire. "I have something to tell you boys."

Luke dug in the cooler of beer, fished out a bottle of Bud, and asked, "Anyone else need a refill?"

"I'll take one," Sam said. Something about the way their father had called them together for a guys' night and then waited until they were all good and relaxed to make an announcement had Sam thinking he might need the extra drink. Surely, his father wasn't going to drop something crazy on them, like getting remarried. No way. The guy didn't even date. At least Sam didn't think he did.

He accepted the open beer from Luke with a thank you and then gave him a look that said, "I have a bad feeling about this."

"I signed another commercial contract this afternoon. Four shopping centers and two doctors' offices for PPI Management." The old man was beaming.

Sam let out a sigh of relief and lifted his bottle in the air "Congratulations, Dad. I know how much you've been gunning for this. That's great news." *Thank God.* No stepmom Sam had never met.

Luke echoed Sam's sentiments.

"Thank you, boys. This means a lot to me, because I know how much it can mean for you and your families. Well, in your case"—he looked at Sam—"your future family."

Sam sucked down some more suds. He wasn't fundamentally opposed to a family of his own, and he knew that was something his mother had wanted for him, but he wasn't going to marry until he was damn good and ready. Unfortunately, most of his family thought thirty-five years old was past time.

"And," his father continued, "I'm ready to hand over the business, boys."

Changeup, Sam thought, and he straightened, wanting to protest but not sure why or how.

Before he could say a word, his father added, "You'll split it 50-50. Sam, I'm making you the head of commercial landscaping, effective immediately. You've handled the stadium project like a real professional, and I'm proud of you. Luke, I'm making you the head of residential. We'll talk money as soon as I meet with my accountant and lawyer."

"Wow," Luke said. "I can't say I was expecting this."

The words *a real professional* rolled around in Sam's head. Was that what you called kissing Rachel Reed in the middle of right field? *Real professional.* The mouthful of beer he'd swallowed rose up into his throat.

"But what will you do, Dad?" Luke asked.

"What I've always wanted to do: sit back, relax, and watch my boys run things. I'll still be on the payroll, answering phones and drumming up new business, but I'm cutting back. Way back. I think I've earned it."

"You have," Sam said, finally finding some words.

A comfortable silence settled around them, and Sam watched the embers from the glowing fire lift into the night sky. He picked the label off his bottle of Bud and thought, *So this is my future now.* You got what you got when you didn't have a plan, but the idea of spending the rest of his life taking care of a baseball field where some other lucky son of a bitch got to play …

He needed something stronger than beer.

Beyond the trees, something stirred, and he looked around the fire for Babe. She was sleeping on the ground beside his father's chair. Sam glanced at the man lounging with his feet kicked up on the cooler, a look of blissful contentment on his face. Sam wasn't about to be an ungrateful son and tell him he wasn't sure he wanted to be locked into landscaping for the rest of his life.

For some reason, that made him think of Rachel again—and that kiss. And when he randomly caught Luke's eye, he felt guilty. It was stupid. Rachel and Luke were ancient history, but getting carried away the way Sam had this afternoon had been careless. Immature. Anything but *real professional.* If something like that got back to his father and brother, he would have serious explaining to do.

Rachel had been right. They needed to just forget that kiss had ever happened. From this point on, Sam was going to keep his hands away from the Rachel Reed cookie jar—no matter how tempting those cookies were.

When the fire had died enough for Sam to douse it with dirt, the three Sutter men followed Babe to the house. Sam's father said his goodbyes at the bottom of the deck steps. The man was still smiling. After dishing out hearty hugs to both his boys, he left, and Sam wished Luke would follow. He *really* wasn't feeling like entertaining anymore.

"Can I hang for about thirty minutes?" Luke asked. "I don't want to get home until my mother-in-law leaves."

Sam knew Mandy's mom. She was nice but overbearing, and he'd witnessed firsthand the way she treated Luke like a moron when it came to taking care of the kids. "Okay," Sam said, and he led his brother into the house, where they sat at the kitchen table and drank another beer.

Luke lifted his bottle. "Here's to becoming business owners."

Sam didn't bother touching his bottle to Luke's, he simply drank.

"Am I sensing some ambivalence here?"

Sam shook his head. "I'm just tired." He knew Luke wouldn't let that lie, so when Babe scratched at the back door despite having been outside for the last three hours, Sam got up and let her out.

Feeling restless and unable to pin his thoughts down, he stood on the deck in relative darkness while Babe moved in and out of the beam from the security light mounted on the back of his house. To his surprise, the dog peed quickly, and he reluctantly went back inside, hoping Luke would be willing to change the subject.

And he was. But the new topic wasn't something Sam cared to discuss, either.

"What's this?" Luke asked. He'd moved from his spot at the table and was standing at the island with one hand atop Rachel's folders, which were clearly marked "coaching candidates."

Annoyance coursed through Sam's veins, and he snapped. "Nothing that concerns you."

Worry lines creased Luke's face. "Did you hear Dad? He said 50-50. If you're thinking about coaching a baseball team, doesn't that concern me?"

"I'm not coaching a baseball team," Sam said bitterly. He was thirty-five, not sixty with nothing better to do.

"Okay, well, whatever it is, I need to know. Dad needs to know. He just gave you 50 percent of his company. Are you or are you not going to be there 100 percent of the time?"

"Of course I'm going to be there," Sam said lethally.

Luke frowned, then put his bottle in the sink, and after a long exhale said, "That comment had nothing to do with Mom. I wasn't insinuating you … just forget I said anything." He roughed a hand over his forehead. "I guess I'm tired, too, man, and … I'm sorry. I am. I only want you to be happy. Always have. I'd just love for you to be happy working side by side with me." He gripped Sam's shoulder and squeezed, infusing a load of emotion into the gesture.

"I am happy," Sam said, but he couldn't make full eye contact, and after Luke had gone, the conversation reverberated in Sam's head. It put him on the defensive. How could he forget what Luke had said?

For ten years, Sam had been everywhere and anywhere his family had needed him to be. But all it had taken was one glimpse of a folder marked "coaching candidates" for Luke to assume the worst—Sam was going to toss the family aside and go back to baseball. He snatched the dishtowel off the counter and flung it against the stainless-steel refrigerator. The impact was slow and soft and ineffective.

He spied the stack of folders that had caused the trouble in the first place and thought about throwing those, too. But Babe was watching.

"Everything's okay, girl," he said. "Everything's fine." It wasn't like someone he loved was dying ... or had Alzheimer's. And as much as he didn't want to disappoint Rachel, he knew—he didn't have the time or luxury to be helping her build this ball team.

Chapter Nine

Liv flopped on the plastic couch in Rachel's hotel room and brought a travel mug partway to her lips. "Richard drives me crazy. He treats me like I'm a lowly assistant. I was so glad when you asked me to come back to Arlington."

"You are a lowly assistant," Rachel said, looking up from her iPad with a smile. "But you're my lowly assistant, and he has no business treating you poorly. I'll make sure he gets the message loud and clear."

"Thank you," Liv said.

"My pleasure. Now, we need to get down to business. Wes had to push back the tree cutting again." Rachel sighed. "I tried to talk to my father about our options, but he's been in a depressive funk for most of the last week. If I can't rely on him for something simple like that, I can hardly expect him to help me with these interviews."

"So you called me."

"Yes, and ..." For a split second, Rachel hesitated before mentioning her enlistment of Sam. That kiss had done more than complicate things between them; it had royally screwed up her usually flawless focus. His heady eyes. His hungry lips. His solid body and big hands. She was at the point where she didn't even need to close her eyes to conjure those images.

"And?"

"Oh. Sorry about that. I, uh, asked Sam Sutter to give me some perspective on the coaching applicants," Rachel said in a rapid but matter-of-fact tone that belied the mental replay of the flirty way she'd enlisted his help and the searing kiss that had followed.

Liv's eyes narrowed inquisitively. "Really? You asked the landscaper's opinion?"

Her tone was incredulous, and Rachel chuckled. "Sam used to play in the minor leagues."

"Oh," she said. "Wait, I thought the interviews were just a technicality because your father had already listed who should be hired based on their resumes."

"The lists are a mess." And as much as she didn't want to go out on her own, Rachel was going to have to if her father couldn't clearly and consistently talk to her about what he wanted. Getting Sam involved was a calculated move. "I'm hoping the baseball bug will bite him, because having a hometown guy in the mix would be great publicity."

"You're right!" Liv perched on the edge of her seat. "Maybe you can sneak him into the coaching mix? Or do you think he'd be better in the front office? Assistant GM, head of personnel scouting? Wait. Do they even have scouts in this league?"

"I have no idea," Rachel said, returning her attention to her iPad. "Before you walked in, I was reading league news, and I didn't see anything about scouts. I did see that Elvis Landry took a coaching job in Virginia, however."

"He was on our list, right?"

Rachel swiped her finger to move up the screen and nodded. "Yep, another one gone. We are so behind the other teams when it comes to hiring, I'm starting to worry nobody good is going to be left."

"Then you really should talk to your dad about getting Sam involved."

Something on the screen caught Rachel's eye: the age of veteran players had been increased. Before she knew it, she was fully engrossed in an article about the Independence League owner's meeting and holding up a hand to silence Liv.

According to the article, each team in the league now had the right to designate "one 'veteran' player who may have attained forty years of age prior to January 1 of that playing season."

Her pulse kicked up as she reread a couple paragraphs just to be sure she was understanding things correctly, because if she was, that meant Sam could play.

Would he even want to after all these years? She glossed over that consideration and imagined the story this would make. A thirty-five-year-old former professional baseball player getting his shot on the field again. What if he was still good—good enough to win a championship? Disney made movies about stuff like that. Talk about inspirational. Surely, the Arlington media would eat it up, and the free publicity would help the ticket office put butts in those seats.

The whole idea gave her chills, and she passed the iPad to Liv. "Look at this."

Liv studied the piece for a minute. "What about it?"

"Why should Sam coach or sit in the front office when he can play?"

"*Can* he still play?" Liv wondered, looking skeptical. "I mean, is he physically capable of it?"

"Of course he is," Rachel said with a wave of her hand. "Why wouldn't he be? He's in great shape, and it's probably like riding a bike. He just needs to pick up a bat again." That part might prove tricky, though, considering his ambivalence toward baseball every other time she'd raised the topic.

"I don't know," Liv said. "Those guys train for years. Besides, isn't Sam kind of … old?"

Rachel glared at the twenty-five-year-old sitting across from her. "He's thirty-five. That's not old. Come on! Didn't you read that article? The Independence League's new age increase for veteran players gives Sam five more years to rewrite his history where baseball is concerned."

Ooh! She liked the sound of that and made a mental note to use that phrase when she pitched him this idea later.

Again, Liv's eyes narrowed. "You're awfully interested in Sam Sutter."

"Correction: I'm interested in what Sam Sutter can do for me."

Liv's look turned sly. "We're still talking baseball-related things, right?"

Rachel's face heated, because there were a great many things the man could do for her off the field, too, and those things kept jockeying for space in her mind until she lost control of her mouth and blurted, "He kissed me."

Liv's shocked expression gave way to a raucous laugh.

"It's not funny," Rachel hissed.

"Did you kiss him back?"

"Of course I did," she said, and when that sent Liv into a further paroxysm of giggles, Rachel softened and smiled, too.

"Wait, where did this happen? And when? I want details."

"Yesterday. In the middle of the field. In the middle of the workday." Rachel shook her head and closed her eyes, indulging in the split-second memory of that positively sinful liplock. "I lost all composure and went after the man." She groaned. "Ugh. Do you realize what this means?"

"You're interested in more than his baseballs?" Liv laughed harder.

"No! Yes. I mean …" She winced. "It means I've officially taken on too much, and I'm cracking up. All this stress, all the deals I'm missing in Philadelphia, my father's health, drama from my family, putting together this team when I know nothing about the business of baseball …" She exhaled loudly. "All of this has rendered me incapable of making reasonable decisions. At least where Sam is concerned."

And that scared the hell out of her. She couldn't remember another time in her life when she'd felt so off-kilter.

"I think it's cool," Liv said. "He's hot. For an older dude. I think you should go for it, Boss."

Leave it to someone dressed in a crinoline skirt and Betsey Johnson platform heels to think that. Was this what things had come to? Spilling her guts about her sex life to her assistant in the middle of a strategy meeting? "It is not cool." Her voice turned steely. "It is unprofessional, and it has become a distraction. I don't do distractions."

"Everybody deserves a distraction now and then, especially you, especially now. I don't see what the big deal is. He's not married, and he's not that much younger than you."

Rachel groaned. "Enough! How the hell did we get so off topic?"

Liv bobbed her brows. "Just one more question."

Rachel decided to allow it. She looked at Liv expectantly.

"Is he a better kisser than his brother?"

Rachel was the one to laugh hard that time. "No comparison. When I kissed Luke, I kissed a boy. When I kissed Sam, I kissed a man." She absentmindedly touched her lips. "It was amazing."

"Then I say kiss the man whenever you want, because you look happier talking about this than you've looked talking about anything else since I met you ..." Liv gulped suddenly, as if her own candidness had taken her by surprise. Then she added a somewhat chastened, "Boss."

Rachel rolled her eyes and snatched back her iPad, but couldn't suppress a smile. "Maybe you're the one who's cracking up after too much time with Richard."

A visibly relieved Liv made a gagging sound while Rachel scanned the article again. *This* was her best plan yet. "I just need to find a way to confirm that Sam still has the skills, and then I have to convince him it's in his best interest to play again." She shot a pointed look at Liv. "I am definitely talking about baseball here. I don't need to kiss him again to accomplish any of that."

Liv chuckled. "Whatever you say, Boss. But if I were you, I'd use any excuse I could to let him into my batter's box again."

• • •

Monday morning, Sam drove the utility cart along the warning track, the rubber band-bound stack of unread folders on the bench beside him. If Rachel came down to talk to him—like he expected her to—he would give them back and apologize.

He'd considered lying, telling her he didn't see anything worthwhile in the stack, but that wouldn't be fair to the guys hoping to coach this team. Instead, he would tell her she was right and, in an effort to keep things strictly professional between them, he was returning the folders unread. It seemed like a reasonable explanation to him.

But two hours later, when Rachel strutted down the warning track with a glorious smile on her face, nothing seemed reasonable anymore. The woman was mouthwatering.

"Good morning," she said. Two simple words, and his pulse raced. The sheer blouse, showing hints of lacy bra, didn't help.

"Morning." He took a step closer and told himself he was dead if he took another one.

He didn't have to, because she came to him. "How was your weekend? Relaxing, I hope."

You know what was relaxing? Orgasms. Slow-building, long-lasting orgasms that left you spent in the end. Too bad he hadn't had that sort of weekend. With her.

He cleared his throat. "My weekend was good. How was yours?"

"Mine was good, too. Did you have a chance to look over those resumes?"

And there it was, the real reason she was talking to him, the only reason he should be talking to her about anything outside of field care. "I did not," he said. "I got sidetracked."

"Oh," she said, her beautiful face momentarily crumbling, but when she regained her composure, her expression hardened. "I was counting on your input, Sam. This puts me in a real bind." She glanced away from him and was silent for several seconds.

As he stood there trying to think of a way to better justify his behavior, she added, "Could you look them over quickly at some point today, and then"—a solitary eyebrow rose suggestively—"we could discuss it tonight?"

Between the brow raise and lowered voice, Sam figured their discussion would turn into other things—things he'd been dreaming about for weeks now, things he was still dreaming about despite his father's announcement and his brother's suspicion that baseball was going to drag him away again.

"I'll see what I can do," he said, but there was more ambivalence behind those words than he'd wanted.

She must've detected it, because she nodded and took a step back. "Thanks for even considering it."

The stilted interaction bothered him all day.

"She's got nice legs," Ian said as they raked the clay between the dugouts and home plate.

"Who?" Sam asked.

"Her." Ian lifted his rake and pointed the handle toward the outfield bleacher seats, where Rachel and Liv were staring up at the scoreboard.

"Which one?" If Ian said Rachel, Sam might have to hurt him.

"The little one. What's her name? Liz?"

"Liv," Sam said with a shake of his head. "And how can you tell how nice her legs are from all the way back here? I can't even tell it's a woman."

"'Cause you're old, man. You need glasses. Like the kind my grandma wears around her neck on a chain."

"Those are bifocals, idiot, and they're for reading. I can see just fine. I was exaggerating."

"Oh yeah? Can you read the number on the center-field wall?"

"Four hundred and ten feet," Sam said without looking. He'd memorized the number after spying it for the first time two weeks ago and wondering if he still had it in him to crank one that far.

"How about the words on that faded advertisement?"

"Shut up and rake," Sam said. "I'll go get us some waters."

He snatched a bottle from the cooler strapped to the flatbed and called a heads up to Ian before he tossed it his way, then he cracked open another bottle and sucked down more than half of it. All the while, those folders kept calling his name. Taking a look at them was the only way to assuage the feeling that he'd let her down. Sam sat behind the wheel with the cart top shielding him from the afternoon sun and pulled the stack of resumes onto his lap. Contrary to what Luke thought, it didn't mean he was heading down a slippery slope toward a job in baseball. Sam was just keeping his word and helping a friend—if that's what he could call her.

He had no idea how long he'd been sitting there leafing through the papers before Rachel called his name. It must've been a decent chunk of time, because he was more than halfway through, and as he pushed the stack off his lap and back onto the seat, he felt a little dazed. The feeling only multiplied when he saw her. She was standing amid the seats behind home plate with her long fingers curled into the protective netting, and she wore a wide-eyed look of anticipation that had him more than a little curious.

He went to her and asked, "What's up?" in a calm voice he hoped covered the havoc she wreaked inside of him.

"We never made specific plans to talk. What time's good for you?" Her mouth was perfectly framed by an opening in the net, and he imagined leaning up to kiss her. After a hit. A walk-off home run. With the crowd cheering and his teammates gathering. He would cross home plate, high-five his teammates, and end up here, with his mouth on hers. The perfect ending to a perfect game.

"What time?" she asked again, and he snapped out of the disturbing fantasy.

"Now?"

She glanced at Ian, who had moved down the third-base line to talk with CJ, who was watering the base path. "Well, I'd like to talk alone. Can you hang around after they leave?"

His lips twitched, because professionalism be damned, he liked the sound of being alone with her anywhere. "Whatever the lady wants." And when she returned his full-wattage smile, he had a feeling he was about to get very lucky.

It took forty-five minutes for the guys to get cleaned up and off the field. Sam did more work than he normally would have simply so he could get them out of here. When he made his way back into the stadium after helping them load up CJ's truck, he found Rachel standing on the mound. Wind tore at her hair and her dress clothes, plastering the flimsy blouse to her breasts. *Jesus.* Sex on the pitcher's mound? He had to fight his legs from breaking into a dead sprint. *Keep it semi-professional, okay, man?*

"So, I've been thinking," she said, when he was a few feet away.

"So have I."

"I have a proposition for you."

With his skin tightening and his heart rate climbing, he glanced around the empty stadium, wondering if any witnesses were left.

"If you hit a home run off me, I'll spare your trees." She brought her hand out from behind her back, and in it was a baseball.

Her words hit him like a fastball meant to maim. "And why would you do that?"

She smiled. "I have my sights set on something even bigger than a parking lot."

Him? The way she was staring him down with laser-beam intensity made him think so, but there was no need for some half-assed home-run derby to get him into bed. Another kiss would have him hauling her home faster than a lobbed pitch could travel 410 feet.

He glanced back at the white number on the center-field wall and felt his palms itch. "I'm not sure what's going on here. I thought we were going to talk about coaching staff."

"Do you want to save the trees or not?"

"Of course I want to save the trees, but I don't want to sell my soul in the process. What are you up to, Rachel?"

"I'm just trying to prove a point," she said, tossing the ball into the air a few inches and catching it. "I think there's still some good baseball left inside you."

Sam's muscles tensed. "I'm sure there is, but I don't see why that matters."

"It matters if you want to save the trees."

He shook his head. "I'll pass. Something doesn't feel right." He looked past her to home plate, where six bats lined up against the fence. Waiting for him.

Again, his palms itched.

"Are you afraid I'll strike you out?"

"No. I doubt you can literally throw a changeup. I would be more afraid of me taking your head off, even with the pitching screen. There's no way in hell you can make the throw from anywhere near this mound. You'll have to be right on top of me."

She grinned. "Sounds good to me."

"What the hell are you up to?" he asked again, but his eyes were trained on the lineup of bats, and already his hands were flexing in preparation of picking the perfect one.

"How about it? Home run for the trees?"

"You're serious?"

"Absolutely."

"And there are no strings attached?"

"None. I just want to see you hit." She bobbed her brows like maybe this was some warped version of foreplay.

"You might be disappointed."

"I highly doubt it." She gave him the once-over. "You don't look like the kind of man that could ever disappoint a woman."

This was crazy. Rachel wasn't making any sense, and still he was considering playing her game. Because he wanted sex? Hell, he could get it a lot easier and a lot less twisted than this. But apparently he liked twisted, because his blood was already pooling between his legs.

"I want it in writing," he said.

She laughed. The sounded carried on the wind, filling the charged air between them, stoking the heat in his belly. "I figured you might say that, so"—she reached behind her back and pulled a folded piece of paper from her pocket—"I brought this." She stepped off the mound and offered him the paper.

When he took it, his fingertips dragged across her palm, and her body shuddered. So help him God, he was going to get more than a few acres of trees out of this deal.

"Good enough?" she asked when he'd unfolded the paper and read her loopy handwriting.

"Good enough for me." He refolded it and stuffed it into his back pocket, then he eyed up the bats again and took a deep, settling breath. "How 'bout you throw a few warm-up pitches so I can get a feel for you?"

Her eyes twinkled as she took her place behind the pitching screen, where a bucket of balls waited. "Feel away."

He almost detoured to where she stood just so he could take her up on the offer. Instead, he watched her toss a ball overhand toward home plate and thought, *Not bad*. "Aim for the dirty smudge on the padded wall." If he could get her consistently throwing strikes at that slower speed, he should be able to hit a home run with no problem.

She bent down and snatched another ball from the bucket, her eyes trained on the smudge behind home plate, and then she released a pitch that landed a foot off its mark. "How many warm-up pitches do I get?"

"As many as you need." He was already wondering how many warm-up swings he was going to need to get used to the feel of a bat in his hands again.

As another pitch popped against the padding, Sam reached for the shortest bat in the lineup, but right before his fingers reached the grip, he pulled back. His heart thrashed around wildly, his tongue glued to the roof of his dry mouth.

Pop. Another pitch. And then she whooped. "That was definitely a strike!"

Another deep breath and he reached out again, telling himself he was saving the trees. But the lump in his throat wasn't there for the sake of some birds. No, the lump was about the boy who still loved this game.

He grabbed the bat and steadied his breathing. All good. Nothing to fear. It was heavier than he remembered. Powerful. He took a few light swings with nothing more than a flick of his wrist. Back and forth. Back and forth. Lulling him into a trance. Before long, he was swinging the bat behind his shoulders, rotating his wrists in a familiar warm-up pattern. He set his feet, squared his hips, and settled his gaze on the ball as it left Rachel's hand. *See it Hit it.* He swung, sending the bat whizzing through the air in a warm-up swing that knocked the breath out of him.

Rachel whooped again. "I'm ready!"

Was he? He adjusted his grip and stared at the snow-white rubber. *Four hundred and ten feet.* He'd wanted a shot at that since he'd walked into this place. Now was his chance.

Sam took his place at the plate, and with surprising ease, his body fell back into old routines: tapping the head of the bat on the insides of both feet, bending his knees, and bouncing three times exactly, before he brought the bat behind his ear and adjusted his grip. Locked and loaded. He watched the ball leave her hand fought the urge to blink, and followed it in all the way until it met his bat.

Whoosh. Crack.

Foul ball.

His hands burned from the vibration.

"Another one," she called out, and he reset, exhaling the nerves.

See it. Hit it.

That ball sailed over his head.

She laughed. "My bad."

And yet for some reason, it made him smile. Rachel Reed was throwing him batting practice. Never in his wildest dreams …

This time when he set, the smile lingered as he watched her fake spit on the ball and shine it in the untucked hem of her blouse. "Nothing but heat, slugger," she teased, and he laughed even while the ball sailed toward him.

He reacted without thought, transferring his weight forward, dipping his back shoulder the slightest bit, pulling with his hips, leveling out, finishing long, and swinging up and through.

The crack was nuclear, splitting atoms in the air as the ball soared over the infield, higher and higher, until it didn't cast a shadow on the outfield grass. He stood there breathless, vibrating with power, watching the ball clear the fence right above the *410 feet* sign.

The good news? He'd saved the trees. The bad news? He still loved baseball.

A lifetime of mowing lawns looked less appealing than ever.

Chapter Ten

Rachel charged home plate, fueled by the rush of being irrefutably right.

Sam Sutter still had some good baseball left in him—maybe even great baseball.

"Oh my God!" She flung her arms around his neck. "That was amazing."

"Four hundred and ten feet." He wrapped her up and lifted her off the ground with ease. Pure strength. Pure heat. Their bodies pressed together in silent celebration.

"You have to play again," she said, her mouth against his ear. "Try out for the Aces."

He set her down and let her go, and his glorious smile slipped away. "You said no strings."

"I know. I meant that. You get the trees. Fair and square. But come on, Sam! After seeing that, how can you not want to play again?"

He flipped the bat toward the ones she'd lined up earlier. "I'm not interested in letting baseball wreak havoc on my life again."

"It wouldn't. You're older and wiser. You can rule baseball this time. And in a league like this, in your hometown, you would have more power than most. Don't you see? It's a chance for you to rewrite your history with baseball."

He stared into the outfield. "You're crazy."

"I'm the sanest person you'll ever meet."

His golden gaze landed on her face and dropped to her lips. "Is that why you kissed me?"

"*You* kissed *me*."

When he smiled, the technicalities didn't matter. Nothing mattered. She felt sixteen again, with an overactive imagination and raging hormones.

"It was mutual," he said.

"Mutual curiosity." Not that they weren't mutually attracted, too.

"How 'bout we throw in a little mutual satisfaction, too?" he asked, stepping closer.

Regardless of what Rachel had said to Liv about not kissing him again, she wanted to, and she would have if she hadn't thought he was just trying to throw her off topic by bringing the kiss up in the first place. "Sam, I want—"

"Boss! I'm sorry to interrupt, but your phone has been ringing nonstop." Liv stood on the wide walkway between the box seats and the grandstand. "It's your mother."

"What do you want?" Sam asked Rachel, his gaze locked on her, as if Liv wasn't even there.

"Like right now," Liv said. "She's calling again."

All the heat Rachel had been feeling gave way to inexplicable anxiety. "I'm coming," she said to Liv, and then she looked at Sam, who waited expectantly for her answer. "I want you to seriously consider trying out for this team."

Shadows slashed his chiseled cheekbones, and his eyes darkened. "Is that all you want?"

"No. I'd like you to go through those resumes in your cart and give me your honest opinion, too."

He smiled. "Anything else?"

"Not that I can think of."

"You're sure?" He drilled her with those sexy eyes.

"For now." Then she scrambled toward Liv and her incessantly ringing phone, knowing they still had unfinished business to settle.

Her gut was telling her that, right now, she had bigger things to worry about.

● ● ●

Rachel Reed was driving Sam crazy. She wanted more from him than he was able to give. First, his opinion on potential coaching staff. Now, his butt in the lineup on opening day. Why couldn't she be happy with his butt, period?

And yet here he was with a cold beer in hand and the stack of resumes in his lap, wondering what it would be like to put on a uniform after all these years. Maybe he was too old. Jeter had played at thirty-five. *But you're not Jeter.* Franco had been forty-nine in his last appearance for the Braves. *You're not Franco, either.*

But he had hit the crap out of that ball this afternoon. Drilled it dead center. Four hundred and ten feet, which was short of the four hundred and thirty-six feet needed to belt one out of Minute Maid Park but more than enough to clear the three hundred and ninety feet at Fenway. Sam had never gotten to play at either place. And while that sucked, it didn't fill him with enough regret to fire him up and make him want another shot at those big-league dreams.

He took a long pull on his beer and dropped his left hand to smooth Babe's head. So, what did he want? The same thing he'd been doing day in and day out for the last ten years: he wanted to do right by his family. But for some reason, that didn't feel like enough anymore.

His gaze settled on the mantle, where a picture from his high-school graduation day sat beside a silver urn containing one third of his mother's ashes. In the picture, she stood on his right side, his father on the left. She was looking at Sam. Marveling at him. And that look of blind love and admiration said, *This young man can do anything and everything.*

Another pull. A long, slow stroke along the sweet spot between Babe's ears and then down her back. "I saved your trees, Mom," Sam whispered. But he wondered what it would cost him in the end. The sense of peace he'd cultivated all these baseball-free years, that was for sure.

He opened the top folder and scanned the first resume. Before too long, he found himself fully engaged, picking out men he wanted to play for, looking for guys with outside interests that made them seem human. Arnie Slater volunteered at a local food bank and insisted his players did, too. Jack Kent played oboe in his local orchestra during the off-season. There was an avid sailor, a classically trained painter, a father of eight girls, a master chef, a published author, and an ordained minister. Men with lives outside baseball. The kind of man Sam wished he'd been when he'd played.

Two hours later, he grabbed the stack of folders and his keys off the hook by the door and decided to deliver the results to Rachel in person. He was excited about the list but even more excited to see her again.

Unfortunately, it wasn't the flirty, sexually charged meeting he'd been hoping to have.

"How long has he been missing?" Sam stood on the Reeds' wraparound porch scanning the lush landscape. At least three acres of pristine grounds stretched between the front door and the road. A long, winding, gravel lane led to a circular driveway where three Arlington Police cars and an ambulance waited. The men who'd driven the vehicles were out looking for Danny Reed.

"Since we were at the field today," Rachel said, clearly worried. "That's why my mother was calling. He was supposed to be showering and getting dressed, but when my mother went to check on him, she found the French doors in the master bedroom open, and he was gone." She white-knuckled the edges of an oversized cardigan sweater, shielding herself against the evening chill. "The police think he's lost in the woods behind the house." She looked sick and sad, and every part of Sam wanted to fix this for her.

"We'll find him." He smoothed a reassuring hand up her arm to her shoulder, where he squeezed, then he jumped off the porch and headed to his truck, where he grabbed a sweatshirt and a flashlight because darkness was closing in.

Rachel remained frozen in place, a shell of the take-charge woman he'd come to know.

"We got this," he said confidently.

To up their odds, he called his father and then his brother, asking Luke to bring Babe to help with the search. Then Sam ran toward the trees. In the distance, he could hear other searchers calling out to Mr. Reed. As their voices faded, an eerie silence settled over the land, and Sam prayed Rachel's father hadn't wandered far enough to reach the gorge. Two waterfalls and a 150-foot cliff weren't things a seasoned hiker wanted to come across after nightfall. He didn't even want to think about the threat this landscape posed to a mentally compromised man.

Once inside the cover of trees, Sam took the path of least resistance, thinking it highly probable Mr. Reed had done the same. With his flashlight exposing the darker sides of fallen trees and mounds of earth, he covered as much ground as possible while keeping his eyes and ears open for any movement.

Twenty minutes into his search, Babe found him, along with a text from Luke that said he and Dad were in the woods, too.

"Come on, girl. Let's find Mr. Reed."

Images of Rachel worried and worn filled Sam's head as he led Babe closer to the mouth of the gorge. With each step, his own worries magnified. He did not want to find a dead man.

Every so often, Babe would take off, leaving Sam hopeful. But when she didn't cause a ruckus, only to return to him, his heart would sink again. By the time Sam reached the gorge, it was good and dark. He drew in a deep breath and called out for Mr. Reed. Nothing but his echo answered.

Maybe the man had tricked everyone and wandered out the front of his house, taking off in the opposite direction. Route 19 was busy, but Sam would take his chances with drivers who were used to encountering deer in the middle of the road over terrain like this.

He shone the beam from his flashlight into the abyss. In the distance, water gurgled over the rocky creek bed, sparkling faintly. If Mr. Reed had fallen, there was no way Sam would know without making his way to the bottom, and that would be suicide without a headlamp and some rope.

Babe bolted from his side again, causing Sam to jump. "Be careful," he called out foolishly. The last thing he needed was to lose her, too. And then he skirted the edge of the gorge, hoping to find an easier way down.

In the distance, Babe barked.

Sam froze, his attention pinned on the sound.

A yip and a growl followed.

She'd found something. And although it was entirely possible that something was a deer bedded down for the night, Sam sprinted toward her, hoping to find Mr. Reed alive and well.

A few yards into the darkness, the barking stopped, making it infinitely harder for Sam to know if he was traveling in the right direction. He slowed his pace and called out to Babe. When the branches cracked up ahead and her shadowy form emerged from the darkness, his heart sank again. Another false alarm.

Except, Babe circled him, whining as she went, running a few feet in front of him and then circling back around as if she wanted to show him something. Something important.

"Mr. Reed!" Sam hollered, moving swiftly behind Babe, who was surging forward and doubling back at a frantic pace.

No answer. Not a sound except Sam and Babe stomping the undergrowth and Sam's heart thudding out of his chest.

"Mr. Reed!" he called again, only to have Babe veer off toward the gorge and stand barking at the edge.

Shit. Sam swallowed a rush of panic and dropped to his knees. With his flashlight in hand, he took a fortifying breath and peered into the abyss.

To his surprise, a generous ledge of rock protruded from the side of the cliff, and on it was a huddled-up man dressed in boxer shorts and a T-shirt.

"Mr. Reed!" Without thought for his own safety, Sam scrambled over the edge and lowered himself to the outcropping of rock.

There was give in the ground around him, and as he moved carefully in the confined space, he heard the rattle of stones breaking away from the ledge. A jolt of fear ripped through him, intensifying when he realized Mr. Reed wasn't moving.

Sam hesitated, a prayer on his lips, and then he touched the man's shoulder, hoping to rouse him. Once. Twice.

"Help." The word could barely be heard

Thank God! "Are you hurt?"

Mr. Reed shook his head and struggled to sit. "Cold," he said through chattering teeth.

Sam helped him—always mindful of their precarious position—and then he whipped off his sweatshirt and pulled it over Mr. Reed's head. He lifted the man's ice-cold arms one at a time to thread them through the armholes. Finally, he lifted the hood and tied it beneath Mr. Reed's chin.

In a swath of moonlight, their eyes connected, and Danny said, "Thank you."

Sam didn't normally cry, but the tears spilled freely as he ran his hands over Mr. Reed's arms and legs, checking for any major injuries. They needed to get off this ledge to safer ground.

"Did I miss dinner?" Mr. Reed asked.

He'd missed more than dinner; he was missing his socks, too.

Sam hurried out of his work boots and wool socks. "You did, but I bet they'll have a feast waiting for you when you get home. Here. Let's put these on you." He rolled one sock down to its toe and slid it over Mr. Reed's frozen foot. Then he did the same with the other and asked the man to stand. "I'll help you."

"You're a power hitter, aren't you?" Mr. Reed asked while he straightened on shaky legs.

Considering their current predicament, it was an odd question, but for the first time in ten years, Sam felt like he could answer—and answer with a smile. "Yes, I am." A 410-foot shot out of Mr. Reed's stadium was proof of that.

"You play for the Cubs."

Sam frowned. "Not anymore." He gripped the man beneath his elbows and said, "It's very important you stay right here. Do not move."

"I own a baseball team. Do you know that?"

"I do."

"You should play for me."

Apparently that thought ran in the family.

Sam ignored the comment in favor of explaining how he planned to hoist Mr. Reed to safety, but he wasn't at all convinced it would work without someone getting killed.

Somewhere in the distance, Babe barked, followed by the muffled sound of Luke calling Sam's name.

Relief flooded Sam's body. "We're down here!" And then to Mr. Reed, he said, "My brother is coming to help."

"Hang on, Sam!"

"And that's my dad," Sam said, damn near euphoric. "We'll have no problem getting you out of here now."

The lift off the ledge went smoothly, and as soon as Sam was up, he dialed 9-1-1, followed by a call to Rachel. They didn't talk long. He didn't say much, just, "We got him," and, "He's okay."

Rachel's joyful cries fueled Sam's desire to get Mr. Reed out of the deep woods to where the paramedics were waiting with a stretcher. Of course, Rachel and her family were waiting there, too.

She ran to her father first, and when everyone followed Mr. Reed to the waiting ambulance, she doubled back and came to them.

"Thank you all! So much. I don't know how we'll ever repay you."

"Repay him," Sam's father said. "He's the one who found your father. Babe just found us and showed us the way."

Rachel latched on to Sam, pressing her cold cheek to his warm neck. "Thank you!"

"You're welcome," he said, holding on a little tighter and longer than necessary.

Then she was gone, striding over the lawn toward her family and the ambulance.

"Good job, boys," Sam's father said, throwing an arm around the shoulders of each son. "I'd say that deserves a beer. We'll stop by your house first and drop off the dog."

Which meant Sam could grab another sweatshirt and a pair of socks. He'd taken the phrase 'give the shirt off your back' quite literally. And he didn't mind one bit.

He was starting to think he'd do just about anything for Rachel Reed.

Chapter Eleven

Rachel moved into the chair her mother had vacated when she'd left her husband's side to find a ladies' room. Since Helen Anne had gone home to relieve Liv, who'd been staying with Macy, Rachel was alone in the ER with her sleeping father. He was covered in a heap of warm blankets with wires monitoring his every move. Except for a bruise on his forehead, a scratch on his right cheek, and a few cuts and scrapes on his feet, he was in decent shape. Physically. But dehydration, hunger, and exposure, coupled with the usual Alzheimer's symptoms, left him drifting in and out of rational thought and conversation.

Thank God for Sam. She texted him to share that sentiment and to tell him her father was okay. Short and sweet. But before he could respond, Rachel was pulled away by her father's weak and raspy voice.

"Jackie?"

She grabbed his hand, careful of the wires. "It's me, Dad. Rachel. How are you feeling?"

"Terrible." He groaned, but it sounded more emotional than physical. "I'm so sorry I worried you."

"I'm just glad you're okay."

"I don't know what happened."

"I know."

"I'm scared."

She fought the tears for no other reason than not to alarm him.

"I don't know why I can't remember some things," he said.

"Because you have Alzheimer's," she said. It seemed particularly cruel that he had to be reminded of the very thing that was crushing him.

"Yes." His voice trailed off with a hint of sadness. "I'm so sorry," he said again. "Maybe we should sell the baseball team."

It was like someone pressed rewind, and she vacillated between wanting to sob and wanting to shake the disease right out of him. "I'm trying," she whispered, and then she dropped her head to his chest, closed her eyes, and let the beating of his heart soothe her. He could've died tonight, but he didn't. That was what mattered now.

"Danny! You're awake." Rachel's mother stood on the other side of the hospital bed, smoothing the hair off her husband's bandaged forehead.

"I'm so sorry," he said again, and Rachel couldn't bear another minute of it.

She excused herself and escaped to the ladies' room, never having felt so helpless before. She'd always believed that if you worked hard enough, you achieved. It wasn't magic. It was cause and effect. She'd amassed power and fortune before she'd even turned thirty, following her father's lead. But all the hard work, money, and power couldn't have saved him today.

And it might not be able to save her in the future.

She hated that, hated this feeling of impotence. Rage so thick and deep stole her breath and challenged her balance. She leaned against the wall and grasped for composure, knowing anger wasn't going to change anything. And that's what needed to happen. *Change.* For starters, they couldn't assume he was safe at home anymore. Fortunately, money could help with that. She would research and buy the best alarms and have the locks altered on the doors so that he couldn't escape without someone being notified. She'd hire additional help if that's what her mother needed. Whatever it would take to keep her father safe and comfortable, Rachel would buy it.

With any luck, it would be enough to make her feel comfortable again, too, because when the rage died, she was left with a horrible fear that all the control and care in the world wasn't going to make a damn bit of difference. One of these days, he wouldn't recognize her. He would forget his kids, his wife, his successes and failures, and there was nothing anyone could do to stop it.

An hour later, Rachel didn't argue when her mother suggested she go home and get some rest. She headed across town in the blinding rain through the blur of tears, wishing to be numb. She didn't want to think anymore. She didn't want to feel. Too many worries. Too much emotion. More than she had ever let in before. And she didn't know how to bottle them up again.

Her brain kept whirring and churning until thoughts of Sam appeared. She owed him more than those trees after what he'd done tonight, but she didn't know what to give him that would come remotely close to proving her gratitude. He'd become more important to her than he could possibly know.

Maybe she should start by telling him that.

•••

Sam wrapped a towel around Babe and rubbed her dry. Five minutes in the backyard to do her business, and she was soaked through. When she was dry enough to stop the incessant shaking, he grabbed a couple more towels from the linen closet to clean the kitchen floor.

That's where Sam was, on his hands and knees in the hallway between the kitchen and living room, when a heavy knock sounded on the door, followed by the ringing bell.

Babe howled and beat him there. She rounded back, trying to tell him what she'd heard. "I know, girl," he said. "I'm right behind you."

He looked at the hand-carved mantle clock his father had given him as a housewarming gift. *Ten thirty p.m.* Who the heck would show up this late and on a night like this?

Rachel. He could feel her presence, and that was just about the strangest thing that had ever happened to him. It probably colored the way he looked when he opened the door, but then he saw her, sopping wet, droplets falling off her bangs to her clumped lashes, where they dripped down her cheeks, and he didn't stand a chance in hell of hiding his concern.

He grabbed her hand and pulled her out of the rain and into his arms. "How long were you standing there?"

She shook her head against his shoulder, soaking his shirt. "I couldn't decide whether or not to actually go through with this."

He lifted her face to his. "With what?"

"Coming here. To you. I don't know. I don't know what I'm doing."

Her teeth rattled. Her body shook. Her face was as white as a sheaf of paper.

"I'm glad you came," he said, snatching a clean towel off the pile, wrapping it around her hair, and wicking away the moisture with a massaging motion that made her close her eyes and sway gently with his movements. Then he cupped her cheeks in the soft terry cloth and dabbed her face clean. "How does a fire sound?"

"Heavenly," she whispered without opening her eyes, and he was beyond powerless. Leaning forward, he brushed his lips against hers in the sweetest kiss.

Rachel opened her eyes. "Thank you. For everything."

He wasn't interested in rehashing what he did or didn't do. He just wanted to get her warm and settled. After he wrapped her in a blanket and left her on the couch, he headed to the back porch for some wood. Normally, he would've split the kindling right there, but between the wind and the rain and his worry, he returned to the family room and used a hatchet to section thin pieces of larger logs to start the fire.

She didn't say a word, but every so often when he looked at her, she was watching him.

"Are you hungry?" he asked.

She shook her head.

"Thirsty?"

Her head tilted thoughtfully. "Got any wine?"

He chuckled. "Beer and bourbon."

"I'll take a bourbon," she said with a weak smile. "No ice."

There it was, a hint of the gutsy woman he'd come to admire, and … as he smiled back at her, he knew there was something more than admiration. Instead of trying to pin down his feelings, he lit the fire and headed to the kitchen, where he poured her bourbon and grabbed a bottle of beer. When he returned to the living room, Babe was snuggled against Rachel in a primal show of protection.

"She's sweet," Rachel said.

"She probably senses you're chilled. She has incredible instincts."

"They came in handy today."

"Exactly," he said, taking a seat on the chair angled toward Rachel. "How was he when you left?"

"Okay. Some cuts and bruises, but considering what happened, he's miraculously fine."

"How are you?"

"Scared out of my mind. And I hate it." She took a hearty swallow of the amber liquid Sam had poured into a juice glass. "My whole life, my father has been the one with the grand plan, the one I looked up to and followed like a dog." She glanced at Babe and smoothed a hand down her side. "Sorry, girl. Not that there's anything wrong with that. Look how successful it's made me. But now, the man I follow doesn't even know where he's going. How sad is that?"

"Sad," Sam said, because it was, and he sensed she had more to say.

"And what if I'm next? I'm forty, you know? Sixty-five will be here before I know it, and there's a genetic component to this stupid disease."

"You're not next."

"You don't know that." She took another drink, swallowing it without a struggle. "I spent my whole life managing my career while I mismanaged my personal relationships because that's what my dad did, and it worked out okay for him. All the traveling, all the missed opportunities to have a conversation with his family about something other than business. We all still love him madly, so why couldn't that work for me? But it didn't." Her laugh sounded slightly unhinged. "I'm rich. I'm powerful. And I'm completely alone. Unless you count Liv, which I don't, because she's on my payroll, and I highly doubt I will be able to pay her enough to take care of my crotchety old ass when I start losing my memory."

He watched her polish off the bourbon and realized he hadn't taken a drink of his beer. Then again, he hadn't had the day she'd had. He probably would've sucked down an entire case if the tables had been turned.

Sam set his beer down and laid a supportive hand on her knee. "In your dismal version of what's to come, you have twenty-five years before it all goes to hell, right?"

Her eyes widened, but then she agreed.

"Well, then I say you're lucky. You've still got twenty-five good years. Focus on that."

"I can't. Not when I know what's ahead. I've done so much research, Sam. At this point in the game, exhibiting these symptoms, my father could only have four or five years left. There's nothing lucky about that. This disease will kill him, and before it does, it will make me a stranger to him." She held out her glass. "More please."

He obliged, figuring she could spend the night if she got carried away. Under different circumstances, he'd be all kinds of thrilled about that. But it was surprisingly easy to keep the libido in check when someone you cared about was struggling. He wasn't exactly sure why he cared, considering she'd roared into his life wielding a figurative chainsaw, but he did. He didn't want to see her broken. She had way too much to live for. And the more he thought about that, the more he wished someone had said something similar to him in the days and weeks and months and years following his mother's death. Maybe he could be that person for Rachel.

After her returned to the room and handed over the second glass of bourbon, he watched her stare thoughtfully at the crackling fire, wondering what he could say to make her feel better.

"You know what really bothers me?" she asked, surprising him. "For as close as my father and I are, we aren't. I mean, we're business partners, and I can tell you what he will do in a boardroom before he even does it. He could tell you the same thing about me, but …" She balanced the glass on her pulled-up knee. "We don't share anything outside of work. I've always suspected he has that sort of relationship with my sister. Helen Anne was always allowed to be the daughter. I needed to be the son."

"Have you ever tried to be just his daughter?"

Creases lined her forehead. "I don't think I know how to do that." She lifted the glass to her lips but paused. "And I'm out of time, now."

"No. You're not." He knew what if felt like to really and truly be out of time. "I'm the one who's out of time. My mother is dead, and there's not a damn thing I can do to make up for the things I regret."

"What do you regret?" she asked hesitantly.

"Not coming home to say goodbye. I wasn't here when she died, and I should've been. I should've jumped the minute she asked me to. Now, it's literally too late. Your dad is here, Rachel. He might not remember everything, but you still have time left.

Do something with it. If anyone can, you can. The woman I'm looking at is unstoppable."

Finally, she smiled. "Why are you so nice to me? I broke your brother's heart."

"You were eighteen, and he's recovered."

"They all do."

"Heartbreaker." He grinned.

"Me? How about you? Former professional athlete turned perpetually tanned-and-buffed landscaper. There has to be a line of women hoping to make an honest man out of you."

"Nope. Too much pressure. My mom always wanted to see me married with kids. Somehow, I figured I would fuck that up, too. Single is easier. Less responsibility."

"More fun," she said saucily.

"It can be."

She set the glass on the ponderosa pine table beside her and dropped her feet to the floor. "Sam, I was serious when I said you should try out for the team."

He pressed back in his chair and chuckled. "You are ruthless."

"Determined."

"Crazy." Their eyes locked, and he thought, *But apparently I am, too, because I can't stop thinking about it.*

A slow, confident smile brightened her face, which was bathed in an ethereal glow from the fire. "Come here," she said. "I'll show you something really crazy."

He slipped off the chair and onto his knees, grabbing her by the hands and pulling her toward him. She went easily, kneeling in front of him, the blanket hugging her shoulders. He tucked her still damp hair behind her ears and soaked in every plane and curve on her beautiful face, and then he slanted his mouth over hers with a hunger he could no longer contain.

She met him more than halfway, heading straight for the button on his pants. But before she could find the leverage to release it he had her arms raised and her blouse sliding overhead. Soft and warm. He brushed his lips against her throat, fit his hands to her waist, and breathed in the scent of roses on a summer day. "You overwhelm me."

Her hands tangled in his hair, guiding his head lower to the fleshy mounds that overflowed her lace bra. He licked the cavern between them.

"Sam." It was a breathless plea that went straight to his groin.

But then she reached back to release her bra, thrusting perfection in his face, and he was the one who was breathless. Breathless and aching. Hot from the fire to his back and the woman to his front. Hard from the throaty sounds she made when he took her breasts in his hands. Heavy and full. Tight at the tip. Wanting him.

He swirled his tongue around one nipple while he brushed the other with this thumb, loving the way her back arched, urging him to take more. He opened wider while he pushed her silky dress pants to her knees.

A thin scrap of triangular fabric was all that stood between him and sweet release, but she had other ideas. She stood briefly, shedding her pants with an elegant kick, giving him a praying man's view of an angel. He growled in appreciation, and she was back on her knees, brushing her breasts against his chest, nuzzling his jaw, his ear, guiding his T-shirt over his stomach, grazing her fingernails over his lats.

He sucked in a breath as she rid him of his shirt and boldly admired him. Tracing the path of his muscles from his shoulders, to his pecs, to his abs.

"Let's try this again," she said, smiling. And this time she made short work of the button on his jeans. "Better," she whispered against his lips as she reached inside his boxer briefs and wrapped a warm hand around his pulsing erection.

He held the back of her head, drove his tongue into her mouth, and guided her to the floor beneath him.

"I want to be on top," she said. It wasn't a request.

Sam wrapped her in his arms and rolled them until Rachel was straddling him, nothing but that flimsy thong in his way. Bypassing the lace with his fingers, he slipped one between her folds, sliding it back and forth over the hardened nub.

She closed her eyes and moved against his hand, giving him a show to beat all shows. And right when he thought he had her ready to explode, she stretched out to reach her purse.

"Condom," she rasped.

For some reason, that made him laugh. "I have some, too."

"We only need one."

He might have argued with her if she weren't already stroking the sense right out of him.

"Are you going to take this off?" he asked, hooking his finger around the elastic of her panties, drawing it down over her hips.

Then she was on all fours above him, wriggling out of them, while she planted saucy kisses on his lips. "How's that?" She slid along his erection, and he nearly lost control right there.

"Condom," he said through gritted teeth, but he should've known she would want control of that, too.

Rachel sat back across his thighs and took her good old time rolling the protection into place. He grinned and bared it, knowing he was about to watch her become unglued.

He caressed her hips, her sides, her breasts, his mouth watering. And then he was inside her, filling her completely, closing his eyes and letting the pleasure carry him away.

While she rode him expertly, he stroked her core, toyed with her breasts, and feasted on her mouth when she offered it. Her body tightened and her rhythm painfully slowed as his fingers continued their slide.

"I can't wait for you," she said, raspy and ready for release.

"Good," he ground out, and then he thrust deeper, lifting them both while he maintained the pressure on the swollen folds between her legs.

"Sam!" She tossed her head back and screamed while glorious spasms milked his erection from the inside.

Fucking incredible. Watching her was almost more than he could take.

He grabbed her hips and rocked slowly, savoring the pulsing of her body until she crashed back to earth—to him—with her hands on the floor beside his head and her breasts teasing his mouth. Faster and faster they moved.

Then, with a groan ripped from his chest, he tumbled over the edge, too.

...

Sex with Sam had been just what Rachel needed. She was already starting to feel like her old self again. Calm and clear. Challenges be damned.

While he was cleaning up in the bathroom, she dressed, then finished her bourbon by the fire, reveling in the warmth both inside and out. There was nothing like an orgasm to banish emotional fog from the brain. Thank God that oppressive, dark cloud had finally lifted.

Sam reappeared, and he was underdressed. His unbuttoned and unzipped jeans hung loosely around his waist, giving her a peek of the navy-blue band of his boxer briefs, flat against his happy trail. She stared. Blatantly. Letting her gaze roll over his corded stomach to his chest.

"Are you rethinking that crack about only needing one condom?" he asked.

Yes. But what would it prove? That she was needy? Nope. She set the empty glass on the hearth and stood. "As great as that was, it probably won't happen again."

He stuffed his hands into his pockets, riding his pants a little lower, eyeing her up suspiciously. "*Probably* leaves room for persuasion. I can be very persuasive."

"I'm sure you can be," she said, smiling. "But I'll be leaving soon, so odds aren't really in our favor. From here on out, I need to focus my energy and limit my risks."

"Sounds romantic," he said in a sarcastic tone that managed to still sound sexy.

"I'm not interested in romance, Sam. I'm only interested in—"

"The bottom line," he said while he tilted his head for a better look at her ass. "Me, too."

She chuckled. "You think you have me figured out, but how did you know I wasn't going to say something like, I don't know, orgasms?"

He grinned. "If that's what you're interested in, I can definitely help with that."

She felt every inch of her body soften as she looked at him. "You've helped with a lot of things tonight, Sam, and I'm very grateful."

"I'm glad."

Rachel was glad, too. She felt refreshed and renewed. Sam had been a lifesaver—literally, with her father—an escape from the turmoil, and a sympathetic ear. He'd also been a surprising source of wisdom. He was right: Her father was here. She still had time. If baseball was one of her father's few sources of enjoyment these days, then while she was in Arlington, she was going to involve him with the team as much as possible. And maybe in the process she would find a way to be the daughter she'd always wanted to be.

Chapter Twelve

Whoever said a man's home was his castle wasn't a businessman.

Rachel watched her father stake his claim on the stadium office she'd been using since she first arrived in Arlington. Yes, the office being positioned at the end of the hall allowed for a brilliant view of the uncut trees beyond the original parking lot *and* the emerald-green baseball diamond, but it wasn't the biggest office. She tried to point that out, while holding back the fact that he wasn't actually going to be working here for long, so what did it matter? It was almost April. Tryouts were in a few weeks, and Opening Day was a little more than a month after that. Once they reached that point, the team would be self-sufficient, running on Mark Oleans's orders, and Rachel would be back in Philadelphia, entertaining potential buyers from afar. Who else but her would be willing to put up with her father underfoot?

"Dad."

"I need to face the door," he said. "Grab the other side."

Oh, what the hell. Rachel did as he asked. She'd brought him here. Her idea. Well, Sam's idea actually. *You still have some time left. Do something with it.*

She repositioned the chair behind the desk. "How's that?"

Her father sat, nodded, and smiled. "Perfect. What time's our first meeting?"

"No meetings, today. Paper products are being delivered. I'll oversee that and the stocking of the concession stands around noon. Then a photographer is coming to take pictures for the ... portfolio." She was purposefully vague. Some days he acted like she was the devil, trying to sell his team out from underneath him. On those days, reasoning with him, telling him it had been his idea in the first place, didn't work. She didn't want today to be that kind of day.

Rachel walked to the widow and admired Sam's work. "The field looks great."

"I played on a field like that once." In the silence that ensued, her father came to stand beside her.

Surprise mixed with hope that this could be something personal for them to share. "As a boy?" she asked, wanting to keep the conversation flowing.

"Boys don't play on fields like that. I played in college."

"For UPenn?" She'd followed in her father's footsteps to the Wharton School of Business, much to Luke Sutter's chagrin. He'd wanted her to go to Penn State, where he was set to major in agricultural sciences. The thought of being married to a farmer bothered her only slightly less than the thought of disappointing her father. She had no regrets.

For some reason, that made her think of Sam.

"No," her father said. "I played in a summer wooden-bat league in Cape Cod."

"I never knew."

He shrugged. "You never asked."

Very true. Very sad. But she was asking now, because it wasn't too late, especially for conversation like this. Her father's long-term memory was blessedly still intact. "Why didn't you play for UPenn?"

"I was there to study, not mess around. My father wouldn't have had it any other way. Baseball was the fallback for boys without brains. I had a brain." He frowned.

Was he thinking about the Alzheimer's now?

"What time's our first meeting?" he asked, and this time, she frowned.

"No meetings today, Dad."

He threw up his hands. "How can we get this team ready for Opening Day if we aren't having meetings? Where's the … ?" His brows knitted together at the top of his nose in a sort of startled confusion. "I want to talk to … Who's in charge?"

"You are? I am?" She wasn't sure what he was asking.

"No! You're not a goddamn coach."

She bristled at the disappointment in his voice. "We hired a general manager, but not a coach."

"What kind of baseball team doesn't have a coach?"

"We will. We're close to hiring. Candidates are being contacted."

He walked back to the desk and sat. "Tell Monica to bring me some coffee."

Rachel sighed. When he was agitated like this, there was no reason to tell him Monica wasn't here. "Okay." Instead, Rachel stepped out into the hall and texted Liv, who was down in ticket sales, helping the new hires get a handle on the software.

Can you bring me up a cup of coffee? Black.

Her father walked past her down the hall at a clipped pace.

"Hey, where are you going?"

"Down to the field," he said in a perfectly normal tone of voice. "Why don't you come with me?"

Like she had a choice.

Never mind, she texted Liv as she followed after him. Maybe bringing her father to the stadium had been a bad idea.

Then again, he seemed perfectly normal the entire way down to the field. At one point, he even gave her shoulder a squeeze and said, "This is our best business collaboration yet."

It made Rachel's heart sing, like the old days, when he would come to the Philadelphia office and praise her over lunch for meticulously following his directions and making the business thrive.

That's where her focus was when they turned the corner and heard, "Good afternoon!"

Sam's rich voice rumbled right through Rachel, littering her skin with patches of heat.

Several days had passed since she'd last seen him—naked. She'd expected some awkwardness, but she hadn't expect this instant flood of desire. It coursed through her, wild and teeming.

"Hello," she said evenly.

"Mr. Reed, how are you?" Sam nodded and reached forward, offering his hand.

Rachel almost took it just to touch him, which was alarming. She wasn't normally this interested in a man. Then again, none of this was normal. She was out of her element, working closely with a very hot, slightly younger man. No suit. No tie. No agenda.

She watched his thick forearm as he shook her father's hand. Noticed his ragtag jeans. His easy smile. The genuine interest in whatever her father was saying. Sam mesmerized her, persuading her to spend more time with him without even saying a word.

Speaking of not saying a word ... nothing in the conversation alluded to what had happened in the woods. No mention of the search or the hospital. Maybe her father didn't remember. Maybe Sam figured as much and went with the flow. He really was a good listener.

The conversation focused on chalkers, liners, and field spray. It was a snippet of normalcy, and Rachel felt something blossom beneath her breast that she hadn't felt in a while: joy. She was still wallowing in it when she suggested they let Sam get back to work.

"Of course," her father said. "I could use another cup of coffee."

She made a mental note to steer him toward the downstairs break room, where she could grab them both a cup, but before she headed off in that direction, she glanced back at Sam, who was smiling at her. The sexy, satisfied smile of a man who was thinking about a woman naked. She smiled back, infusing the same damn thing in her expression. And then he winked, as if to say, "I'll see you again soon. Very soon."

She would have to seriously consider that.

· · ·

Liv was leaving for Philadelphia in the morning and Rachel had finally conceded to staying with her parents rather than at the hotel, so the pair hit up Foley's to toast their recent burst of progress. Their to-do list was shrinking, the front office staff was in place, and she had a workable list of coaching candidates to hand over to Mark Olean, thanks to Sam.

Of course, the minute she thought about Sam, he walked into Foley's, wearing a sinfully fitted pair of jeans and a thin, gray, crewneck sweater.

Sam's gaze locked onto her as if she were magnetic.

Rachel smiled, to which Liv glanced over her shoulder and paled. "He's with Ian."

"He's always with Ian."

"Let's go." Liv slid toward the edge of the booth.

Rachel looked at their untouched buffalo-chicken salads and ruby-slipper martinis. "No."

"He's going to come over here, and I'm going to say something stupid."

"So what?"

"He'll know I think he's hot."

"I don't see how that's a bad thing. You have an empty hotel room right next door."

"I would die."

"A very happy death."

"I mean, I wish I could, but I'm just not confident like that. I overthink everything."

"A good lover will make you forget your name."

Liv blushed. Rachel laughed. And the guys ambled toward them like a dessert platter.

"Ladies," Sam said, holding a bottle of beer.

"Gentlemen," she returned.

Ian smiled down at Liv, who was inordinately fascinated by her salad. "Hi," she managed, adding a little wave of her fork.

"Why don't you guys join us?" Rachel asked. She was evil. She made no excuses. Instead, she tapped the toe of her heel on Liv's. "Wouldn't that be nice?"

"Sure!" Liv said, sounding slightly deranged.

Ian either didn't notice or didn't mind the awkwardness. He dropped his bottle to the table and slid into the booth beside Liv with a playful nudge. He probably said something funny, too, but Rachel didn't hear it, because Sam moved into the booth beside her, pressing the full heat of his body against her side, from knee to shoulder. All she could hear was the whooshing of her heartbeat in her ears.

She was too old to be feeling like this. Wasn't she?

"Hey," he said, smiling. "It was nice seeing your dad at the field today."

"It was nice having him there."

"Speaking of the field ..." Ian raised his bottle. "I have an announcement to make. I'm trying out for the Arlington Aces."

Rachel looked at Sam, who seemed to be stunned silent.

Well, well. At least someone at this table was trying out for the team. Ian wasn't the local guy she wanted and needed, but he would definitely help—maybe even to get Sam to play.

"I didn't know you played baseball," she said, lifting her martini glass.

"I'm nothing like this one"—Ian hitched a thumb in Sam's direction—"but I can play.

"Good for you," Sam said. "I hope you make it." But his voice sounded strained.

Rachel was about to ask him why he didn't join Ian for tryouts as moral support, when Ian said, "Air hockey table is open!" like an overgrown kid.

"Um …" Sam looked at Rachel, and something intimate and pleasurable shot through her. "I'm going to hang out here for a little bit. Why don't you take Liv to play?"

"Do you play?" Ian asked.

"She sure does," Rachel answered with her gaze locked on Sam's and her foot nudging Liv out of the booth.

"She doesn't play, does she?" Sam asked when the odd couple had gone.

"I don't know. I doubt it."

"Trial by fire." He slid a hand up her thigh, and she melted.

She was definitely too old to be feeling like this, but for the time being, she didn't care. He was just that good. Too good. "Is there anything you're not good at?" she asked.

He laughed. "Yes."

"What?"

"Let me think about it."

She laughed, too. "Well, we know it's not sex or baseball."

He raised his brows. "You've experienced both once. How do you know they weren't flukes? You should definitely see me in action again before you make any rash decisions."

"I never make rash decisions."

He leaned back long and low in the booth, slinging his arm across the edge of the seatback behind her. "Excellent."

She angled toward him, propping her elbow on the table, so they could be eye to eye. And when she leaned closer, his pupils dilated, taking her in, turning her on. "I have an idea."

"So do I. Let's hope it's the same idea."

"If you try out for the team, I'll get to see the full breadth of your talent as a ball player."

His face wrinkled. "Not what I was thinking."

"Don't get pouty," she said, poking a finger at the corner of his mouth and lifting his lips into a lopsided, deranged smile. "There's more to this proposal."

"Thank God."

"The new workout facilities are sitting there empty. You have my permission to use them to get ready for tryouts."

"Oh. Thanks." Sexy sarcasm dripped off the word.

"You look disappointed."

"Aren't *you*?"

It was a loaded question better circumnavigated, but she tackled it head-on. "Sam, I'm a grown-ass woman here to do a job. If we get intimately involved on a regular basis it will just … complicate things when it's time for me to leave."

"I'm not asking for complicated, Rachel." His mouth was inches from hers, his beer-scented breath tickling her lips. "I'm just asking to make you weak again. Seems simple to me."

Very, if her pulse was any indicator. And she was tempted. So tempted to kiss the man right here. But then an ice-cold bucket of water in the shape of Luke Sutter walked into the bar and up to the sign marked "takeout."

"Maybe some other time," Rachel whispered and excused herself from the booth.

• • •

Sam watched as Luke turned away from the bar, putting him in Rachel's path. They seemed cordial enough, but then Luke looked Sam's way, and the tick in his jaw made things clear. Sam was going to hear about this later. Whatever *this* was. He wasn't sure how it had looked from the outside, but he sure as hell knew how it had felt.

"Hey." Ian plopped into the booth across from him. "Do you think she's going to eat this?" he asked, staring longingly at the barely touched salad.

"Order your own," Sam said, even though he was pretty sure the ladies wouldn't be back.

"Shit." Ian had turned his attention to his phone. "Well, that sucks."

"What sucks?" But Sam had his own idea when he saw Rachel huddled up with Liv in a conversation that no doubt involved discussion about leaving.

"Watts is sick. We're playing the first-place team this weekend. We need … Hey! Do you have any interest in subbing for us?"

No. But he heard himself ask, "What position does Watts play?"

"First."

Funny coincidence.

"Nobody should squawk about us bringing in a former professional, because you're pretty rusty and out of shape."

Why was everyone worried about his shape? Sam glanced down at his well-formed chest and shook his head. "I'm in great shape."

"So you'll do it?"

Maybe, but again he heard himself saying something different. "Sure. I'll give it a shot."

"Awesome, man. Maybe your next step can be trying out for the Aces."

Of course, that's when Luke walked up. Sam could've convinced himself his brother hadn't heard any of the conversation if it weren't for the steely set of his jaw.

"I figured I would come over and say hello," Luke said, eyeing up the table, which included two pink drinks in martini glasses. "Didn't mean to interrupt anything."

"It's all good," Sam said, even as he snuck a peek at Rachel, who was talking to the waitress, probably squaring away her bill so she didn't have to come back to the table. "How's Mandy?"

"Craving wings, and cravings can't be denied," Luke said with a smile, but there was wariness in his eyes.

"Exactly!" Ian said loudly. Then he picked up Liv's fork and dove into her salad.

"You're a piece of work," Sam said.

"Order for Luke!" called the kid behind the bar.

"That's me." Luke nodded a couple times and looked at Sam as if he had something more to say, but all that came out was, "Take it easy. See you guys at work."

This wouldn't be the end of it. Luke was either worked up over seeing Sam in a semi-compromising position with Rachel, or he'd heard enough of the conversation to think Sam was considering playing baseball again. He wouldn't be wrong thinking that. The minute Ian had made his announcement, Sam's chest had grown heavy with a desire to do the same damn thing. That's why he'd agreed to fill in for Ian's rec team. Sam wanted to play ball. It didn't matter where. Baseball had been eating at him ever since he'd walked onto that field.

Something else was eating at him, too. He watched Rachel leave the bar without a backward glance.

"Okay! It's all set," Ian said, finishing off a text and then shoving his phone aside in favor of the salad again. "You're officially a Bloody Bandit," he said with his mouth full. "Well, for the weekend at least. Let's hope you don't suck, man."

Yeah, Sam thought. *Let's hope.*

Chapter Thirteen

"What's going on between you and Sam Sutter?" Helen Anne asked.

Rachel had known eventually she would regret her decision to leave the hotel and stay with her family. Eventually had simply come faster than she'd expected.

She rolled her eyes over the rim of her coffee mug and said, "Let me guess. Someone saw us last night and couldn't wait to text you the juicy details."

"Jaime Klein. She was behind the bar." Helen Anne split an English muffin apart with a fork and dropped the halves into the toaster. "But she didn't give me any details."

"Because there aren't any. Liv and I went to grab a bite to eat, and we ran into Sam and Ian. End of story."

Helen Anne didn't look like she was buying it. "People saw you holding hands and dancing at the festival."

"So what?"

"These people are bored and hungry for distraction. They'll be more than happy to move on from cracking jokes about the fat Reed sister who couldn't keep her hot husband to the older Reed sister who is sleeping with a younger man." More hints about the divorce and the toll it had taken on Helen Anne. Rachel was just about to broach the topic and refute her sister's self-reproach when Helen Anne shut her up with, "Don't be their distraction, Rachel. Don't give them any more reasons to talk about how the mighty Reed family has fallen."

Had the Reeds really fallen? Rachel wasn't sure she could agree with her sister on that. In fact, Rachel didn't care if people talked about her. She would rather have them talking about her and Sam than talking about Helen Anne's divorce and their father's

Alzheimer's. "Everybody needs a little distraction," she said. "I don't mind being theirs. Let them talk about me."

Helen Anne stared at her, butter knife pointing at Rachel in accusation. "Who are you? Everybody needs a little distraction? Since when? You always said you couldn't afford to be distracted. Wasn't that what you told me when I asked if you wanted to be at Macy's birth?"

Ouch. And yes. But in Rachel's defense, she'd been under pressure with a deadline from her father to lease every last retail space in a King of Prussia outlet mall they'd recently purchased. Not to mention seeing her sister's lady parts torn to bits hadn't ranked high on Rachel's list.

Helen Anne dropped the knife into the sink with a huff and a clang.

Was that when things had gone drastically wrong between them? Rachel didn't know for sure. They'd never been best friends, but they'd been closer than this.

You still have some time left. Do something with it.

"I'm sorry I wasn't there," Rachel said. If only for the distance the decision seemed to have put between them.

Helen Anne nodded but didn't look at Rachel. "It's water under the bridge."

Rachel didn't believe her, and she sensed it was going to take more than an apology to fix whatever had gone wrong between them. More than words. Actions. And time, too. For the first time in recent memory, Rachel was willing. Someday—sooner than she'd been willing to admit—it would be just the two of them left.

"Mom!" Macy slid into the kitchen in a pair of knee-high fuzzy socks, her mobile phone in hand. "I have to go see Mr. Fry play baseball today. I totally forgot, and the game is at eleven. You can take me, right?"

"Of course not," Helen Anne said. "It's Saturday. I open the store at nine."

Macy's eyes widened. "But this is important. Mr. Fry said we can get extra credit for going. You own the store. Can't you just not open it until after the game?"

Helen Anne laughed. "No, and you don't need extra credit for fourth-grade P.E."

"But everyone is going!"

"So now we get to the truth. This is about hanging with your friends, not seeing your gym teacher play baseball. Isn't it?"

"Maybe you can go with a friend," Rachel interjected.

Helen Anne's eyes widened just like Macy's had, and then she grinned. "That's an excellent idea! Aunt Rachel is looking for distractions these days. She can take you."

"Yes!" Macy fist-pumped with her phone-free hand.

The know-it-all voice in Rachel's head whispered, *Here's your chance to make actions speak louder than words.* "Sounds like a plan," she said. And a few minutes later, she realized it was actually a good plan. She could spend the day with her niece, doing something that would hopefully mend a little of the rift between her and her sister, and while she was at it, she could scope out more of the local baseball talent to see if anyone else was worth recruiting.

A few hours later, Rachel and Macy walked carefully down the grass-and-gravel hill toward the Arlington Parks field complex. The paved parking lot was full, so Rachel had pulled onto the grass and left her BMW under a tree beside the picnic pavilion. When in Rome …

But now, it was all she could do not to slip on the soles of her favorite ballet flats, which were entirely impractical here. Macy did much better in her little white tennis shoes. They were covered in eyelet and secured with bows. Cute, stylish, but definitely capable of off-roading. Rachel made a mental note to pick up a pair. Then, she squashed that plan with the simple reminder that she wouldn't need something like that once she was back in Philadelphia.

"Can I sit with my friends?" Macy asked when the bleachers were in sight.

So much for spending time with her niece. But Rachel had been ten once, too. "Where are your friends?"

Macy pointed to a pack of six preteen girls sitting behind the first-base dugout.

"If you leave that spot, you need to tell me. I'll be at the top of the bleachers over there." She pointed to the metal-and-wood structure behind home plate and nearest the snack bar, figuring the placement would give her a good view of the field and Macy, who would only have two possible places to go—the snack bar or the restroom—if she chose to leave the bleachers. "And watch the game. Don't be talking the whole time about boys."

Macy made a prune face. "Aunt Rachel, boys are weird. Besides, I like baseball."

"You do?"

Macy nodded. "*Duh.* I play softball, which is almost the same thing as baseball, and Pop-Pop has taken me to lots of games."

Rachel stopped at the bottom of the hill and faced her niece. "He has?"

"Yep. We go see the Pirates all the time, but ..." Her green-eyed gaze flashed to the ground. "Well ... he can't do that now."

"No. I suppose not," Rachel said with a heavy heart. "But maybe your dad will take you."

"Probably not," Macy said. "He's always busy."

Like Rachel's dad had been when she was little. "Well, I bet your mom will."

Macy laughed, reddening her cheeks. "No way! Mom hates baseball. She says it's long and boring, and she doesn't like the way they scratch and spit."

Yep, that sounded like Helen Anne. "Well, then I'll take you. I like baseball." The guys weren't bad to look at, either—despite the scratching and spitting. She grinned.

"Would you really take me?" Macy asked.

"Absolutely. We'll look at the schedule and make a plan. But don't forget about the Aces. They'll be playing baseball right here in Arlington. You can go to every game and sit right behind home plate."

"You think?"

"I know. Pop-Pop owns the team."

"Yeah, but you're selling it." There wasn't any accusation in Macy's eyes like there had been in Helen Anne's.

"That's the plan," Rachel said, feeling oddly conflicted.

She was grateful when a redhead called out and waved to Macy.

"I gotta go," Macy said. "I'll see you later. Oh, and Mr. Fry is number ten."

Hopefully the guy had a good game, because there were kids crawling all over this place. Adults, too. Maybe she should've brought Aces' season ticket information. Yes, she definitely should have. This was a targeted audience, and she was missing a great opportunity to help the newly hired marketing team boost generally lackluster sales. What was wrong with her?

Rachel caught a whiff of fresh popcorn as she passed the snack bar, and her mouth watered. When was the last time she'd had salty, crunchy, artificially buttered popcorn? *Oh, what the hell?* she thought and detoured for a bag and a bottle of water. Then she climbed the bleachers, using the warped, wooden seats as steps, and settled at the top.

The players were in their respective dugouts while the coaches and the officiating crew met at home plate. Mr. Fry was number ten and presumably on the home team, since that was the dugout the kids were gravitating toward. She would root for the home team and hope Mr. Fry put on a show.

"Play ball!" the home plate umpire yelled, and the home team spilled from their dugout, wearing ugly pea-green-and-mustard-yellow uniforms with a cartoon image of a large duck wielding a pitchfork on their chests. *The Devil Ducks.*

Rachel chuckled around a mouthful of popcorn. This was bad. No self-respecting man should wear pea-green pants, especially not the pitcher, who wasn't in the greatest shape … *Ooh.* She cringed as he turned away. *Hello, number ten.*

But Mr. Fry had some serious zip on that ball. During warm-ups, it whizzed in over and over, landing with a sharp pop in the catcher's mitt. *Never judge a ball player by the way his pants fit.*

"Batter up!" the umpire called, and the little guy who'd been warming up in the batter's circle walked toward the plate. He looked about fifteen and ridiculous, wearing a baggy black-and-red uniform with the image of an old-time burglar on his chest.

She squinted to read the team name. *The Bloody Bandits.* Nice. What was with this league?

"Strike him out," she said around another mouthful of popcorn. Sitting this one down shouldn't be too hard. Mr. Fry was twice his size. But the first pitch was a ball. The guy in front of Rachel said it was because the strike zone tightened up when the batter was smaller. It made sense, and it seemed to really rattle Mr. Fry, who quickly fell behind in the count—three balls and no strikes.

The kids along the first-base line started chanting, "Strike, strike, strike, strike." And whether that egged on Mr. Fry or messed with the batter's head, the ball whizzed over the plate to make the count three and one. On the very next pitch, a foul ball made it a full count, and you would've thought the entire game was riding on this one pitch by the sounds of those kids.

Windup. Fast pitch. Swing and a miss.

"Ring him up!" yelled the guy in front of her.

Rachel shoved another handful of popcorn into her mouth so she could clap. Good for Mr. Fry. Hopefully, he would have an easier time with the next two batters, who were probably normal-sized gu …

Sam Sutter strolled out of the dugout looking startlingly sexy in his silly uniform. Rachel's popcorn stuck in her throat, and she hacked.

The guy in front of her turned and asked, "You okay? You need help?"

She shook her head as she fumbled with her water bottle. "I'm good," she managed between coughs.

But she wasn't. Seeing Sam in a pair of perfectly fitted baseball pants was very bad … for all the right reasons.

•••

It's just like riding a bike, Sam told himself, even though he had a hunch it wasn't quite the same. Before the game, he'd warmed up, hit well, and fielded decently. There was nothing left to do but put it all together in real time.

He swallowed the nerves and dug his feet into the dirt around the plate. *See it. Hit it.*

He set his stance and relaxed his eyes in an effort to pick up the ball when it released. *No changeups, please.*

The first pitch was low and outside. Sam sat back on his heels and let the umpire call, "Ball."

Nerves rattled in his chest, and he imagined them as thoroughbreds behind the gate. The minute he swung, those nerves would release in an explosion of power, driving the ball over the wall. *See it. Hit it.*

He swung and missed. *Fucking changeup.*

Now, those nerves taunted him. He was old, rusty, washed up, and delusional. He stepped out of the batter's box and acknowledged that all of that might be true, but it would take more than one strikeout to prove it.

He stepped back into the box and settled into his stance. *See it. Hit it.* And when he exhaled he added, *Just have fun.*

The ball barreled toward him high and hanging, curving slightly at the last possible second. He opened that gate and swung with the strength of all the pent-up nerves.

Crack! Sam could've sworn he heard the ball rip the air as it ascended into the outfield at an alarming rate. He dropped the bat and focused on the first-base coach who was swinging his arm wildly. Sam's feet hit the ground with such force he felt the vibration all the way to his neck. Faster. Faster still. And then he saw the umpire behind second base give the universal whirly motion for home run.

The weight of ten long years lifted off his chest, and he felt free. No more pounding the ground. The rest of his run was effortless. He floated around third with a smile on his face.

Bright sunshine split the clouds as if to say, "What took you so long? Welcome home."

"Old man's still got it," Ian said as they crossed paths and high-fived at the plate.

"You bet your sweet ass I do."

And that's when he saw her. *Rachel.* On her feet at the top of the bleachers. She was framed by clear blue sky, and she was beaming. But it was what she did next that lit something deep and dangerous in his chest. She pressed her fingertips to her lips and blew him a kiss.

He steadied his breathing, tipped his hat beneath his helmet, and smiled.

There was no reason to overinflate the meaning of her being here. He had a fan in those bleachers, which was cool. Fans made everything better, including the way he played.

Sam ended up four-for-four with six runs batted in, and he more than held his own on first base. The Arlington Aces didn't seem like such a long shot now. And as he packed up his bag, he found himself shuffling work schedules in his mind, delegating tasks to new hires who showed promise, explaining his decision to his father and brother.

But he still wasn't sure. Could he competently run his half of the landscaping business while he spent four months of the year playing baseball?

On his way to join the team for a victory toast at the tailgate of Ian's truck, Sam detoured to where Rachel was waiting alongside the snack bar.

"What are you doing here?" he asked, hoping she would say she'd come to see him.

"Well ..." She looked down the first-base line, where a crowd of kids was talking to the pitcher through the fence. "That's my niece's gym teacher. She wanted extra credit, so we came."

"Seeing me must've been a surprise."

She smiled that sultry smile that made him want to back her against the snack bar for a victory kiss. "You're always a surprise, Sam Sutter. But now that I know what you're truly capable of, I won't take no for an answer."

He gave her a slow, smoldering look. "I could say the same thing about you, you know?" Visions of her flush and full in front of the fireplace bombarded him until he had to ask, "Are you busy tonight?"

"I'm always busy." But her crooked grin made him think he stood a chance.

"Too busy for a little uncomplicated fun?"

She glanced at the kids again. "You really are persuasive, aren't you?"

"Depends on how you answer my question. What do you say?"

She laughed when he bobbed his brows, and then she nodded. "I guess I could spare some time for fun. I'm actually long overdue."

Chapter Fourteen

"Where are you going, pretty lady?"

Rachel smiled at her father, who was sitting in an armchair beside the fireplace with a Grisham novel in his hands. Behind her smile was worry that he'd called her "pretty lady" because he couldn't remember her name. "I'm going out with a friend."

"Be home by curfew," he said, adding to her worry, but then he laughed. "I guess you're kind of old for curfews."

"Just a little." She kissed the top of his head, and then said, "I won't be out too late."

Helen Anne, who was in a matching armchair with a Brontë novel turned over on her lap, made a scoffing sound under her breath.

Rachel ignored her, but a few seconds later, Helen Anne caught up with her in the entrance hall.

"Are you going out with Sam?"

"Yes," Rachel said firmly. She wasn't going to argue, and she didn't need a lecture.

Helen Anne seemed to mull that over, pursing her lips and wrinkling her nose. "What do you think Luke will say about that?"

"I don't care what Luke says. This isn't 1996, Helen Anne. Nobody cares about that anymore."

"I do." She looked away, and when she looked back, her eyes sparkled with unshed tears. "Do you know *that* was the last time we really talked? The night you broke up with Luke and you sat on the end of my bed telling me about it. But the next morning, Mom and Dad drove you to school, and you never looked back. Not once. It …" She struggled for words. "It hurt. I always figured I had that in common with Luke. So yeah, I care what Luke will think, even if it's just because I want you to talk to me the way you used to."

Crud. Rachel gave in to her own swell of emotion and wrapped her sister in a hug. "I'm so sorry. I really am. I don't know what happened. If I could go back knowing everything I know now, I'd do a lot differently … but not the Luke part." She pulled out of the hug and looked at Helen Anne. "I like being with Sam. I like being with you and Macy, too. I'm going to make more time for that even after I go back to Philly. I promise."

Surprise and something softer registered on Helen Anne's face. "Thank you for taking her to the game."

Rachel took a few steps toward the door and said, "You're welcome. I'm going to take her to Pittsburgh to see a Pirates game one of these weekends, too."

"That would be great."

"You can come, too. I heard how much you like the scratching and spitting."

Helen Anne's laughter echoed in the hallway. "I can't believe she told you that."

"Kids." A pang of nostalgia for their own teenage years suddenly filled her. "If you wait up for me, I'll sit on the end of your bed and give you details," Rachel added.

Helen Anne didn't hesitate. "Deal."

As she left, Rachel hoped tonight would be particularly good so she didn't have to embellish anything. She should've known Sam was way ahead of her.

"Should I be nervous?" she asked, studying his strong, handsome profile as he drove the truck down a narrow dirt road.

He smirked. "Nah. It's not like it's something you've never done before."

"I'm way overdressed for camping."

He looked her over. "You're way overdressed for what I have planned, too."

"I'm not skinny-dipping in a water hole. I've watched Discovery Channel. People get brain-eating amoebas doing stuff like that. If you want me naked in water, I'd prefer a hot tub."

"Well, now I know what we can do on our second date."

While Rachel was wondering where and when they could get private access to a hot tub, Sam parked and then opened her door.

She looked from his smiling face to the soft ground, rutted from trucks and ATVs. "I wore heels."

He glanced at her feet. "I see that. I told you to wear something comfortable."

"These are comfortable, and I wore jeans. I tried to be practical, but it's hard when you don't know where you're going." She gave him a playful angry eye.

He patted her thigh and said, "Hang tight."

From the bed of his truck, he pulled out a bottle of wine, a box of crackers, and two plastic cups, which he put into a reusable grocery bag. Then he was back with a smile, lifting the bottle so she could see. "You wanted wine the other night, and I couldn't deliver. That didn't sit right with me."

"And they say chivalry is dead."

"If they say that, then this will really floor them." He wrapped his arm around her waist and lifted her off the seat.

"Wait!" She tensed, and he stumbled, nearly dropping her, but he regained his balance easily enough. Probably those athletic tendencies kicking in.

"Hang on. I'm going to carry you over this mud."

She was in shock. That was the only way to explain why she didn't insist he put her down so she could walk like the able-bodied woman she was. Instead, she let him hoist her high on his shoulder, so her belly bounced against him as he jogged. It was so ridiculous she laughed.

He stopped a minute or so later and deposited her in the middle of a clearing. "How's that?"

She could stand without sinking, which was good, but … "What exactly are we doing here?" Probably a picnic. Which was sweet and completely opposite of her experiences with other men.

Sam's bold brows rode high on his forehead as he took in their surroundings. "I used to come here as a kid … to play Wiffle Ball. I thought it might be fun, but you can't play in heels."

That sounded like a challenge.

"I can play in these," she said with a definitive nod.

"You're going to hurt yourself."

"Then you can carry me back to the truck again."

"I'm going to do that anyway," he said with a grin and a pat to her butt.

She would've been offended if she'd been anywhere but here. With him. She couldn't imagine any circumstance back in Philly where a man would take her out and swat her ass without getting the toe of her Manolos in his crotch.

"The game's called Wipe Out," Sam said as he walked around, digging lines into the dirt with a stick. "This line is the pitcher's mound. That line is home plate. One of us will pitch, and the other will hit. Every time you make contact with the ball, you get five points. Every time you swing and miss, you lose a point. You get twenty pitches, and then we switch. You have to swing. There's no such thing as a ball. You either swing and hit, or you swing and miss. It's called Wipe Out because if the pitcher catches the ball, the batter's score is wiped clean. Got it?"

He looked boardroom serious. "I think so," she said.

Finally, he smiled. "Good. Now, let's have a drink as a show of sportsmanship."

"Sportspersonship," she corrected.

"That's not a word."

"It should be."

He crouched to open the wine and fill both cups. She stood over him, feeling the waning sun on her face and the sweet breeze in her hair, and sighed. For once, she wasn't thinking about the stack of things back on her desk she hadn't finished or the list of appointments overflowing on her calendar for tomorrow. She was just here, living in the moment for a change. Rachel took a long, deep breath, pulling the fresh forest air into her lungs, as she idly admired Sam's strong hands and thighs.

He rose, handed her a cup, and then lifted his. "To changeups." He really had a hang-up about that pitch, but before she could ask him about it again, he added, "And to beautiful women who play Wiffle Ball in high heels."

"I'll definitely drink to that."

The cheap clink of flimsy plastic on plastic was as satisfying as any crystal stemware's ding. And the oaky Cab tasted heavenly on her tongue. But it was the company that stirred her insides into a pleasant frenzy.

Five minutes later, Rachel had scored minus five points, and no matter what Sam said, she refused to blame the shoes. "I found the one thing you aren't good at," she teased. "Pitching."

"Hey, now. It's hard to pitch accurately with a Wiffle Ball. That's what makes this fun."

She could argue that he was the one who made things fun, but she didn't want to go getting sentimental. It would definitely mess with her game.

Eventually, she made contact, but the ball didn't travel very far. Even so, Sam tried to make a daring catch, which amounted to him diving headfirst into a patch of grass.

He missed. She cackled. "That was very graceful."

After he dusted the dirt off his jeans, he eyed her up like he was either going to toss her over his shoulder again or kiss her. She would've been okay with either, but not yet …

"Back to the mound," she said, sticking the bat between them. "I get ten more pitches."

She ended her turn five points up, though she was under no illusion that it was good enough to beat him.

Sam took his sweet old time handing over the ball and getting positioned at the imaginary home plate. He did a lot of wiggling and flexing and preening, which she rolled her eyes at. But on the inside, she was buzzing. He looked amazing no matter what he did.

"I'll try not to take your head off," he said cockily.

"I'll do the same." The devil was in her eyes, and she liked how that made him laugh.

Rachel cranked her arm around in windmill fashion and drilled it in there underhand.

Sam swung and missed. "Lucky break," he said.

"Mad skills," she countered.

"Do it again," he challenged, looking mighty sexy when he did.

The ball left her hand, whizzing through the air, but then a gust of wind whistled through the holes and sent it sailing off hard right. To her surprise, Sam chased it down, all grace and strength, hitting the ball with the tip of the bat.

"Five points!" he yelled.

But Rachel had the ball in her sights, and it was reachable. She sprinted, heels and all, arms outstretched. And when the ball hit her hand, she curled her finger into a hole to make sure she didn't lose it. "Wipe out!" Her voice cracked with the thrill of it.

"You've got to be kidding me."

"Wipe out," she said again, teasing him with the ball overhead and her own gyrations.

He watched intently, a smile on his lips but heat in his eyes. "Beginner's luck," he said. "But I'm not holding back anymore. I'm coming at you with all I've got."

"Bring it on, big boy."

His brows bobbed, and his hips circled as he took a couple warm-up swings.

She spit-shined the ball on her untucked blouse and rolled her shoulders for dramatic effect. Then, she let it rip. The wind made a funny whirring sound through the holes of the ball as it left her hand. But then the air stilled, and the ball seemed to hang there, begging to be hit.

He launched this one like a rocket, straight into the air above him, higher and higher, until it caught on the breeze and carried into the trees.

"Five points," she said.

"Game over," he said. "I bet it's hung up in the trees."

"So, tie game?" she asked, trying to keep the disappointment out of her voice.

He rested the silly yellow bat on his powerful shoulder and studied her. "I get the feeling you're not okay with that."

"I like to win." Truth be told, she liked the game, too. She liked this day, the company, the way her chest had opened up and she could breathe. No stress. No fear. No important deals or health scares. "And I didn't want it to end yet."

Understanding graced his smile when he said, "Then let's hope we can find the ball."

Five feet into the woods, it was clear their chances sucked. Rachel stood on an overgrown path in her heels, peering up at the dense, leafy cover, looking for anything white to catch her eye, while Sam wandered farther into the brush.

"See, if you were dressed appropriately, I could show you how beautiful it is off the beaten path."

He already was, and that surprised her. She'd never learned much from her previous lovers. They were a means to an end. Utilitarian. But Sam was different. And if she was honest, that scared her.

Rachel ventured deeper into the trees, careful where she stepped, surprised to find a bench in the middle of a tiny clearing. Carvings marred the weathered wood. Initials, hearts, a swear word or two, but what really caught her eye was the three-by-five rusted metal plate attached to the back, bearing a Thoreau quote: *To be awake is to be alive.*

In the middle of the woods in a pair of $300 heels with her heartbeat echoing in her ears, Rachel had finally opened her eyes.

"See anything?" Sam asked from somewhere in the distance.

"Everything," she whispered. For the first time in forty years. She'd been doing more than selling her lovers short; she'd been selling herself short, too. There was more to her—and life—than professional goals and executive decisions.

"Is everything okay?" She heard him coming through the brush toward her.

"Did you know this was here?"

"Nope." He ran his hand along the carved-up back and then sat. "It's a great place for a little bird-watching." He tilted his head to look at the treetops, and she admired the curve of his throat and strength of his jaw. *The little things.* "There," he whispered, motioning with an outstretched arm and wiggling fingers for her to join him on the bench. "A wood thrush."

Rachel sat, his arm warming her upper back, and scanned the trees.

"See its white belly?"

She looked harder. "No."

"Relax your eyes," he said, his soft breath fluttering against her cheek, and she knew he was looking at her. "Relax your focus. That's the key to hitting a baseball, too. If you stare at one point, you lose the power of your peripheral vision, and that's where you'll pick up the pitcher's release point—or in this case, the bird."

She took a deep breath and exhaled, willing her eyes to relax. Her vision hazed. Sounds grew louder. The whistle of the wind. The rustle of the leaves. The creaking of the limbs. The rush of Sam's exhale. And then a flash of white drew her focus higher. But it wasn't the wood thrush. "The ball!" Way too high for either of them to reach.

"Good find," he said. "Bad break, though. We aren't going to be able to get it down from there."

"Now what?" She faced him, her mouth inches from his.

There was hunger in his eyes. "I can think of a few things."

"Do you have a condom?"

He wrapped a loose strand of her hair around his finger. "In my truck."

"Too far," she said, her hand already moving up his thigh to the apex of his jeans.

He dropped his mouth to her throat and nuzzled her neck. "So what do you propose?"

"Second base," she said, moaning when his hand slid inside her blouse to cup her breast. "Maybe third. Right here on this bench."

He drew her onto his lap, cupped her face in his hands, and said, "You make me want things I never knew I wanted."

"Like heavy petting on a park bench?"

"Yes. But mostly just you. Anywhere and everywhere." He paused and smoothed his thumbs over her cheeks, looking deeply into her eyes, creating a whirlwind of emotion deep in her belly. "And I want to play ball again."

The air whooshed from her lungs, and she almost screamed. "You're going to try out for the team!"

"Sweetheart, you could get me to do anything."

That was a lot of power to have over somebody, and normally, Rachel wouldn't think twice about it. But everything was different with Sam. She didn't want to hurt him. Unfortunately, life was unpredictable—no matter how hard you planned.

• • •

Monday morning, Sam drove down the dirt road toward the equipment barn with a smile plastered on his face and Sam Hunt blasting on his radio. Luke was already hitching up the trailer, and

Sam's bass must've been loud, because Luke made a face wrought with disgust.

"What?" Sam asked innocently when he was out of his truck.

"It's five a.m."

Acres of grass and trees stretched out around them. "Who's going to care? Dad's sure not sleeping. He's probably got CNN on so loud he couldn't even hear me driving up."

Luke yanked on the safety chain. "I take it you had a good weekend."

"Actually, it was a great weekend."

"Because it involved Rachel? Something's going on between you, and it's more than her being grateful you found her dad."

There was an accusatory tone in his brother's words that Sam didn't like. He stopped midway to the garage, feeling an angry heat climb up his neck. But before it could reach his face—and his mouth—he decided it wasn't worth an argument. "Yep."

He was almost safe inside the garage when he heard Luke ask, "Do you think that's wise?"

So much for no argument. He about-faced. "Christ, Luke! I'm thirty-five. She's forty. We're adults. We're single. And you're happily married. What's the fucking problem?"

Luke broke eye contact long enough for Sam to think maybe he'd get an apology. "She's … I don't know," Luke said. "She's not your type."

"I didn't know I had a type. I haven't exactly been looking."

"Well, let me tell you what type you should be looking for. It's sweet and uncomplicated. Like Grace."

Sam groaned. He'd dated Mandy's friend Grace for a couple months last year. She'd hung on his every word, even wanted his approval when it came to ordering at restaurants. "I'm not you, man. I go for something a little more exciting."

Luke flinched, and before Sam could tell him that wasn't a hit on Mandy, Luke asked, "So it's just …" He cleared his throat. "Sex?"

"Are you mad because we had sex with the same woman?"

"No. Not at all. I never had sex with Rachel," Luke said awkwardly. "We were … I had planned to"—he fidgeted uncomfortably—"the night she broke up with me."

Though Sam knew it shouldn't matter, that bit of information made him very happy.

"But listen, man. If all she had to do was sleep with you to get you to play ball again, I'm worried."

Sam narrowed his eyes. "What are you talking about?"

"I know you played for Ian's team. I also know you're trying out for the Aces."

"So what?" Sam shoved his hands in his pockets and shrugged.

"What about the business? What about Dad? When were you going to tell him?"

"I haven't even made the team, yet. But when I do, we'll sit down and figure this out together. I'll delegate when I'm away, and I'll be here when the team plays at home. I can do anything and everything." Sam knew his mother would agree.

Luke snickered. "Jesus, she must've been one hell of a lay to get you to buy that crap. Life doesn't work like that, Sam. You have to make responsible choices. You can't just pick up and leave when you have obligations."

Anger heated Sam's blood. So this was what his seemingly affable brother had been holding in all these years? The idea that Sam was *still* irresponsible. There'd been hints of that opinion when they'd been kids, and then again when Sam had chosen baseball over college, but after their mother had died and Sam had come home, he'd thought he'd done a damn good job of growing up and taking life seriously. Maybe even too seriously. And for what? So Luke could treat him like this. "Fuck you," Sam said, and he headed for the garage.

"Wait," Luke said. "I'm sorry. Shit!" The expletive reverberated in the early-morning quiet. "I'm saying that way too much lately, but I *am* sorry." That got Sam to stop. He didn't turn around, though, until Luke said, "I'm not trying to be a dick. I swear. It's just ..." He shrugged and shook his head. "I like having you here, man. Things have been good. Really good. I don't want you running off to Philadelphia or moving across the country to play ball again. It's selfish, but it's true."

Sam exhaled his anger. "I'm not going anywhere, Luke. Maybe a couple of road trips a month, but we're grown men. We can handle that, can't we?"

"Yeah, but can you handle it if baseball ends badly again? You forget I was the one who was here after you quit playing the first time. I saw what it did to you. I even tried to talk you into going back, thinking it would help. Remember? But you said you just wanted to move on and get past it, and that's exactly what you did—until Rachel rolled into town. I don't know. Something about it worries me. You just changed your mind awful damn quick, which means she must've been pretty damn persuasive, and that makes me think she knew what she was doing all along."

"You're paranoid."

"I'm practical. What's that saying about a tiger not changing its stripes? Look, I'm telling you, Rachel has always had a complicated agenda. Trust me. She lives and dies by her daddy's grand plan."

So what? Sam still didn't see how that mattered. "Does it make you feel any better to hear I don't give a fuck about their grand plan? I'm only after her for the fun of it."

"You say that now, but later ..."

Sam only had now. He wasn't going to worry about later. Unless later involved Rachel naked in his bed. That was the kind of later he could worry about all day long. But first, he had to set his brother straight on this. He was glad they'd talked some of this out, but the Rachel that Luke remembered wasn't necessarily the same woman Sam knew now. "Do you remember how I tried to come between you and Rachel back in high school?"

Luke shrugged like maybe he didn't.

"Well, I do, and I remember you telling me to back off, because you liked her and she liked you, and I was too young to understand something like that. You used to tell me I was too young for things all the time." Sam still felt the sting of how inconsequential those words had made him feel. The hurt made his spine steel. "Well, I'm grown up now. So *you* need to be the one to back off where Rachel is concerned."

Sam could handle Rachel, baseball, and the business. He would handle every damn thing and prove his brother wrong.

Chapter Fifteen

The next week and a half flew by in a blur of ticket sales, marketing meetings, stadium preparations, and personnel introductions. Mark Olean still couldn't pull himself away from whatever crisis was keeping him in Minnesota, so Rachel—with her father by her side whenever possible—acted as general manager and met with the newly hired coaching staff. They seemed like knowledgeable, likeable men who had winning on their minds. Sam's stamp of approval had resulted in some great staffing for the Aces.

Sam. Thoughts of him were never far from her mind. He'd been an integral part of the last ten days. His fun, his games, his laugh, his body. All distractions, for sure, of which she was taking full advantage. But by the end of next week, the roster would be settled, Mark would be in Arlington, and Rachel would be back in Philadelphia. She ignored the irrational disappointment that arose when she thought of that deadline.

The desk phone buzzed, and Adele Packer, the newly hired secretary to the general manager, said, "Rachel, there's a Mr. Schumer on line one. He asked to speak to you directly."

Rachel had talked to so many people during the last several weeks, it didn't surprise her she didn't recognize the name. "Rachel Reed," she said after pressing the button for line one.

"Rachel, hi, this is Mike Schumer. I represent a Midwest investing conglomerate that has shown interest in the Arlington Aces baseball team. You're the broker, correct?"

For some reason, there was a flash of panic, but she managed an even, "I am."

"Excellent. My clients are involved in racing and boxing, and they're very serious about moving into baseball. Could we schedule a time for a more detailed discussion? We would also like to see the operation in person."

Where was the spark that normally ignited a blaze of focused adrenaline whenever Rachel had a credible bite on a major property? She had no clue, so she faked it, enthusiastically pawning Mr. Schumer off on Adele for scheduling purposes. Then, Rachel sat back in her chair and stared out the picture windows at the pristine field below her. She should've gotten the name of the investment group. She should be researching them right now. Instead, she was thinking about pouring a fresh cup of coffee and taking a walk down to the field, where she could sit on the dugout roof in the sunshine and clear her head. *Awake and alive.*

The phone buzzed again. "Mark Olean is on line one."

Rachel exhaled. "Thanks, Adele. Did you get the meetings set up for Mr. Schumer?"

"Yes, the phone call is tomorrow at three, and as long as that goes well, they will be in town April 27. That was the soonest they could be here, and since that's your last day on the schedule I figured you would rather squeeze them in than come back to Arlington a week later."

April 27 was also the last day of tryouts. Somehow it seemed smarmy to be potentially selling the team the same day a whole slew of guys would be signing on. "Okay. Thanks."

"Don't forget Mr. Olean on line one," Adele said.

Hopefully he was calling to say he'd be on the next plane. "Mark, how are you?"

"I've been better." She could tell by the tone of his voice that getting on a plane was not in his near future. "I gotta be honest here. I haven't given details up to this point, because it's killing me to even talk about it. My daughter was recently diagnosed with Hodgkin lymphoma."

"Oh, no!"

"She's a strong kid, stronger than her dad, that's for sure. I thought maybe things would be better by the start of the season down there, but it's not looking like that's going to happen, and … well, an opportunity has come up for me to coach at the college level here, which means I can be closer to my family while still providing for them. I'm sorry to do this to you."

"I'm sorry, too," Rachel said. "You were our first choice, but we understand. Your family will be in our thoughts and prayers, and if there's anything we can do, let us know."

"Thank you, Rachel, and good luck. I'll be rooting for the Aces."

After she hung up, she banished her growing panic and opened the file containing the final ranking of applicants for the GM job. *Contact the second choice. Get his ass in here ASAP.* But the second choice hadn't been a unanimous decision. In fact, the second choice hadn't been on Rachel's father's list at all. Rachel had plugged the name into the spreadsheet only after Mark Olean had been hired and after hearing it from Sam and doing some research that revealed Benny Bryant was in the market for a GM position. It would mean the world to Sam to have this guy involved with the team.

Grabbing her purse from under the desk, Rachel let Adele know she was going to be out of the office for a couple hours, then she headed home to talk to her father. When she walked into the kitchen, she found her parents baking cookies and had to do a double take.

Danny Reed had never lifted a finger to do anything but eat and drink in this kitchen. Today, he was wearing a floral apron.

"You're just in time to test the first batch," her mother said. "They should be cool enough."

A rack of uniformly sized chocolate chip cookies graced the marble countertop.

"Rachel!" her father said in a booming voice that didn't quite sound like him. "Grab an apron and you can help."

Surreal. These personality changes were almost harder to take than the lapses in memory. "I can't, Dad. I'm working. I actually need to talk to you about work."

"Try a cookie, dear," her mother said.

Rachel sighed, grabbed a cookie, and took a bite just so they could hopefully move on. "It's good," she said as she chewed, tasting warm chocolate and hints of vanilla. "Very good."

"Bring me one," her father said.

She gave her father a cookie and sat beside him. "Dad, I need to tell you some things." He worked the cookie over, making satisfying sounds. "We may have a buyer for the team."

"It's not for sale."

"Yes, it is," she said gently. "That's why I'm here."

"I'm not selling my team!"

Rachel looked at her mother pleadingly, hoping for some help, but her mother balled up cookie dough as if this conversation didn't concern her.

"Dad, please …"

"What's going on?" Helen Anne stood in the hallway, her chin up, and her lips in a hard line.

"We're baking cookies," their mother said.

"We may have found a buyer for the team," Rachel said.

"Nobody's selling my team!"

Helen Anne put her arms around his shoulders from behind. "Of course not, Dad."

Rachel wanted to scream. How was she supposed to do her job and take care of her family when nobody would back her up? "Mark Olean quit today, too," she said. "I want to hire Benny Bryant to replace him."

Her father's forehead wrinkled with confusion. "Who?"

"Let's not do this today, Rachel," her mother said.

"You know what we need?" Helen Anne asked. "We need some milk!"

Rachel sat there, stunned. What was she supposed to do? Wait until her father had a better day to discuss their next step? That would only drag things out more. She had the legal power to make this decision, which would keep them on track and get her back to Philadelphia, where she had more work than she wanted to think about. But hiring the GM was a major deal, and she felt like a villain sneaking Benny Bryant into the role without her father's explicit approval.

She needed to get out of here, clear her head. "Enjoy your cookies," she said. And then she left, headed for the one person who was as interested in this baseball team as she was.

"Hey," she said when she'd reached her car and dialed Sam.

"Hey yourself. What's going on?"

"Where are you?"

"Messing with Mrs. Applebee's rose bush." He chuckled. "It's perfectly innocent despite how it sounds."

And despite the shit she was wading through with her family and this team, she smiled. "Do you ever take a lunch break?"

"Are you asking to see me in the middle of the day?"

"Maybe."

"Then, yes. I can take a lunch break."

"Your place?"

"I'll meet you there."

Twenty minutes later, she was naked in his bed, flat on her back, with his head between her legs. Her life was officially out of control. Maybe this was the proverbial midlife crisis.

Rachel gripped the cold, metal headboard and tried to concentrate on the steady stroking of Sam's lips and tongue as he teased her, filling her belly with a luscious heat that displaced the upset of that morning.

"So good," she said, her voice scratchy and low.

His fingers circled her entrance, dipped in and out. One. Then two.

She rocked against him, close to release, wanting it strong and long—enough to make her forget her own name.

"Sam!" she screamed when he pulled her sensitive nub between his lips. That little trick proved to be the epicenter for her orgasm, shattering her into a million glittering pieces. She hovered nowhere and everywhere. No thoughts. Just feelings.

"Again," she finally said when the ecstasy wore off enough that she could feel her limbs. But then the distinct sound of her phone buzzing in the front pocket of her purse, which was on the chair in Sam's bedroom, distracted her. She propped up on her elbows, even as he planted kisses on her inner thighs. "That's my phone," she said.

"So?" He was near her belly button now, rounding it with his tongue, while his fingers extracted a few more tremors from the swollen flesh between her legs.

"What if it's important?"

He looked up at her, eyes dark, mouth never leaving her skin. "This is important."

Too important, maybe. She'd never had sex in the middle of a workday, not to mention a workday as fucked up as this. "I have to get it," she said, swinging out from underneath him.

She scrambled to her phone in time to miss the call from Liv, and then she stood there, watching the screen, waiting for the voicemail. Behind her, she could hear him moving, probably getting dressed, probably pissed she'd turned her back on him.

"Hi, Rachel. Nothing new here. I'm bored. You sure you don't need me back in Arlington?"

So much for the call being important. Rachel returned the phone to her bag and faced Sam, who wasn't dressed at all. He was under the sheets, propped up on pillows with his arms behind his head. Beautiful. Strong. Dark against the white sheets, and despite the thin layer of covering, clearly still aroused. So much for being pissed.

"Sorry," she said.

"Don't be. It's one hell of a view." He looked her over and licked his lips, and she decided, *Screw it*, and crawled under the sheets with him.

He wrapped an arm around her shoulders and held her close, while she kissed his chest and took her time exploring his erection.

"Was it important?" he asked, sounding pained and pleasured all at once.

She teased his nipple with her tongue. "Not as important as this."

In a flash, she was beneath him, her mouth covered with his. The kiss was hot and deep. All-consuming. She shuddered when his fingers found her folds again, and she lifted her hips eagerly when he was sheathed and ready.

He drove into her. Hard and long. Over and over. Branding her with his body in a way she'd never experienced before. Dominant. Possessive. And yet, when she opened her eyes on a swallowed moan, she found him staring at her, something soft and wondrous in his eyes.

He slowed his pace. Cupped her face. And said, "You are … amazing."

More luscious and addictive kisses followed. Their bottom halves moved in sync. And when they pulsed together, wrapped in sweet sweat and delicious aftershocks, Rachel truly felt amazing, too.

This time, she didn't rush to dress. She waited in his bed when he left to clean up. There was no use in pretending to be a hard-ass who'd had another lapse in judgment. This was more than that. She was more than that.

"Hey." Clad in his boxer briefs, his hair curling wildly at the ends, he looked pleasantly surprised to see her there.

"I'm not quite ready to go back to the real world," she said.

"Well, then, you're in luck, because as the head of commercial landscaping for Sutter & Sons, I'm fully within my managerial boundaries to send my crew to finish out the day without me. Which means"—he slid into bed beside her—"I'm all yours."

It sounded wonderful, but she didn't have that sort of freedom. "I lost my GM today."

"Olean?" he asked, clearly remembering their past conversations.

"Yes. And I want to hire the second guy on the list … Benny Bryant."

She saw the shock in his eyes even before he said, "No fucking way!"

"I looked him up after you mentioned him, and I found an interview where he said he was interested in moving into the front office at a lower level. Well, you can't get much lower than this." She smiled sadly. "Unfortunately, Benny is not who my father would hire. His list defaults to Gordy Stallman. Do you have any idea how hard it is to have your guiding principle be 'what would Dad do' when Dad isn't even himself anymore?"

"Here's a thought," Sam said. "Make your guiding principle 'what would Rachel do?'"

She smiled and snuggled closer to his chest, liking the simplicity of that. But it was too good to be true. Too easy. She had to reconcile the wants of two Rachels now. Business-minded Rachel would sell the team, bank the commission, head back to her life in Philadelphia, and assuage her guilt by knowing she'd done what she'd been asked to do. But the Rachel lying in Sam Sutter's arms couldn't get excited about that scenario, because she wanted … *this*.

She closed her eyes and steadied her breathing. But what was this, and where would it lead? Marriage. Kids. She almost laughed. That train had barreled past her ten years ago. Could she really see herself married and starting a family at this point in her life?

Imagine the sacrifices it would take. She tensed, because she wasn't at liberty to make a single one. Her father was counting on her to follow his business plans. It was the last thing he would ask of her.

Loosening her grip on Sam, Rachel said, "I really should go." And this time, when she left the bed, she gathered her littered pieces of clothing and got dressed.

"Ready to tackle the real world?" He looked as relaxed as ever.

"I don't have a choice."

"You're the boss, Rachel. You always have a choice." He smiled, extra wide and alluring, patting the sheets beside him.

"Maybe, but this boss has to hire a GM."

A thoughtful look crossed his face, and she braced herself for the enthusiastic speech on behalf of Benny Bryant. She suddenly wished she hadn't said anything.

Instead, Sam asked, "And then?"

"I have to prepare for a meeting." With prospective buyers, but she didn't feel like divulging everything. She wasn't required to simply because they were sleeping together.

Thankfully, he didn't push. Of course he didn't. This was a little uncomplicated fun. Those had been his words, and she needed to hold them both to that. In fact, she needed to pull back and put some space between them. Although, she didn't feel the need to tell him that, either. It was her body, her decision. It was also time to get serious.

One week was all she had to hire a GM, court prospective buyers, and see that a team was ready to take the field for Opening Day.

•••

Over the next five days, Sam and his crew worked long hours getting the field into playing shape. He didn't need to stop by dressed in his jeans and work boots at 6:15 a.m. on the first day of tryouts to double-check anything. No, that wasn't why he was here. He was here hoping to calm his nerves and absorb some of the peace he could only find on an empty baseball field … or in the trees. That's why he'd walked over, figuring the one-two punch would do him wonders.

He climbed onto the roof of the dugout, like a king admiring the view from his watchtower, and took a deep breath. The newly risen sun filtered the scene like an artsy photograph, and he thought about pulling out his phone to capture it. Instead, he took another deep breath, held on to the soothing scent of healthy grass and damp dirt, and let everything else slip away. He could do this. He wanted to do this. He'd spent the last week dealing in hypotheticals, figuring out the logistics, when he would be gone and who would pick up the slack. It was complicated by the fact that Ian was trying out, too. But they'd hired enough people to make things manageable. And his father was on board—happy, even. That was the most important thing. Sam wanted to play ball again, but this time, he wouldn't forsake his family. Not even Luke, who was handling things much better since they'd both blown off a little steam.

"Sam?" He turned to see Rachel behind him, clutching the rail and looking at him like he was a ghost. "What are you doing here this early? Tryouts aren't until three."

"Focusing," he said, thinking she looked even more beautiful than usual dressed in a pale-blue pantsuit with her long hair piled high on her head.

"Good luck today."

"Thank you."

Her pink lips parted, and her lashes fluttered like she wanted to say something else, but then she just smiled.

"Will you be at tryouts?" he asked.

"I'll be watching from up there." She gestured to the wall of windows overhead. "My father will be, too."

"Good. You know I perform much better when you're around."

This time, her smile was livelier and a little wicked. "I'm sure you're wonderfully capable on your own."

The sun had barely risen, and already he could feel a full day's heat between them. He wanted to make her writhe right here on top of the dugout, but that ever-present phone made its presence known, and he knew she wouldn't ignore it—not even if his mouth were on her body.

"We'll talk later," she said before she answered the call, which gave him hope they could keep this thing going right up until the last minute. He hated that the thought simultaneously buoyed him and dragged him down, so he hopped off the dugout and wandered the field, breathing in and out. Refocusing. Until tryouts were over, he couldn't afford to be distracted by any more changeups.

Eight hours later, Sam walked onto the field dressed in an old practice uniform.

Ian was at his side, a bag slung over his right shoulder. "It's a busy place."

At least a hundred guys littered the ground they'd babied for the last two months. "I hope to God this sod can handle two hundred feet."

"Is that a woman?" Ian stopped short of second base and dropped his bag. "*That* is a woman on the mound."

Sam was about to argue that some men had ponytails, too, when the pitcher turned, and her profile sported obvious breasts. "That is a woman," he confirmed. That was a first.

"You've got to be shitting me."

Sam shook his head. "Who cares? As long as she can throw, I have no problem with it."

"That's because you won't have to catch for her. Maybe she won't make it."

Maybe Sam wouldn't make it, either. He took stock of the competition while he and Ian warmed up. Some of the guys looked barely out of high school and green around the gills. They misread pop-ups and overplayed grounders. Other guys were seasoned. They were strong and sharp, snagging anything that came near them.

"Sutter?" He caught the last toss from Ian before he turned to see Benny Bryant striding across the outfield toward him.

Holy shit!

"Good to see you, son," the man said as he gave Sam's ungloved hand a hearty shake. "I heard you put in a good word for me, and I wanted to thank you."

"Coach! I'm speechless." Partly because he'd never seen the guy dressed in a suit, which was indicative of his position in the front office rather than the dugout. "I can't believe you're here. I don't know what else to say."

"Just play hard today. Nothing you've done before this moment matters. Only what you prove on this field."

It was a warning. There would be no favors. And that was fine with Sam. He'd never been the kind of guy who skirted by on who he knew.

He glanced up at the glass high above home plate and thought about Rachel. Something akin to pride swelled in his chest. First the trees, now Benny Bryant. And how about the fact that Sam was even here, getting a second shot at this? Rachel had given him more than he deserved. But why? Unless … she felt more for him than he realized.

"Dude, let's go!" Ian said. "Time to meet the coaches."

Sam rolled through the next four hours of tryouts with his feet never touching the ground. He made every play. He hit every ball.

"You've got this wrapped up," said Matt Fry, who, at twenty-seven, was one of the only guys even close to Sam's advanced age

"I don't know about that," Sam said.

Matt laughed. "Hell, I knew that when you tattooed my slider—and just about everything else in my arsenal—two weekends ago. My students still rag me about that."

Sam smiled. "You're looking good today, man."

"It's hard to tell. And to think if we're lucky, we have two more days of this."

Sam couldn't wait. He was surer of his future with baseball now than he'd ever been. And he was considering something else, too. Once he had a spot on this roster, he was going to march into Rachel's office and claim a future with her, too.

Chapter Sixteen

"Arlington is a baseball market. A full 80 percent of residents will attend at least one Pirates game or Phillies game every season."

Sure, Danny Reed had been relying on the notes in front of him since the meeting with the Midwest conglomerate began, but he was confident and coherent. More like the man Rachel had admired and patterned her entire life after. Seeing him like this after the turmoil of the last two months gave her a huge swell of hope. She prayed it wasn't some fluke but rather something longer lasting brought on by Dr. Rictor's latest medication adjustments. If that was the case, she could head to Philadelphia tomorrow morning with some semblance of peace.

"If Arlington is such a baseball market, then why are season ticket sales so poor?" asked Mike Schumer, who looked like Ichabod Crane with a goatee: lanky and awkward, the sleeves of his suit coat too short. And that nose, as long as the nostrils were wide. Rachel got a bad vibe from the man, who hadn't let his clients get a word in edgewise.

She looked at the men sitting on either side of Mike. Farris Keller was bald and pale. William Adair was short and fat. They'd made a big deal about being "sports guys" during an earlier round of small talk, but Rachel doubted either one had ever played a single organized game. They were investors. Plain and simple. And she knew how to handle them.

"Season ticket sales will come," she said, alternating eye contact between the two. "What you see as lackluster ticket sales, I see as meeting our goal for the inaugural season. The expectation should be to double that number next year, and again the year after and so on and so forth. All it will take is one season for people to understand the unique, cost-effective, family-entertainment opportunity presented by the Aces. After that, they will buy in droves."

The arch of one brow belied Keller's interest in her statements, while Adair nodded with understanding. Unfortunately, Mike sighed. "That's an opinion, Ms. Reed, and you'll have to forgive me for questioning its accuracy. Our walk around the grounds made us suspicious that, by the looks of the limited parking, you've undersold on purpose. That's a bit disheartening, and I have to take that into consideration when advising my clients. I certainly wouldn't advise them to base a major financial decision on speculation."

Well then, why are you here looking at an unproven baseball team? Speculation was all she and her father had. *And heart,* which was irrelevant when it came to business. She had no idea why she'd even thought that. But when she looked at her father, who was already trying to get them to see things his way, she knew it was painfully true. Maybe the idea that this could ever be a profitable venture was an illusion. Maybe passion wasn't enough.

"You would be buying a piece of Americana," her father said, fervidly, as if that ideal alone would thaw Ichabod's opinion and excuse the speculation the Reeds were peddling.

Of course, it wouldn't. In fact, the longer this meeting went on, the clearer it became they were short on hard facts and lacked the upper hand. An advantageous sale at this point in time was a long shot. Rachel's gut told her if these guys offered, they were going to lowball, which was frustrating, to say the least. This had been the riskiest, most uncharacteristic investment her father had ever made, and if they couldn't sell the team, they'd be screwed. His latest medications might provide a reprieve from the more troubling symptoms and rapid decline but not a cure. Danny couldn't be depended on to ultimately oversee this team, which left Rachel, the sole special power of attorney, handling everything. She didn't want to do it all anymore. But what choice did she have?

"The potential for money-making is definitely here," her father insisted, and then he read word for word from the paper in front of him. "No expense was spared updating the stadium, making it a unique architectural offering in the tri-county area. Leasing inquiries are fielded daily. We are close to an agreement with the PIAA to host high school play-offs. The county fair committee is interested in the venue, and the community college has expressed interest should they reestablish their baseball team. This stadium could be a hub for community entertainment and, as such, a very lucrative asset."

None of the men on the other side of the table looked impressed.

"My clients are only interested in the baseball side of things," Mike said.

"Then why don't we take a closer look at that?" Rachel stood. She'd had enough. All she wanted now was to pull her father aside and tell him these weren't the buyers they were looking for. They needed to sit on the team awhile longer. Let the season start and fill the seats. They could leverage those numbers when the right buyer came along.

Adele knocked on the doorjamb. "Lunch has been set up in Box A."

"Thank you," Danny said, smoothing a hand down the buttons of his blazer.

Again, Rachel thought about how good he'd looked and sounded when he had the script in front of him, but as he stepped away from the desk, she noticed the slight wobble in his gait. He was tired. A lunch break would be good. Maybe then she could convince him to head home and leave the rest to her.

While the out-of-towners converged on the luxury box's buffet table, which had been set up with the complete stadium snack-bar offerings, Rachel joined her father in the open-air rows of seats beyond the glass. She'd tried not to dwell on Sam these past three days. What good would it do? After all, she couldn't wish him onto the team. Making the roster was up to him—and the coaches, of course. But she couldn't lie to herself, either; she'd been praying for a solid tryout. She'd been watching him, too. Off and on, all three days. By now, she could easily pick him out of the dwindling crowd, which had suffered cuts at the close of every day.

In a matter of seconds, she zeroed in on his broad shoulders and powerful legs as he stood on first base. Someone lobbed a ball from third, and Sam stretched beyond the limits of what she'd thought was humanly possible, especially for a man, to snag the ball. He flipped it to the woman on the pitcher's mound. The whole exchange made her smile. Sam on first. A woman on the mound. The warm breeze. Her father by her side. But then she remembered the freaks in the room behind her.

"Dad, this doesn't feel right," she said.

"Where's Olean? Why hasn't he come to talk to me today?"

Rachel sighed. She'd already explained on several occasions why Mark had to decline the job offer. "His daughter is sick."

Her father nodded, and she felt relief only to have it ripped away from her a moment later. "When will Olean be here?"

"He's not coming. We hired Benny Bryant as his replacement."

"Who the hell is Benny Bryant?"

Rachel shot a worried glance in the direction of the men behind the glass. They were stuffing their faces and watching tryouts through the far window bank.

"He used to coach in the minors. I talked to you about this." Multiple times in the past week. But they were obviously conversations he didn't remember. "Dad, I was in a bind. I had to move quickly. I thought—"

"You thought I wouldn't notice if you pulled a fast one." His voice was tight and high, angry but also petulant.

"That's not what happened. I would never do something like that. I've followed your orders explicitly." Except for this one.

He got quiet. Sullen. And she wondered how long it would take him to forget this conversation, too.

"I'm tired," he said finally.

"I know." She had the urge to lay her head on his shoulder, but she didn't dare. Not now. Not here. "Helen Anne is going to come get you."

When he didn't argue, Rachel sent the text Helen Anne had been waiting for, and then she texted Adele, who'd been alerted to the possibility of having to sit with Danny at some point today while Rachel continued this meeting alone.

"Perhaps there's a little promise out there," Mike said from somewhere above her.

She didn't turn, but she noted the interest in his voice, and she hated it … hated the position it put her in. She had explicit instructions to sell the team and all the assets as high and as fast as possible. If her father was upset over Benny Bryant, she couldn't imagine his anger if she made the executive decision to ignore an interested buyer. She couldn't imagine her guilt.

Her stomach heaved, but she squared her shoulders and lifted her chin. "Dad, Adele's coming out to watch tryouts with you while I finish up this meeting."

"What meeting?" he asked.

"I'm here, Mr. Reed," Adele said, sliding into the open seat beside him.

Rachel stole one last glance at Sam, who was trotting away from first base toward home plate. All things considered, she didn't regret hiring Benny Bryant. She liked the guy. Sam loved the guy. It was the least she could do after Sam had saved her father's life. But they were even now, weren't they? She wasn't going to veer from her father's written instructions again. *What would Rachel do?* was irrelevant. It always had been when it came to Reed Commercial Real Estate. She'd spent the last twenty years of her life smothering her own instincts because she'd been convinced success meant emulating her father. Now was definitely not the time to try and revive them. She would have time to do things her way—someday.

At the moment, she didn't know whether to be happy or sad about that.

• • •

And then there were thirty-five.

Sam glanced around at the ashen faces gathered outside the dugout. Some he knew better than others. Ian. Matt Fry. Hank Carlyle, another guy from The Sandlot League. The rest, he'd come to know over the past three days. He'd talked to most of them. Learned he'd played in the minors with Andy Pullman's brother, a guy who was now career military. Enjoyed the perspective of Paulina "Pauly" Byrne, the rare woman in professional baseball, who was keenly aware that most guys didn't want her there. Calmed Roy Willet, who was stressed out about making the team and the impact road trips and abysmal pay would have on his wife and two young kids. And shared a couple beers with Reece Yourdon and Giovanni Caceres, two guys who'd driven all the way from California for a shot at a spot on this team.

None of them had six-figure contracts and major-league accommodations to look forward to, but every one of them was committed. This game … it didn't let go once it had you.

"Gentlemen!" Coach Slater said, but when the pitching coach, Louis Howland, cleared his throat and inclined his head in Pauly's direction, Coach Slater corrected himself to something more accurate. "Players!"

Pauly grinned, while Ian said, "That's stupid," under his breath.

"If I call your name, have a seat in the dugout. If I don't call your name, you can leave. I won't bore you with the speech about how well everyone did and how hard it was to fill the roster. We had one goal, and that was to put together the best team possible. If you didn't make it this year, we hope you'll try again next year." He cleared his throat and looked back down at the list in his hands. "Pauly Byrne, nice tryout. Now, sit your ass in that dugout."

She whooped. A couple guys rolled their eyes. Sam smiled broadly. He had a feeling Rachel and Pauly would get along.

"Matt Fry."

Sam heard an audible exhale beside him, and then Matt jogged across the third-base line to shake Coach's hand.

Two pitchers. Coach was calling names in order of position. Eight more pitchers took their place on the dugout bench before Coach moved on to catchers, naming Reece Yourdon first.

Ian fidgeted on the other side of Sam, chewing his dirt-riddled fingernails. They wouldn't need nearly as many catchers as they did pitchers. Two, three at the most.

"Ian Pratt."

Sam slapped his buddy's back before he could get away.

Five outfielders were named next, including Giovanni Caceres. The guy immediately high-fived his traveling buddy, Yourdon.

"Hank Carlyle." The best shortstop in the bunch, which meant they were on infielders.

Sam stood at attention while two more names were called. He looked around at the remaining faces and felt confident but anxious. He wanted a spot on that bench. Even more so now that Benny Bryant was standing amid the seats above the dugout, watching the drama unfold.

"Roy Willett."

And then there was one spot left. The first day of tryouts, they'd been told the roster would cap at twenty-five. Twenty-four people already sat in that dugout.

"Old man," Coach Slater said, smiling at Sam, adopting the nickname some of the younger guys used freely. "Welcome to the team."

Sam didn't think he'd ever heard sweeter words.

He shook hands with the coaching staff, waved at Benny, who gave him a thumbs-up, and then headed into the dugout where he went down the line, smacking hands with his new teammates, feeling like he was reborn.

Baseball was officially part of Sam's life again. And while he'd made the team on his talent alone, he would've never been at tryouts if it hadn't been for Rachel. He wanted to make sure she knew that—how important that was to him. How important *she* was.

The first chance Sam got, he headed to her office, still dressed in his dusty, grass-stained practice uniform. He didn't care. Good news shouldn't wait for a shower. Besides, time was running out, and he didn't know exactly when she planned to head back to Philadelphia.

He stepped off the elevator and saw the empty reception desk, so he headed back to the room where he'd presented his exterior grounds plans all those weeks ago. A lifetime ago, really. He felt like a different person now. Not so hell-bent on protecting the past and forsaking the future. There were so many things to look forward to.

Her voice stopped him.

"What are your terms?" she asked, sounding off somehow.

Either she was on the phone, or she wasn't alone.

Sam stepped closer to the open door but remained well out of sight of the room's inhabitants.

"My clients want to see a 10-percent increase in season ticket sales before the opening game." A man was with her. He had a deep voice with a bit too much arrogance for Sam's liking. "In your opinion, is that doable?"

There was a lengthy pause, during which Sam slowed his breathing, and then Rachel said, "Yes. We expect sales to increase substantially once the roster is announced. There should be a few local names on there that will draw people in."

A few local names? Like his. To sell tickets. No wonder she'd been so persuasive. The grand plan. Nothing personal.

Sam felt sick.

"We also want to be guaranteed that no league residency minimum will restrict the relocation of this team should Arlington not be the viable market you expect it to be. Should my clients wish to move the team as early as next season, can that be accommodated?"

Another sucker punch. Sutter & Sons would lose the stadium contract.

"Yes," Rachel said again, sounding like a goddamned robot.

"Excellent. And finally, the lack of parking. We perused the land survey, and it's clear you have the space to expand. Am I correct?"

Sam feared her answer. He almost walked away, but a part of him couldn't imagine her selling him out so completely.

"You are correct," she said. "An expansion was in the original building plans."

"Very good. Then, as far as my clients are concerned, if you can increase sales by 10 percent, provide proof the team is able to relocate as early as next season, *and* expand the parking lot to your original specifications, well, then we'll have a deal, and the Aces will be under new ownership."

Jesus. So this had been the bottom line? The Reeds were selling the team. Not that he couldn't see how it made sense considering Danny's health. But … it broke his heart. Seeing Benny get the chance to call the shots for a team that might only be around for a year. Had Rachel even told the guy that was a possibility? Probably not. She hadn't even had the decency to tell the man she was sleeping with. *Son of a bitch.* She'd convinced him to open himself up to baseball again, despite knowing he might be faced with a choice between staying in Arlington with his family or moving God only knew where with his team.

The bottom line, he thought again. The only thing she cared about. Her words. Not his.

"It's been a pleasure doing business with you, Ms. Reed."

Sam didn't hear Rachel's response, but from the definitive sound of the man's voice, he imagined a handshake had occurred somewhere in there. And he hated that Luke had really and truly been right about her.

Looking down at the glove in his hand, Sam wondered what the hell he was doing, getting wrapped up in another dead-end dream, letting his name be used as a ploy to crush the hopes of other people. These guys—and that girl—came from all over the U.S. for a shot at playing professional ball again. To think they could play their hearts out just to be told they wouldn't have a team to report to next year. They deserved to know the truth.

A lanky man with a miserable face nearly bowled Sam over as he left Rachel's office. He never even said, "Excuse me." Which meant Sam could've left without Rachel ever knowing he'd been here. But slinking away had never been his style.

He took a seething breath and stepped into plain sight to find her seated behind the desk, her forehead in her hand and her phone pressed to her ear. She was still the most beautiful thing he'd ever seen. But now he couldn't erase her from his brain fast enough. Too bad the deep ache in his heart told him that wouldn't happen easily.

"Rachel," he said, gruff and unforgiving.

She looked up, startled, eyes wide, lips parted. Whoever was on the other end of the phone must've answered, because she said, "Can I call you back?"

"Don't bother," he said, not caring one bit if he was overheard. "I just wanted you to know I heard about the plans for the team— or should I say the bottom line." He sneered. "Thanks for nothing."

Before she could hang up the phone and manipulate him any further, Sam walked away.

Chapter Seventeen

Rachel caught up with Sam in the parking lot. "Will you please wait?" she asked for the umpteenth time since she'd run after him. But his head start and his long strides had made it a losing battle until now.

He threw his gear bag into the bed of his truck with a murderous thud.

"Will you just listen to what I have to say?" she asked, stopping short, giving him plenty of distance.

"I heard everything I needed to hear while I was standing outside your office." He bolted for the driver's-side door, and she made a mad dash for the passenger seat. She wasn't going to let him get away without hearing both sides of the story.

"Get out of my truck," he said, seething.

Rachel didn't move. "At least tell me if you made the team."

That seemed to piss him off even more. "Are you kidding me? After everything I heard back there you expect me to believe you didn't already know I made the team? Wasn't I your grand plan? Some local guy to make you look good … so you can sell the fucking team?"

She weathered the blow of his words, her hands folded in her lap and her gaze locked on the setting sun. "I'm glad you made the team, and despite how bad this looks, I didn't know you made the team until you told me. I thought you would make it because I saw some of the tryouts, but still. What do I know?"

Crises of confidence were rare for her, but at this moment, she questioned everything. Maybe she should've done things differently. Been up-front about the fact the team was being sold. That probably would've been a good place to start. But she knew in her gut they wouldn't be here now if she'd told him everything.

And aside from this dark spot, missing out on everything else would've been a real shame.

Silence filled the cab of the truck until it almost pushed her out. "Sam, you have to believe me when I say that conversation wasn't easy, and it's not a done deal. I have a plan …"

He bristled. "I don't need any more of your goddamned plans, Rachel."

"The deal you heard back there is not what I want. It's what my—"

"Don't finish that sentence."

"Why?"

"Because you're forty years old. You should be thinking for yourself. Period."

"You don't understand the position I'm in. If the tables were turned and this was your mother asking you to do something difficult, you'd do it, no questions asked." She closed her eyes and wished she'd closed her mouth before that last bit had come out. It was a low blow after he'd told her his biggest regret in life was not coming home when his mother had asked him to. "Sam …"

He leveled a glare at her, then crossed his arms and looked away. When he spoke again, he sounded beaten instead of furious. "I may not understand the position you're in, but I think I finally understand the position I'm in. I was played." His laugh was hollow. "Every step of the way, you played me. From the minute you walked into my father's office and made him an offer he couldn't refuse to that afternoon in my bed. It was all strategy to you, a means to an end. And then once I was locked into tryouts, you checked out."

"That's not true." She reached out, but when he recoiled, she returned her hand to her lap. "That's not what happened. I …" She took a painful breath and studied his angry profile. So handsome. So devastated. And she couldn't blame him. She was devastated, too. But the words stuck in her throat. "I … have genuine feelings for you."

"Genuine feelings?" He looked at her, incredulous, shaking his head and casting shades of pity in her direction. "Don't do me any favors."

"Sam, come on. We're way too old to be acting like this. We knew this thing had a shelf life. You live in Arlington. I live in Philadelphia. We're in two different places, literally and figuratively. You'll want a wife and kids, and I don't know if I can ever be that and give that to anyone."

His eyes roved her face, losing their hardened edge as they went, and all the resolve in the world couldn't keep her from wanting him despite the mess they were in. "You really thought you had this all figured out, didn't you? Too bad you never thought to ask for my input, because if you had, I would've told you that I never wanted you to be or give me anything but you."

"Sam." She fell deeper into his wounded gaze.

"To think I let myself fall for you." They were beautiful words, spoken with such honesty and sadness.

If she kissed him, would anything change? Would he understand she felt the same? But then what? Her father's demands would still need to be met. The team would still need to be sold. She would still be heading back to Philadelphia.

Whatever he'd been thinking in their shared moment of silence must've been as dismal as what she'd been thinking, because he looked away and said, "You might want to tell the buyers there will be one less local name on the roster, because I'm quitting."

"Don't."

This time when he looked at her, all she saw was contempt. "Have a nice life, Rachel. Make sure you guard that bottom line. We wouldn't want you to lose sight of it and actually have to follow your heart for once. You do have one of those, don't you?"

Shades of Helen Anne.

Rachel didn't feel like defending herself anymore—she wasn't sure she could—so she slipped off the passenger seat, but before she closed the door, she said, "Baseball makes you happy, Sam. Please, don't turn your back on that again." When she was in Philadelphia taxed with the impossible project of closing out and liquidating her father's other assets, she wanted to think of Sam hitting home runs and rounding the bases.

Then, at least, something good would've come from all of this.

• • •

Later that night, Sam met Benny Bryant for a beer at Applebee's. Normally, he would've suggested Foley's, but he didn't want to run into Rachel on the off chance she was still in town.

"I have a feeling you didn't ask me here to celebrate," Benny said.

Sam stared at the talking head on the television behind the bar and figured it best to cut to the chase. "Did you know the team was being sold?"

"Yes," he said.

Sam didn't try to hide his shock. "And still you took the job?"

"Of course I took the job. I want the job."

"Didn't you think the players deserved to know this before trying out?

"No. What the hell would that have proved?"

"What if the team gets moved next year?"

Benny took a sip of his beer and rolled his gaze toward the television. "Sutter, this is indie ball. Nobody's guaranteed a next year."

Harsh words. Honest words. Said like that, Sam felt foolish. Then again, Benny and the rest of the team hadn't been as wrapped up in Rachel's scheme as Sam had been. "I'm not interested in playing anywhere but Arlington. My family needs me."

"That's your prerogative."

"I'm also not interested in getting involved with all of this again if it's only a one-year deal." He was starting to realize he didn't handle heartbreak well.

"So what are you saying?" Benny looked at him, and Sam's resolve shook.

"I should quit," he said. "Open up my spot for somebody else."

After another sip of his beer, Benny said, "I can't tell you what to do now any more than I could all those years ago."

"Yes, you can. I should've listened to you then." God how he wished he had. "If I'd listened, things would've been different." He wouldn't have carried around this guilt for the past ten years, that was for sure.

"Sutter, you're one hell of a ball player. Always have been. But you're not a spring chicken anymore. There's not a whole lot a thirty-five-year-old can get out of this experience other than personal satisfaction and some good, old-fashioned diamond joy. If that's not enough, move on. Life is too damn short."

The sad thing was, it *was* enough. Before Sam had stood outside Rachel's office with the walls closing in on him, he couldn't have imagined a better way to spend the next five years than by playing baseball for the Arlington Aces—expect maybe if the next five years included Rachel, too. That thought grabbed hold of his heart even as it disgusted him.

"I don't know what to do," Sam said, staring at his untouched beer.

"Well, normally I would pick up the tab and send an indecisive guy on his way with my blessing, but we go way back, don't we?" Benny said. "And I'd be lying if I said I wasn't looking forward to watching you play another year. But nobody can guarantee us anything more than one season. You could get hurt. I could move on. The team could end up in Poughkeepsie. That's the nature of the beast. You either take the risk and go along for the ride, or you stay safe at home and wonder what might have been. Your choice, Sam. Just let us know what you decide by the start of practice on Monday."

Sam left the bar shortly after that, deciding to sleep on the decision. Instead, he tossed and turned. He looked and felt like hell by the time he showed up for work Saturday morning.

His father was already in the equipment barn, tinkering with a gas-powered edger. He took one look at Sam and said, "Those bums cut you? Are you fucking kidding me? I'll never step foot inside that stadium."

"I made the team, Dad."

"Oh. Well, you look like hell, and you're late. Plus, you never called to give me the verdict last night, so it was an honest mistake. But if you made it, why the long face?"

"Because I'm thinking about quitting."

Paul set his needle-nose pliers on the top of the toolbox and gave his son a good hard look. "Why?"

"It's a long story."

"I've got time." Paul leaned the edger against the workbench and grabbed an old white T-shirt out of his back pocket to wipe off his hands. "You want to talk here or in the house?"

Sam looked over his shoulder, down the long and winding gravel driveway, across the expanse of grass. Nobody was around. Everyone else was out working, including his crew, who were already at the stadium, getting the field ready for Monday's practice. "Here is fine."

"What happened?"

Rachel Reed happened, but he didn't want to spend another minute of his life thinking about her and how she'd completely screwed him. It was bad enough he had to wash his sheets twice and endure the stench of way too much bleach in a wayward attempt at obliterating her memory.

"I found out the team is being sold," Sam said, shoving his hands in his jean pockets, trying to pull off healthy indifference. "There's a possibility it won't stay in Arlington."

"And you're worried about the business." His father sighed. "I never wanted it to be a noose around your neck. Luke and I will manage just fine."

"No. That's not it." Not completely. "I want to be here. I want to help. I'm not going to get dragged into moving around again. Being away from home. A two-week road trip is bad enough, you know? But at least with the team based in Arlington I know I'm always coming back here."

"But you love baseball," Paul said.

Sam couldn't deny it anymore even if he wanted to. "I do, and I can play sandlot."

"Not much of a challenge."

"Maybe not, but at least I'll still be playing. And I'll be home." That was the most important part.

Paul's left eyebrow twitched.

Great, Sam thought, *here comes the quivering upper lip.* Ever since he'd been a boy, his father had given telltale signs of his impending emotional breaks. Sometimes anger. Sometimes tears. Paul Sutter wasn't the kind of man who held things in.

Right on cue, Paul's lip quivered. "Your mother used to say home is where the heart is."

Sam wasn't sure he'd ever heard her say that, but the mention of her had him steeling himself against an onslaught of emotion, too.

"*Your* heart is wherever baseball is, son," Paul said.

Sam balked. "That's not true. I've been without baseball for ten years, and I've done just fine."

"Fine isn't living. It's getting by. You deserve better than that."

Sam wasn't so sure. Maybe this was his penance for turning his back on his mother when she'd needed him most. "I should've come home a long time ago," he said, hating the way his voice broke but hopeless to stop it.

The next thing he knew, he was wrapped in his father's strong arms and surrounded by the scent of lawn-mower grease and freshly washed flannel. Childhood memories roared back at him. Travel games he'd blown. Grandparents he'd lost. Honor rolls he'd made. Records he'd broken. The same hug was exchanged. Comfort or congratulations. Except after his mother had died. There'd been anger, distance, and total devastation on Sam's part, and he'd pushed his father's open arms away, too guilt-ridden to accept comfort. He hadn't realized how much he'd needed this hug until now.

Holding on to his father, Sam let it all go. With each breath, he softened his muscles, settled his mind, and finally forgave himself.

"Thanks, Dad."

"I love you, son."

The magnitude of the moment was chased away by the sound of tires crunching along the gravel driveway as Luke's truck barreled toward them.

Sam didn't want to rehash what had just happened with his brother, so he said a quick goodbye to his father and then headed to his truck. But he wasn't fast enough.

"Hey!" Luke said, hopping out of his vehicle and heading straight for him. "Did you make the team?"

"I did."

"Congratulations?"

"Don't hurt yourself with all that enthusiasm."

"No, man. I'm happy for you. I really am." Luke raised his brow in suspicion. "I'm just wondering why you don't look happy."

"I am happy."

Luke narrowed his eyes. "What did she do?"

"Nothing, man," Sam snapped. He wasn't sure why he felt the need to protect Rachel after everything she'd done.

"Sorry. That wasn't cool. You're right. You're all grown up. Rachel is your business now. I knew her a long time ago. You know her better than I ever did."

Yep, that's what Sam had thought, too. *Sucker.* He nodded and said, "Thanks, man. See you later." And then he closed his door, knowing he'd protected her yet again. Wondering if maybe he'd been protecting himself, too.

It didn't matter. She was gone. Out of his life. And he had a choice to make.

As he backed up and pulled around, pointing his truck toward the main road, he realized the decision had been made in the midst of that hug.

His heart was with baseball. At least half of it was.

Hopefully, that would be enough.

Chapter Eighteen

"Richard sent these over," Liv said, having walked into Rachel's Philadelphia office with a smile on her face. "They're the originals of the copies he emailed you last week when you were in Arlington. He wanted me to tell you he outdid himself this time. Whatever that means."

"Thank you," Rachel said, distracted by a text from Macy that detailed all the weekend dates Helen Anne had approved for a trip to Pittsburgh to see the Pirates play. "You can leave them on my desk."

Liv set the fat stack of property disclosures on the corner and asked, "Are you feeling okay? No cracks about Richard today?"

Rachel opened her calendar and nodded. "I'm fine."

"Really? I don't believe you. What's wrong? You haven't even mentioned his hair."

Richard had changed his hair? Rachel looked up and shrugged. "I didn't notice anything."

"He got highlights!"

"Good for him."

"They look ridiculous."

Well, Richard was ridiculous, but he knew this business inside and out, and he'd done one hell of a job keeping things together in her absence. Rachel's phone vibrated, and she looked down to find another text from Macy:

I'm going to see Mr. Fry's first game!!!

It was followed by six thumbs-up emojis and one with tears coming out of the eyes. Rachel could never figure out if that meant happy or sad. She was going with happy this time.

"Seriously. What is going on with you?" Liv asked.

"Nothing." Rachel shook her head clear and put her phone facedown on her desk. "That was Macy. She's going to the Aces' home opener."

Liv tilted her head. "Are you?"

"No."

"Is your father going?"

"As long as he's feeling up to it. I talked to Helen Anne and my mother. They've agreed to take him."

"If you want to go, I'll go with you."

"I don't." But she did. She'd been trolling the site for the last week, waiting for the roster to be posted, and sure enough, Sam Sutter's name was listed. Just to make sure it wasn't a mistake, she'd called Benny Bryant with some concocted excuse and asked him to send the final roster to her.

Thank God Sam was on there. At least she hadn't screwed up everything.

Liv sat, and Rachel shooed her away with one hand. "I don't have time for a girly chat."

"Who said anything about a girly chat?"

"I can see it in your eyes."

Liv chuckled. "Real quick. Have you talked to Sam?"

"No. Now get back to work."

"Aren't you going to tell him about the trees?"

Rachel had tried once already. In his truck. She'd considered calling him and trying again after she'd finalized the details with the community college, but maybe it was better to leave things alone. "He'll figure it out soon enough."

"Are the interested buyers pissed?" Liv asked in a lowered voice, as if Mike and his oddball clients could overhear her.

"Yes. But they're more upset we haven't seen a major spike in season ticket sales. Mike left me a message I still haven't returned. He wants to renegotiate the terms."

"What if they back out?"

Rachel had thought about that a lot this week. Having substantial physical distance from her father, who no longer called daily for a breakdown of her accomplishments, gave her some much-needed perspective. "If they back out, they back out. I can't fake ticket sales."

"True." Liv waited a beat before she stood and said, "I guess I'll get back to work now." But she hesitated. "I was sort of hoping you would go to the opening game, because I want to."

Rachel smiled. "Go. Nothing is stopping you."

"Well, you pretty much got that team up and running, but you're not going, which makes me wonder what's stopping you."

Rachel eyeballed the printed roster she kept on her desk and scanned the names until she stopped on Sam. "It's Sam's day," she said. "I don't want to ruin it for him."

"You wouldn't."

"He hates me. He has every right to hate me."

"He said he couldn't believe he fell for you. Right?"

"In a forlorn sort of way," Rachel reminded Liv.

"Because he was upset in that moment. But have you thought about exactly what he meant?"

"God, no," Rachel said. Remembering the misery on his face, the misery she'd put there, was not something she wanted to relive.

"Well, usually when people say they fell, they mean they fell in love."

Rachel choked out a laugh. "That's not what Sam meant. You can fall for someone without falling in love. It's just an expression."

"Are you sure?"

"Absolutely. We weren't together long enough for that."

"I just read a HuffPost article that said it doesn't take long for some people to fall in love, especially at your age," Liv said with a glint of humor in her eyes.

"Well, it takes longer than ten weeks, even for a senior citizen like me."

"So, you don't love him?"

"I"—her throat tightened up—"wouldn't know love if it hit me between the eyes," she said flippantly. "Too subjective."

Liv seemed to think about that, and just when Rachel thought she'd brought this crazy conversation to a successful end, Liv asked, "What's this?" She walked her fingers across Rachel's desk to where the roster laid.

"Nothing," Rachel said, sliding other papers over it. "Just the list of players. For professional purposes."

Liv rolled her eyes. "How often do you think about him during the day?"

Too often. "You should go before I start questioning why I ever hired you."

Liv backed away from the desk with a smile. "You should flip that piece of paper over and start keeping track with hash marks. Every time you think of him"—she sliced her hand through the air—"mark, mark, mark. I bet you fill up that page by the end of the day."

"Goodbye, Liv. Tell Richard I said thank you."

Liv was almost out the door when she added, "If you fill up the page, it's safe to say you love him."

Rachel picked up her empty foam coffee cup and pretended she was going to throw it.

The door closed with a definitive click, and Rachel sat back to enjoy the peace and quiet. Only, the air in the room felt unsettled, and her brain whirred like a radio tuned to white noise. A single word broke through every now and then. *Contracts. Closings. Tickets. Trees.*

Love.

She'd pulled back from every relationship that threatened to go too far. She never let herself love anyone aside from her family members, and even that love was twisted. That love had put her in this predicament. Making promises she was starting to wonder if she could keep. On the day not so long ago when her father had come to her and explained his desire to give her special power of attorney because of the disease, she'd felt crushed by the expectations, yet honored, determined to do him proud. It had always been that way. Prove to him he didn't need that son. Maybe forty years of living like that had finally taken its toll.

God, what *had* she been doing all these years? Closing deals and making money. Worrying about the bottom line.

It wasn't enough.

She'd been so sure of her decision to follow in her father's footsteps. She'd seen the freedom he'd had, jetting off to close deals on a moment's notice, while her mother was stuck in Arlington with sick kids and PTA obligations. No, thank you. That was never going to be Rachel. She chose to be like him instead. He controlled the money. He had all the power. She laughed cynically, because he still did. Despite the Alzheimer's. Despite the special power of attorney. She continued to give him control over everything.

You're forty years old, Rachel. You should be thinking for yourself.

Fine. She would play Sam's game … hypothetically, of course. What would Rachel do? Her first decision would be to not sell the team to those idiots. Yes, it would piss off some people, including her father. But so be it. She was in charge in this scenario. And when her father snapped at her for going against his wishes, she would tell him she did it *for* him, not despite him. She would tell him Helen Anne was in agreement with her, because holding on to the team a little while longer would give him a chance to enjoy what he'd built. He would argue with her about who would run the team in the meantime and what he should do if another buyer didn't come along, and she would say, "I'll run the team like I have for the past two months with as much or as little input from you. And if money is what you're worried about, if you need cash to continue to fight this disease, then you can have mine. That way we get the team *and* more time together."

The air whooshed out of her lungs as the daydream spun out of control in her head. It was a fairy-tale ending, and fairy tales didn't come true, but still … the idea nagged at her, morphing into something else entirely: What if *she* bought the team?

Rachel's hands shook with the realization that it was feasible. She knew the list price. She knew her net worth. Parting with eight million dollars in one fell swoop would change everything. It would thrust her into the financially precarious position her father was currently in, but it would also allow her to see her father's dream to fruition. Her parents would be able to afford care and treatments. Helen Anne and Macy could stay in the house for as long as they needed to. And Rachel would have a chance to make things right with Sam.

That alone was worth every penny she'd ever made.

Buy a baseball team. Sam's team. She smiled as she lifted the papers and glanced at his name on the roster. It would be risky, dramatic, and life changing.

Wasn't that everything love was supposed to be?

• • •

Sam thought about walking the mile through the trees to the stadium for this afternoon's practice, but it was drizzling. Dark clouds overhead threatened to full-on rain, so he drove, parking in his usual spot at the end of the third row. Every day, for the last week and a half, he'd expected to pull in here and see heavy equipment poised to cut down those trees. Still nothing. The waiting was torture because every time he thought about it, he thought about Rachel.

How could he have been so wrong about her? Why was he still hoping for some sort of redemption, something to change his mind?

Like he always did, he left the questions hanging in the air while he unloaded his gear from the back of the truck and headed to the clubhouse. The locker room wasn't big. It wasn't flashy, but it was newly remodeled, painted blue with a white stripe halfway up the wall. An oversized playing card was painted on the floor. The ace of spades. He walked around it. They all did. Not wanting to wear off any of the shine or show disrespect.

Two weeks in and they already had some superstitions.

Sam loved it. He couldn't believe he'd gone ten years without this—the preparation, the ritual, the competition—in his life. It fed his soul. It made everything better.

Almost everything.

"Gentlemen!" Coach Slater yelled and then shook his head, clearly still struggling with the fact one of his players was a woman.

Most of the guys had lapses. Like last week, when Ian rolled out of the shower without a towel. Sam had to give Pauly props, though, because she didn't even blink. "Three older brothers," she'd said. "It's nothing I haven't seen before." Oh, did Ian take exception to that.

"Just call us Aces, Coach," Matt Fry said from behind his open locker door. "We can all answer to that."

A couple of the guys whooped but then quieted as Coach continued.

"The front office has a request." He pulled his reading glasses out of the chest pocket of his windbreaker and propped them on his nose. Then, he lifted his clipboard and read, "Opening Day, Friday, May 11, presented by The Community College of Huntingdon County—Arlington. Saplings to the first two hundred people."

Trees? Was this some kind of sick joke?

"After the game, a sign marking the"—Coach looked at the clipboard again and then butchered the word—"*arboretum* will be unveiled. They would like at least two players to attend." He looked up. "Can I get a couple volunteers, or will I need to assign you?"

"An arboretum?" Sam wondered aloud. None of this made sense.

"Yeah. It's a fancy word for a bunch of trees. I didn't know what the hell it meant, either. I had to look it up."

Sam knew what it was. He just didn't understand why or … "Where?"

"Behind the parking lot," Coach said. "Supposedly the land was donated back to the community college. Makes no sense to me—why you'd buy something and then give it back to the person you bought it from. But, hey, I ain't rich, so what do I know?"

"I'll do it. I'll be at the unveiling," Sam said, maybe a little too enthusiastically, because his teammates looked at him funny. "What? I like trees. I'm a landscaper, remember."

Coach nodded and wrote something on his clipboard. "Okay. I got Sutter. Who else?"

"Me," Ian said. "I'm a landscaper, too."

"Second order of business." Coach yanked a stack of papers off the clipboard, leaving a few behind. "Finalized schedules. Front office is going to email you a copy, but this'll save you from having to print it so you can hang it in your locker." He started passing them out. "I expect Ws next to every contest."

Sam reached for his copy and scanned the dates and team names. He was still reeling from the news about the arboretum. No wonder he hadn't seen any equipment. During the argument in his truck, Rachel had mentioned a plan, and he'd shut her down. Had she been trying to tell him about this back then? Was there more to the story than what he'd heard standing outside her office? His gut cramped, and he knew the answers to those questions.

Damn. What if he'd fucked this up worse than she had? Not telling him the team was for sale, not telling him she was hoping to monetarily capitalize on his return to baseball. Those were bad things. But not hearing her out, not giving her a chance to explain, and making light of her feelings for him and the position she was in with her father … Those had been dick moves that replayed over and over again in his head. She wasn't innocent, but he'd been selfish. He should at least call her and admit that, apologize, too. He could leave a voicemail if she didn't answer. Just clear the air.

He locked eyes on three games the Aces were slated to play in Camden, New Jersey, in two weeks. Maybe he could follow up the call with a surprise visit. It was a lot harder to ignore someone when they were standing right in front of you.

"Why are you grinning like that?" Ian asked. "Thinking about those trees?"

"No. I'm thinking about the woman I'm assuming is behind those trees being turned into an arboretum."

"Who's that?"

"Rachel, you meathead."

"Oh." Ian laughed. "How should I know?"

"I don't know. You agreed to be at the unveiling, so I figured you had some idea what was going on."

"I'm just hoping there's a party afterward."

"Figures." Sam grabbed his glove off the top shelf of his locker and headed out to the field with Ian by his side.

"So … Rachel."

"What about her?" Sam asked warily.

"Are you guys still"—Ian bobbed his brows—"getting busy?"

"She's in Philly."

"Yeah, but she can visit. You can, too. I'd drive a few hours for …" Sam raised his glove in front of Ian's mouth as they closed in on Pauly. "What'd I say?" Ian asked.

"Nothing yet, but I know where you were headed. Show a little respect."

Ian frowned in the general direction of Pauly and then asked, "How'd you know I wasn't going to say I'd drive a few hours for the woman I *love*?"

"Because that would mean you've actually focused all your attention on one woman long enough to fall in love, and we both know that has never happened."

Ian slapped his mitt over his heart dramatically. "That hurts man. I'm deeper than you give me credit for." They shared a laugh and then split up into positional warm-ups.

Off and on, Sam thought about the weird but welcomed shift in the day. An arboretum. Talk about a changeup. His mother would've been ecstatic. Front and center at the dedication. How he wished she could be here for Opening Day.

When it was time to stretch, Sam laid back in the grass he'd groomed to perfection and stared at the clear blue sky while a mass of black birds flew in V-formation overhead. In that moment, he knew she would be there. In fact, she'd been here all along. Now all he needed was for Rachel to be here, too.

After practice, Sam went home and sat out back with Babe by his side, a beer on the fat arm of his Adirondack chair, his cell phone in his lap. "If she doesn't answer, I'm just going to apologize and hang up. No babbling. You hold me to that." The dog tilted her head as if she understood. Maybe it was silly, but it made Sam feel better.

He touched the screen, placing the call, and was slow to put the phone to his ear. He didn't expect her to answer, but she did.

"Hello."

A startled, "Hey," was all he could come up with.

"I take it you heard about the arboretum," she said, her tone almost teasing.

That was his girl—sharp and to the point. "Yeah," he said, smiling, but then he remembered this wasn't some run-of-the-mill phone call. "I'm sorry."

"For what?"

"For being selfish. For not letting you tell me about the trees when we were in my truck. You tried, didn't you?"

"I did, but I also deserved to be shut down. Sam …" God, he loved it when she said his name. "I'm sorry, too. I made verbal promises to my father and ignored the nonverbal promises I was making to you."

"Nonverbal promises? Does that mean what I think it means?"

She laughed, a breathy sound that thrilled him, and he closed his eyes, dropping his head to the seatback, so thankful they'd cleared this hurdle.

"You weren't some one-night stand," she said. "You deserved better than to find out about the buyers the way you did. And as far as playing you goes, I admit it. I definitely walked into your father's office with an ulterior motive that would get you off my back about the trees. I also recognized that helping you reconnect with baseball could help me fill those seats. But I wasn't trying to exploit you as much as I was trying to make us both happy, and then something else happened." She paused, and a shaky exhale filtered across the line. "I fell for you, too. I hope you can forgive me."

"Forgive you for falling for me?" he asked, his voice calm, but his heart pounding.

"No. I'm not sorry about that part."

"Good, because that's the only part I care about right now."

"Sam, I'm so glad you called, but I really have to go. I have a critical meeting in five minutes."

"Are you just saying that because you want to avoid this awkward conversation?"

"Absolutely not. It's not awkward at all." She laughed. "Well, maybe a little. Why don't we finish the conversation in person?"

"When?"

"How does May 11 sound?"

Opening Day. "You'll be here."

"I wouldn't miss it for the world."

"Rachel …"

"Sam …" He could hear the smile in her voice. "Don't say anything else. Save it for May 11. Okay? I have to go."

He agreed, smiling, too.

May 11 was going to be one hell of a day.

Chapter Nineteen

"Where are we going?" Danny asked again. It was at least the fifth time in the last fifteen minutes.

Jackie fussed with the zipper of his Arlington Aces windbreaker. "To the baseball game."

"Oh, that's right." He smiled at Rachel, who was admiring the way her mother cared for her father. She supposed that was when love really mattered—during the roughest spots. She felt ashamed suddenly for all the years she'd looked down on her mother's life as a housewife and all the years she'd thought she was somehow superior to Helen Anne, who'd skipped college to become a wife and mother. These two women were every bit as strong as Rachel was … in some ways maybe even stronger.

With her husband settled, Jackie turned her attention to herself, fiddling with the belt of her jacket, a royal-blue trench she'd topped off with a white cashmere scarf. "How do I look?" she asked Rachel.

"Very nice. I still think you should wear a hat, though."

"It will flatten my hair."

"You look beautiful," Danny said, smiling.

Rachel couldn't recall ever witnessing simple affection like this when she was growing up. What a shame it had taken a catastrophic illness to slow things down enough that her parents could refocus on what was important. What a blessing she'd finally opened her eyes wide enough to see she didn't have to make the same mistakes. Better late than never.

Helen Anne and Macy joined them in the entrance hall, both wearing Arlington Aces hats like the one Rachel wore, her sleek ponytail pulled through the back.

"We'll meet you there," Helen Anne said.

"Where are you going?" Danny asked.

"To the baseball game, Pop-Pop!" Macy bounced up and kissed his cheek. "Aunt Rachel got me seats behind home plate!"

Rachel smiled and high-fived her niece even as she worried her father might not be able to tolerate the excitement of the day. Lord knows he hadn't wrapped his mind around all the changes. Maybe he never would. Which was fine with Rachel. He could think he still owned the team until the day he died. He would own it vicariously through her.

"Where's Liv?" Helen Anne asked.

"Already at the stadium."

"Is Liv moving to Arlington, too?" Macy had gotten used to having Liv around. When Liv was here, she was the youngest adult in the house, and that earned her major cool marks with Macy. But, unfortunately, Liv was staying in Philadelphia to help Richard in his new, permanent capacity of Senior Vice President and Broker.

Rachel shook her head and was about to answer Macy's question when Danny asked, "Who's moving to Arlington?"

"I am, Dad." Rachel placed a hand on his shoulder. "Remember how we talked about me moving back home and working with the baseball team full-time?"

His forehead wrinkled, and her heart dipped. He didn't remember. But then a sort of recognition flashed in his eyes, and he smiled. "We're going to win a championship."

"You bet we are," she said, sending up a prayer that his memory would remain intact long enough for him to still care about a championship once she was able to deliver one.

He'd said the same thing in the lawyers' office last week, during a particularly lucid few hours in which they were able to hash out the terms of the sale, making sure it was fair and equitable. Apparently a championship had been his personal and private goal all along, and the minute she'd heard that, she knew she would spend the rest of his life trying to make that dream come true.

It dawned on her that maybe she was falling into old patterns, making business decisions based on what her father wanted, but she wanted this as much, if not more, than he did. She wanted it for herself. She wanted it for him. And she wanted it for Sam, who had five years of age eligibility left. *Five years.* She knew the odds of her father remaining fully engaged five years from now were slim, so she'd given herself three years. Max. The Arlington Aces were going to win the Independence League championship, and that was that.

Once the Reeds were at the stadium, ensconced in the modest owner's box above the third-base line, Liv joined them. She was dressed in jeans and an oversized Aces jersey unbuttoned at the bottom and tied at her waist.

"Cute," Rachel said. "Did you have to raid the locker room to get that?"

Liv blushed. "No! I've gotten to know Quincy, the equipment guy, pretty well. He snagged me one that wasn't being used. I hope that's okay. I don't want to get him in trouble."

"It's fine," Rachel said. An authentic jersey was the least she could do for the woman who had been her right hand through all of this. Her right hand and best friend. Somehow, some way, Rachel was going to bring that girl back to Arlington.

Adele appeared a few minutes later, wearing her Aces ID on a rhinestone lanyard around her neck. "The coaches want to know if you're coming down to say a few words of encouragement to the team before the game."

Rachel blinked. "I …"

"Absolutely!" her father said, standing. "I'd like to say a few words to my boys."

Rachel shared a worried glance with her mother, and then she scrambled to her feet. "I'll go with you, Dad."

"Of course you will. You're my co-captain." He smiled at her, an expression that was riddled with deeper meaning, and the longer he stared at her, the more she sensed his gratitude. *Co-captain.* She liked it. The word was gender-neutral, unlike daughter or son, and equal.

She grabbed his hand and squeezed. "Let's go see your boys."

Along the way, Adele shot Rachel looks, as if to say, "What are we supposed to do?"

Rachel answered with reassuring smiles. The coaching staff knew about her father's diagnosis. Sam knew. By now, the rest of the players might know, too. What was the worst thing that could happen? He would forget why he was there? No big deal. She would pick up where he left off. They would do this … together, like co-captains.

The locker room was silent when they walked in. Rachel immediately honed in on Sam. He sat in a folding chair, facing his locker. But he glanced over his shoulder, and a smile lit up his gorgeous face. She tried to play it cool for the sake of professional impartiality, but she hadn't seen him in two weeks, and he looked amazing—better than she remembered. So she grinned. At him. And didn't care if it was inappropriate. She owned the team— or at least she would officially own the team soon, once the paperwork and the assets were cleared for closing, which was a small technicality, really. This team was destined to be hers the minute she'd stepped inside the stadium.

Twenty-four men and one woman dressed in crisp, clean, blue-and-white Aces uniforms sat in folding chairs in front of their lockers, looking at the Reeds expectantly. They were ready to play. Ready to win. Rachel could read it on their serious faces.

Various coaches milled around the room, which smelled warm and oddly chalky, but it was Coach Slater who stepped up and shook her father's hand and then hers.

"Aces," Coach said. "Our owner would like to say a few words."

Danny stepped right up to the proverbial plate, and Rachel didn't try to stop him. Instead, she made eye contact with Sam, but he looked wary, probably because as far as he knew the team was still on the auction block. Little did he know. Rachel grinned at him again, and he looked confused, which made her chuckle.

"Gentlemen," her father said in a booming voice that echoed off the low ceiling and metal lockers.

Rachel couldn't help but look at the sole female and flash an apologetic smile. Hopefully, her father wouldn't forget he lived in a world where women were as capable as men—even on the mound.

"We're going to win a championship," he said.

There was a stunned beat of silence before the room erupted with cheers that went on so long Rachel's father seemed to forget why he was there. When the locker room quieted, he froze, so Rachel stepped up, linked her arm with his, and added, "We're honored to be a part of this journey with you. The people of Arlington are honored, too. Play hard. Win big. We'll be rooting for you."

As far as rally speeches went, it was short and pretty terrible, but she would have other chances to say different words.

This was only the beginning.

• • •

Sam wasn't sure what to think about today. So far, it surprisingly outmatched his minor-league debut in nerves. Possibly because the stadium was filled with people he knew, including his father and brother. Probably because he hadn't suited up and played a truly meaningful game in ten years. Then there was that pep talk Rachel and her father had given. He'd expected it to be a little off, considering his other interactions with Danny Reed, but Sam got the sense something else was going on, too.

Nowadays, he was always looking for that changeup and the excitement it would bring.

When some of Sam's teammates had asked about Mr. Reed, Coach explained about the Alzheimer's, but nobody had said a word about the team being on the auction block. Sam didn't know who—if anyone—knew, other than Benny. He didn't care anymore. Playing for a singular season was exactly the way they all should be playing. Actually, playing for a single game was even better. Nobody was guaranteed tomorrow. All they had was right now.

And right now, Sam stood on first base, waiting for "Fries" to deliver the first pitch to a batter who looked polished enough in warm-up swings to have seen some time in at least the minors. But the big guy whiffed the two-blink fastball right down the middle, looking considerably less skilled in full motion.

Next pitch. Same thing. That got the decent-sized crowd cheering. It wasn't a sellout, but it still sounded good to Sam.

Another windup. Another pitch. And everything went still for a fraction of a second as the beefy guy sat on the pitch too long before making contact. The late swing sent the ball barreling straight for Sam. Pure adrenaline fueled his sudden movement—a lunge to the right of the base, where he snagged the ball after an errant hop, and then a sprint to the bag, where he beat the runner.

One out.

All day, all night, Sam thought, feeling settled in his skin, looking forward to his turn at the plate.

That came in the bottom of the second. Unfortunately, the Youngstown Yardigans had one hell of a starting pitcher, who'd managed to sit the Aces down one, two, three, which meant Sam, who was batting cleanup, strolled out to the mound as the first batter and promptly struck out on a fastball he expected to be a changeup.

Frustration marred his jog back to the dugout. When he sat "Uncle" Pete, the hitting coach, sat beside him, spitting seeds every few seconds. Finally, Pete said, "Keep your weight back."

Sam nodded.

"For as long as possible," Pete added. "Give yourself time to relax." He spit again. "Take it all in. Then you react." With a slap to Sam's back, Pete was gone.

Sam had never realized it before, but baseball was one hell of a metaphor for life.

In the bottom of the third, the Aces rung up two on the strength of Ian's lead-off double and Sam's stand-up triple. After that, the Yardigans fell apart, and the Aces went on to win the home opener 10–zip.

The high was incomparable—except for maybe the moments he'd been tangled up with Rachel. He showered with those moments in mind, which was tricky while naked and hopped up on adrenaline, and Sam would've lingered in the hot spray had Coach not come looking for him.

"Sutter, you're wanted upstairs in the business office."

Probably something to do with the arboretum. "Be right there," he called, then killed the water, and wrapped up in a towel in case Pauly had finally made it back from signing autographs and talking with her family.

Apparently, a lot of Sam's teammates were still out on the field, though, which gave him plenty of freedom and space to dress. He'd been told to look sharp, so he'd bought a new tan-colored suit. Paired with a crisp white dress shirt he'd left open at his throat, Sam felt pretty damn good, and he left the locker room with a spring in his step.

On his way upstairs, his mood continued to rise as he texted with his father and brother, fielding more congratulations. He loved that they could be so closely involved because he was playing in Arlington. Home games had never felt this good in the minors. Sam had never felt this full.

"Hi."

The minute he stepped off the elevator, he saw Rachel, standing in the middle of the reception area, decked out in the same white-and-blue dress that had knocked the wind out of him when she'd walked into the locker room before the game. Only now, the ball cap was gone and her hair fell freely around her shoulders.

"God, you look beautiful," he said.

She grinned, letting her gaze wander over him. "So do you."

He walked toward her, not exactly sure of what he would—or should—do once he was there.

"Care to step into my office?" she asked coyly.

He glanced around them. "Are you the person I'm meeting?"

"I hope so," she said laughing. "Who are you meeting?"

"I don't know. I was just told to come up here. I figured it had something to do with the arboretum."

"Sort of."

He smiled. "Now I'm intrigued."

"You should be," she said, turning and heading toward the open door at the end of the hall, giving him a lovely view of her swinging hips and strong strides.

When she shut the door behind him, he made his move ... only to be halted by her hand on his chest. "We need to talk."

He might've felt rebuffed if it weren't for her fingernails scraping a light rhythm that hummed straight to his core. "Among other things," he said, letting his voice drop in suggestion.

She smiled. "I've missed you."

Screw it. He slid an arm around her waist and pulled her in, keeping her hand pinned to his chest. "If that's the way you're going to talk, we're going to get to those other things pretty damn quick." He brushed his lips against the feathery hair at her temple, breathing in the rich, clear spice of her perfume, and whispered, "You have no idea how much I've missed you."

Her free hand roamed his back beneath his suit coat. "Are you happy, Sam?"

"Ecstatic," he whispered against her ear, loving the way she shuddered.

"Good, because I bought the team."

He straightened and met with her anxious expression. Maybe he'd heard her wrong, because what he'd heard didn't exactly make sense. "I thought the deal was done with those other guys. I thought that's why you made the arboretum happen. It was a consolation prize."

With his grip loosened, she brought both hands to his shoulders. "I don't believe in consolation prizes. Winner takes all. And this time, we all win."

"*You* bought the Aces?" His mind spun with the implications.

She nodded. "Thoughts?"

"I think my brain might explode."

She wrapped her arms around his neck and leaned into him. "Well, we can't have that," she said, brushing her lips back and forth against his. "Nobody wants a brainless first baseman."

He kissed her—open mouths, tangled tongues—and backed her up until she hit the door. "I don't want anyone to want me but you," he whispered harshly.

"Me, either."

He slid a hand beneath her skirt and up her smooth thigh to cup her bottom. "Can we skip this tree thing?"

She pushed against him playfully, only succeeding in grinding her pelvis against his erection. "Absolutely not. You're the one who made such a big deal about those trees in the first place. Don't you wish I had cut them down now?" She slipped a hand between them and rubbed him harder.

"No," he said, the word dissolving into a groan, and then he grabbed her hand and pulled it away before she could cause any real damage. "I have plans for you in those trees. I'm buying a bench."

Her eyes twinkled. "You really are happy, aren't you?"

How could he be anything else? "You make me happy."

She smiled. "Baseball makes you happy."

"And now you're both inextricably linked."

"You *could* have one without the other."

"I wouldn't want it that way. I want it all," he said, tightening his grip on her.

"Because you're greedy," she teased.

"Because I love you." The words surprised even him. They hadn't been part of some grand plan. Just an undeniable feeling put into words. "I want to share it all with you, Rachel. Anything and everything."

Her eyes watered, and she blinked furiously. For a second, he questioned if she felt the same, but then she cupped his face and said, "I love you, too. Everything means nothing without you. That's what I realized these past two weeks."

He kissed her again, so damn happy to have gotten to this place where the past didn't drag him down and the future didn't leave him hopeless.

The future. He couldn't wait. In fact, he welcomed it.

Changeups and all.

Acknowledgments

After thirteen books (Lucky 13!), I'm probably starting to sound like a broken record, but as always, huge props to my editor, Tara Gelsomino; imprint manager, Julie Sturgeon; and the entire Crimson Romance team. I'm so grateful for your support, vision, and patience (when necessary).

I need to shout out a very special thank you to my readers, who've been patiently waiting for this book while I took some time off and slowed my writing schedule. (It has paid off. I promise. My editor says so, too.) Big virtual hugs and kisses to every reader and blogger who sent words of encouragement when I was dealing with life's crazy ups and downs this past year. You're the real reason this book was written. I couldn't let you down.

And finally, I send my love to friends and family who have been with me on this journey from book one. I couldn't do any of this without you.

About the Author

Elley Arden is a born-and-bred Pennsylvanian who has lived as far west as Utah and as far north as Wisconsin. She drinks wine like it's water (a slight exaggeration), prefers a night at the ballpark to a night on the town, and believes almond English toffee is the key to happiness. Elley writes books with charming characters, emotional stories, and sexy romance. For a complete list of her books, visit www.elleyarden.com.

Running Interference
by Elley Arden

Mmm. Mmm. Mmm. There was something about a sunny Sunday morning that put extra spring in Tanya Martin's already speedy steps. No dealing with ornery high school students and excuses about forgotten gym clothes. No football practice. Just hours to spend however she liked at her father's boxing gym.

She lifted her face to the unseasonably warm rays and wished late February in Cleveland, Ohio, always looked like this. But the heaping mounds of filthy snow lining the sidewalk reminded her winter wasn't done with them yet. She didn't care. Today was going to be a great day.

A glass door opened up ahead, and a man backed onto the sidewalk. He was so big his body loomed around the stainless steel framing, and his voice boomed when he laughed at someone inside the coffee shop. Her pace slowed as she took in his profile. Black, fitted ski jacket. Dark denim jeans that clung to his tree-trunk thighs. And a pair of designer work boots that had never set foot on a jobsite. *Not from around.* These new businesses brought in all kinds, sellouts who couldn't get through their Sundays without a double shot of something she couldn't even pronounce let alone swallow.

She put her head down and picked up her pace, wanting to pass before she was forced to say hello. She didn't want her South City neighborhood to change, and she didn't want these people getting comfortable. They weren't wanted. They weren't needed.

What this place *needed* was people with a sense of loyalty and conviction—people like her parents, who both owned mom-and-pop businesses on this stretch of street. For even longer than her mother had been cooking her "almost famous" pulled-pork and holding twice-monthly Free Soup Fridays at her restaurant, Mama Mary's, her father had been taking kids off the streets and teaching them life skills with the help of boxing and martial arts at his gym. Those things were so much more important than overpriced warehouse condos and a chain coffee shop.

"Oh crap!"

The rich rumble of words came first, followed by a splash of something hot along her neck, and then an impact that had her careening toward the icy snowdrift. Her hands jutted out to break her fall, but she never hit. Instead, a crushing grip circled her right elbow and a jolt set her upright. Somehow her shoulder remained attached to its socket.

"I'm so sorry," said the deep voice again. "I … "

She looked from the work boots to the face of the trendily dressed, mammoth man, and her jaw dropped. *Cam Simmons.*

"Tanya Martin?" he asked. "Holy shit!"

Stunned into silence, she reached a hand to her neck and wiped at the droplets.

He pulled a napkin bearing the Coffee Bean logo from his pocket. "Are you okay?" He dabbed the napkin at her neck, then her chest. A little too rough. But the swipes that followed were a little too friendly.

She nodded and brushed his hand away.

How long had it been? *Five years.* Not that she'd been counting … lately. Their friendship had cooled on a barrage of texts and calls that tapered off as he got used to life away from Cleveland. Eventually the distance between them proved too great to cross. Who needed old friends when you had a shiny new multi-million-dollar NFL contract?

And that contract looked good on him, too. It had turned him into an entirely different person from the anxious, overachieving high school boy she'd spent hours with at Pop's gym. Taller and bigger, naturally, but there was also a relaxed confidence gleaming in those deep brown eyes. He didn't just want to be good; he knew he was good.

"What happened to your hair?" she blurted.

He'd had curls that rivaled hers in high school.

He palmed his nearly bald head and smiled. Somewhere angels sang. He'd always been too talented and handsome for his own good.

"I like my helmet to have a snug fit," he said. "And I was tired of messing around with skull caps. Does it look bad?"

Sly dog. Always digging for compliments, but he didn't need the ego boost. "Do you really care what I think?" Again, the last five years weighed heavy on her mind. There hadn't been so much as a Facebook like or a forwarded chain email between them. "I mean, come on. You're the Super Bowl MVP. You hardly need approval from me."

"But it would be nice." He flashed that smile again and her heart spontaneously warmed.

Disturbing. She did not want to have feelings for him after all these years. Their one night together senior year had muddied the innocent friendship, and it had taken years for her to find a neutral place, where she could hear his name, see his face, watch his games without feeling some sense of loss and hurt.

"I can't believe you're here," she said.

"I owed my mama the trip. Been promising for years. Got nothing going on until optional team activities in April, so I figured why not."

That was at least a month away. A month of running into him like this.

Shit. She backed up. "Well, it was good seeing you."

"Wait a minute." He grabbed her arm. Softer than the last time. Even through the layers of her hooded sweatshirt and long-sleeved T-shirt, she felt an unsettling tingle. "Where you running off to so fast? I'll buy you a coffee."

She glanced behind him at the gleaming monstrosity that required the leveling of two locally owned businesses to create. "No thanks. I'm not a coffee drinker. Besides, I have some ring time waiting for me."

"That's right! Pop's Gym & Ring." Deep, loud, and somehow flashy, he sounded like he'd already signed his name on a lucrative sports network announcing career. "I'm going to tag along. Say hey. Do you mind?"

She did, but if she made a big deal out of it, then she wouldn't be neutral. "Come on."

They walked the next two blocks with a safe distance between them, talking about the obvious: his Super Bowl win. It seemed safer than delving into their overly personal past. She'd never been so happy to push open the doors to the gym. Her sanctuary. She breathed in the musty smell of hard work and dedication, and exhaled her restlessness over seeing Cam.

"I'll catch ya later," she said, waving a hand at him and eyeing up the hallway that led to the locker rooms. With any luck, he'd be gone by the time she came out, and if he wasn't, maybe she'd throw on some gloves, challenge him to a few rounds, and teach him a couple things. He might be bigger and stronger, but she wasn't above hitting below the belt if need be. Hell, he deserved it.

It was always good to have a backup plan.

She ducked around a support beam and dragged her hand along the red ring ropes as she passed, smiling at a couple guys who were lifting free weights. This was still going to be a good day. Literally running into Cam Simmons was not going to change that.

Her father's office door opened and out stepped a man in a suit. Business on a Sunday? Or maybe church. That made more sense. She smiled at the man and then at her father, but her father didn't smile back. He looked stricken and pale.

"You okay, Pop?" She went to him, now highly suspicious of the well-dressed man. With all the real estate bullying that had gone on in this "up-and-coming neighborhood" over the past year, she couldn't be too careful.

"I'm fine," he said, and then he flashed an uneasy look at the man and made a gesture toward the door. "He was just leaving."

"Who is he?" She directed the question at the suit, who looked down his nose at her.

"Foreman Keller, from Great Lakes Savings and Loan, and you are?"

A banker. She lifted her chin and looked down her nose at him. "Tanya Martin, Pop's daughter." She looked at her father who was shaking his head like he wanted this conversation to end.

"Well, Tanya Martin, you might want to tell your father to pay his bills. It would save all of us time and money."

"Excuse me?" She puffed out her chest. Habit. Two older brothers, four hundred high school students, and a roster spot as a women's professional football linewoman taught her the bigger you looked the more seriously people took you.

"Stop," her father said. "It's not her concern."

"What do you mean it's not my concern?" She set her sights on the suit again. "Why are you here?"

"Just doing my job. And as long as he does his, I won't be back." He pointed at Pop. "You hear me?"

Smug *and* threatening? Not on her watch. She sort of snapped. The heels of her palms hit his lapels and knocked him back a couple feet.

"Stop!" her father said again.

"You're crazy!" The man scrambled for the door, but she followed.

"Get out and don't come back." She raised her hand for emphasis—not to hit him again—but still he flinched.

A pair of strong arms rounded her waist and halted her forward progress. A second later her back hit something hard and unforgiving, and the banker fled through the double doors.

When the arms released her, she spun around and came face-to-face with Cam. Again.

"What the hell do you think you're doing?" she spit out.

Cam's eyebrows rose. "Stopping you from getting arrested for assault."

"*Please.* I just pushed the guy. And you didn't hear how he was talking to my father." She looked around him in time to see the office door close.

What was going on? There was only one way to find out.

She raised a dismissive hand to Cam, warning him to stay away, and stalked back to the office. Her father was sitting at his desk, face in his hands. "Pop?"

He looked up, and his expression crumbled. "I'm sorry."

"For what?"

"Messin' up."

"How?" She fell to her knees and patted his thigh. "Start at the beginning."

When he exhaled, he shuddered, and her already rattled mood plummeted. Whatever it was, it was bad.

"I borrowed money to help someone out. I put the gym up as collateral, and now I'm behind on payments. I have ninety days to pay in full or they're gonna take it."

Fuck. Tanya swallowed against the lump in her throat. How the hell had this happened? She was in the gym whenever she wasn't teaching or playing football, and her brothers Terrell and Tyler were in and out too. None of them had intimate knowledge of the gym's finances, because that was Pop's thing, but somebody should've seen or sensed trouble.

He rubbed the back of her hand. "I failed everyone."

"No!" Those words didn't belong on her father's lips. He was South City's big-hearted hero. "We can fix this. We can talk to everybody in the family, and whatever you owe, we'll pull together and pay it back. It's the least we can do for everything you've done for us. How much do you owe?"

His voice muffled in his throat as he said, "Thirty thousand."

Damn it. She didn't have anywhere near that much. Neither did any of her brothers or sisters. Terrell was unemployed. Tyler's money was tied up in a messy divorce and custody battle. Tori was raising three kids on her own. And Teresa had just gone back to graduate school.

"Who'd you loan the money to?" she asked. "We'll just have to make them pay you back sooner than they expected. Then we can settle the debt."

Pop crossed his arms and hardened his expression. "Nope."

She squeezed her father's hand in an expression of sympathy and strength. "I know you don't want to call in a debt, but no friendship is worth losing the gym. Who is it?"

He looked at her, and his eyes fluttered as they rolled toward the back of his head. "I gave the money to your mother."

Tanya sat back on her heels and let his words sink in. Talk about worst-case scenario.

After a few calming breaths, she asked, "Why would Mom take $30,000 dollars from you? You haven't owed child support payments in years, and it can't be the restaurant. I live right above it, remember? It's freaking packed on weekdays."

Pop sighed. "The Diazes got an offer to sell the building to developers, so they told your mother they wouldn't be renewing her lease. She came to me panicked, and we put together an offer to buy the building ourselves."

What an unbelievable mess with her mother at the heart of it. Tanya bit back a growl. She'd been so proud of that purchase, thinking her mother had done it while standing on her own two feet. A strong, capable, independent woman. When in reality, her father had helped his ex-wife. Of course he had. His sense of obligation didn't quit. Pop Martin swooped in to save the day with no care for the trouble it would cause him.

Tanya didn't want to take sides. She'd thought she was beyond that. But in times like these, it was hard not to. The anger tossed her back seventeen years to the day he moved out of the family home. She'd been eleven, and convinced her mother was to blame.

Damn it. It just proved her theory on love and marriage. Once you loved someone enough to promise them forever, you were tied to them and their freaking problems even after forever fell apart. That's why she stayed far away from relationship strings.

"What's done is done," she said, grasping desperately at words that would help her remain neutral. "We just have to figure out a way to fix it."

There had to be an idea that would let both her parents hold onto their dreams.

She looked around, hoping for inspiration. Photographs lined the office walls, chronicling the accomplishments of the kids that had worked out in this gym. Some of them actually made it onto the few remaining college boxing teams. Her heart squeezed. This gym was so many things to so many people. Her father had even managed to bring low- and no-cost healthcare to the neighborhood in this very space by partnering with her best friend MJ's fiancé, sports medicine guru Tag Howard.

Wait! Maybe that was the answer. "What about Doc?" She jumped to her feet and pointed at the medical equipment in the partitioned corner of the office. "He's pumped a ton of cash into this place to create the training room. I bet he'd lend us more."

"No." Pop's face wrinkled. "I won't borrow any more money I can't pay back." He slapped his hands on his thighs like he'd done her whole life whenever the situation was non-negotiable. "Enough is enough. I've had a lot of time to think about this. And without any savings, my pension alone can't cover all the payments I already have. Borrowing more money would be irresponsible."

"What happened to your savings?"

Pop shrugged. "The house needed a new roof last summer."

The house where her mother lived. Tanya threw up her hands. "Unbelievable." Her father hadn't lived in that house since her parents had separated and he moved into the apartment above the gym. Sure, Tori and her kids had been living there for years, upping the responsibility Pop must've felt, but still…

How about a little independence, people? Take care of your own problems. There was a novel idea.

More deep breaths. More head shakes. "Okay," she said. "There's gotta be a way to stop this." There had to be.

Think, Tanya. Think. Something would come to her, because nobody threw a block like she did. Protection was the name of the game. They'd be prying this gym from her cold, dead hands.

A knock sounded, and she turned in time to see the door she'd forgotten to close completely swing open.

"Cam!" her father said.

"Hey," Cam said.

Great. For five years, he hadn't been anywhere to be found. Today, he was every-damn-where.

•••

"How can I help?" Cam stepped into the office and closed the door behind him. "I couldn't help but overhear."

Pop stood. "Whatever you heard, forget about it, and get over here and give me a hug, Mr. Cam Damn Simmons." He whistled. "Super Bowl *champeen*."

Cam hugged the little man, letting him slap him soundly on the back. He hated the circumstances he'd walked in on, but it sure felt good to be back. He'd spent so much time here as a teen, Pop had become a surrogate father to him.

"Glad to see you made it home," Pop said.

"Glad to be home."

Cam heard a scoff from someplace behind him. *Tanya.* But when he turned she was leafing through papers on her father's desk, looking uninterested in the conversation.

"Can you give my dad and me some time alone, please?" she asked without looking up.

He nodded. "Yeah. Of course." But as he backed toward the door, he made eye contact with Pop and said again, "I can help … if you let me."

Tanya glared at him. *Woo wee!* Ice cold. And it didn't get warmer until he was back in the gym.

Under the circumstances, he wasn't surprised by her reaction. He wouldn't want his dirty laundry being aired in front of anybody. But he wasn't just anybody—at least he hadn't been. That's why he'd walked in and offered to help. Apparently, five years away changed things. Something else that didn't completely surprise him. He just hadn't thought it would erase ten years of a friendship so close they were damn near family. With one exception—what had happened beneath the bleachers senior year. Thinking about it still made him smile.

They'd always been willing to go the extra mile for each other back then, and after what he'd overheard standing outside Pop's office, he wasn't going to let that change.

When Tanya had time to really talk to him, he'd get her to see he could help.

"Cam Simmons?" A short, chubby guy with moon-shaped sweat marks underneath his man-boobs stood in front of him. "No way! It's me, Goby Klinker, John-John's little brother."

"Holy crap."

They grabbed hands and bumped opposite shoulders.

"It's been forever, man," Goby said.

"I was just thinking the same thing." He looked around the gym. "Is John-John here?"

"Hell no. He's in worse shape than me. Works three jobs now because of the little ones. Hasn't been to the gym in years."

That guy had never made it to a full week of high school classes. How was he holding down three jobs? "Wait. John-John has little ones?"

"Three. Under four." Goby wrapped his hands around his neck.

Damn. "I didn't know that." He'd lost touch with the guys he used to run with too. "What about Joe and Marquis? Are they around?"

"Not around here. Joe's banned 'cause Daria thinks it's a meat market. She don't trust him."

Like Cam's ex-fiancée Sabrina hadn't trusted him. He rolled his eyes. "That sucks." Especially when it was unwarranted. "And Marquis?"

"Workin' in Atlanta. Moved about a year ago. Hear he's doing real good."

Now that was something to smile about. Marquis got out. Hopefully Cam would be saying the same thing about his mother at the end of this trip. Boston was where she belonged. With him.

"Bobby, come here!" Goby waved his hand to attract some guy's attention, and then he shifted back to Cam. "This dude's the biggest football fan. Browns, of course, but we ain't winning a Super Bowl anytime soon." He faced the room and the half-dozen guys who were lifting and practicing footwork. "Listen up, everybody! Super Bowl MVP Cam Simmons is in the house."

Cam smiled as heads turned and eyes widened. Three weeks after earning the title, and he still got a rush from it.

"What's up, gentlemen?" He raised his arms in invitation.

Something about the attention stoked his adrenaline. Always had. Like walking into school Monday morning after a big Friday-night win. Everybody knew your name. Everybody wanted a piece of you. Powerful stuff. The kind of stuff that helped a man feel important.

He signed a few autographs and told a few "war" stories, but when Pop's office door opened and Tanya stepped out, he was too distracted to do much more than listen to the guys rattle on about football. She said something to her father, who returned to his office, and then she walked over to the punching bags and systematically went down the line pounding the hell out of each one.

"Excuse me," he said. "Gotta take care of something real quick.'

He made his way through the small crowd toward Tanya, who was now whaling on a punching bag out of view from most of the gym.

"Hey," he said.

"Oh my God," she mumbled, then shot him a look, but didn't miss a beat with the bag. "You want the bag, you have to wait, Simmons. Super Bowl MVPs don't get special treatment 'round here."

He almost smiled at the exasperation in her voice.

Tanya Mary Martin. Five feet, nine inches of attitude and curves that would get a guy's head bit off if his admiration wasn't discreet. The best female basketball player East High had ever seen. And the most loyal daughter he'd ever seen. This shit with her dad was tearing her up.

"Let me help," he said.

She cut another glance at him, scornful and pitying like he was the biggest moron she'd ever seen. "He won't take your money."

"Why not?"

"Because he's proud." Boom, her fist connected with the canvas. "And we don't need your charity."

"Okay. I respect that. Fine. We'll figure something else out."

She pushed the bag into another and straightened. "*We* won't be doing anything, Cam. This is my family's problem. You are not my family."

"But I'm your friend."

She narrowed her golden eyes. "Are you? Because I thought friends stayed in touch."

Fair enough, but she could've nudged him when his silence had gone on too long. He was a busy man. But now was probably not the time to point that out, so he simply nodded. "I'm sorry about that, and I'd like to fix it. We can move on from here and not lose touch again. Deal?" He held out a hand.

She ignored his peace offering. "I've got a lot to figure out these days, so you're going to have to get in line."

Again, he almost laughed, because it had been awhile since he'd been around a woman who was so clearly not anxious to be around him. "Should I take a number?" She didn't blink at his attempt at humor. "You know, so you can call for me when it's my turn?"

"I wouldn't hold my breath, Simmons. It could take a while." She shot him a snotty smile before she turned and headed toward the hallway, then tossed over her shoulder, "Maybe like five years."

He laughed then. She'd always been a spitfire. And he had a feeling she was just getting started. He was going to be taking a lot of potshots from her over the next month.

The funny part? He kind of couldn't wait.

For more from this author, check out:

Crossing Lines

Keeping Score

Praise for the Cleveland Clash series:

 "Readers need not be sports fans to appreciate the strong female lead Arden has created in Tanya. Adding to the entertainment is the sweat-inducing physicality that occurs both on the field and off." – *Library Journal*

"Arden creates a heroine worthy of the MVP title … this sports romance [is] one to root for!" — Heroes and Heartbreakers

"I love the focus on women in sports, a very underappreciated and underexposed focal point for novels. The contrast between men's and women's pro football was quite poignant. Arden, writing with her usual well-polished, light-hearted style combines this all into an unforgettable package." — Pure Jonel

"I'm a sucker for second chance romances and *Running Interference* did not disappoint. This is my first Elley Arden read and I can guarantee it won't be my last. She has a unique writing style. Simple, yet strong with fluid and easy dialogue, you can't help but dive in and not come up until you're finished." — Eat Sleep Read Reviews

"I devoured the story … Fun, sexy, and filled with smart ass side comments (and humor), this book is a great way to enter the world of the Cleveland Clash series." —4 stars, Art Books Coffee

Harmony Falls Novels

Crashing the Congressman's Wedding

Battling the Best Man

Marrying the Wrong Man

Praise for the Harmony Falls series:

"The ending was my all-time favorite . . . This is definitely an AMAZING book that I recommend to all!" —Marnival's Books

"Good things come when you least expect it—at least I did with this book. I didn't expect to laugh, cry, and fall in love. But Elley Arden did those things to me, and after that short read, I think I'm coming back for more from this author." —Book Freak

Emerald Springs Legacy

Trouble Brewing